ENDOR

Great read! Once I started it I couldn't put it down. I was astonished by the elaborate way Marlene Wise described the setting. I felt I was there riding along with the characters. It was such a captivating and touching story that it brought tears to my eyes several times.

—Patricia Solis

Great story! Could not put it down. Wonderful time era; felt like I was actually in the story. I could actually feel my soul going back to those times. Writing was excellent.

—Leticia Gonzalez

From the moment that you start reading this book, it immediately takes your soul to those places so very well described. It is amazing how what you think you can only see in a movie finally comes to life in a good written book. Very family oriented. A smashing hit.

—Kristopher Perez

Marcy

A NOVEL BY
MARLENE WISE

Marcy
A YOUNG, SPIRITED PIONEER

Tate Publishing & *Enterprises*

Marcy
Copyright © 2009 by Marlene Wise. All rights reserved.

No part of this publication may be reproduced, stored in a retrieval system or transmitted in any way by any means, electronic, mechanical, photocopy, recording or otherwise without the prior permission of the author except as provided by USA copyright law.

This novel is a work of fiction. Names, descriptions, entities, and incidents included in the story are products of the author's imagination. Any resemblance to actual persons, events, and entities is entirely coincidental.

The opinions expressed by the author are not necessarily those of Tate Publishing, LLC.

Published by Tate Publishing & Enterprises, LLC
127 E. Trade Center Terrace | Mustang, Oklahoma 73064 USA
1.888.361.9473 | www.tatepublishing.com

Tate Publishing is committed to excellence in the publishing industry. The company reflects the philosophy established by the founders, based on Psalm 68:11,
"The Lord gave the word and great was the company of those who published it."

Book design copyright © 2009 by Tate Publishing, LLC. All rights reserved.
Cover design by Lindsay Behrens
Interior design by Stephanie Woloszyn

Published in the United States of America

ISBN: 978-1-60799-414-5
1. Fiction / Historical   2. Fiction / Family Life
09.05.29

DEDICATION

To daughter, Christina, and husband, Glenn, who gave their support and encouragement. They believed in my work to fruition. Blessings and thanks to you.

THE OREGON CARAVAN

Marcy and Beth remained close to their brand-new canvas-covered wagon as their parents had requested them to do. They waited patiently for their parents' quick return. So many details had to be attended to before their long, tedious journey could begin. In the meantime, both girls watched apprehensively as they lingered on pins and needles beside their new home on wheels. As they waited, they drank in the view of an awesome scene surrounding them. The panorama their eyes beheld at the present moment would not likely be forgotten anytime soon.

Marcy's wide green eyes had never focused on such a sight as encompassed them at that moment. There were many new covered wagons sitting everywhere around them that looked just like their own. They were stretched out in every direction. Some were fortunate enough to get a place in the shade while others stood soaking up the broiling hot sun.

The disturbed swirling dust filled the dry air and covered everything like a fine brown snow. Heavily built,

MARLENE WISE

creaking wagons busily came and went in both directions on the street. Roaming dogs wandered aimlessly and barked incessantly. Excited children ran and played, cattle lowed, and the horses stomped and snorted, beating their tails against their quivering bodies to drive away the maddening bites of the black flies. The wagons were constantly being loaded and unloaded and made ready for the long, hard journey that was soon to face all the travelers.

A strange vibration and an echo hummed in the girls' ears from the banging and pounding of hammers. There was constant chatter and conversation, some of which seemed to imitate the sound of angry bees. Then, further in the distance, a faint sound of music wafted across the air, probably from a local saloon.

A loud gunshot reverberated from the end of the dirt street causing both girls to flinch. Beth quickly scurried over to the wagon and clutched the top of the big wooden wheel in her small shaking hands. "Oh, Marcy! I wish we were back home. I don't want to go to this strange new land. I'm afraid! I want to stay! Perhaps Mother and Father would let me stay behind with Uncle Ned and Aunt Ruth."

Marcy stepped closer to Beth and put her long, tanned arms around her. "No, Beth. Please don't talk like that. What would I do without you? It is going to be a long and weary expedition, I'm sure. But I'm convinced that it will be a very lonely trip without my sister and best friend by my side. We must stick together as we have always done. We can help each other through the hard, trying times and the frustrating situations we are sure to go through. Promise me that you'll forget about wanting to stay behind."

Beth hung her head fighting back the hot tears, which were ready to cascade down her pale cheeks. She then looked at Marcy with her sad, childlike face and shook her head yes. This brought a big smile to Marcy's face because the girls had constantly been close to each other, even if there was an age difference of five years.

Marcy had turned seventeen in the fall of last year. She was sturdy and strong and had been an immense help to her parents. The Brewsters could have wished for no more even if Marcy had been born a boy. She had aided her father in the fields, assisted him in building their cabin, hunted and fished, labored in the garden, tended to livestock, and had still found time to learn to cook and sew, make candles, cure meat, and help prepare for harsh winters in Minnesota. Marcy had acquired much knowledge in her few short years. Sooner than she realized, she would have to rely upon her skills for survival.

While Marcy continued to hug Beth, she appeared to take on an expression of determination. She made a pledge to Beth that if they journeyed together she would take care of her no matter the consequences or how difficult the situations they would face.

Beth's appearance was that of a small-boned and fragile-looking young girl. She was quite tall for her age. Her long brown silky hair touched the tip of her shoulders. Her twelve years of age did not quite fit her stature. Beth could have easily been mistaken for a young lady of at least fourteen years. Her red-rimmed eyes stared sullenly from beneath her black velvet lashes causing her countenance to take on a teary and sad look. Marcy suddenly felt overwhelming compassion for her little sister. Marcy's eyes smarted and stung, and a sudden urge to weep along with her sister pulled at her with great force. She could not afford the emotion of crying just now. She must be the tough one and keep a clear head as to Beth's feelings and actions. Their parents were too involved and busy at the moment to understand how Beth must be feeling. But Marcy understood her sister very well. Marcy was shortly to find out that she would be the needed adhesive for many emotional conflicts they would have to face together.

One's attention was drawn to Marcy as she held Beth in a motherly way and stroked her soft brown hair. Love and compassion flowed from Marcy to Beth as she willingly drew strength and comfort from her beloved older sister. Marcy was a beautiful and caring young lady. She was strong and sturdy but very feminine too. Right now she looked exceptionally so. Her slightly curly auburn hair was pulled back with a blue shiny ribbon. Her green eyes had the hue of beautiful sparkling emeralds with just a touch of blue to them. She wore a blue-checked gingham dress fitted in at the waist. It was plain but well made and would wear well. Marcy's complexion was somewhat darker then Beth's, as Marcy was more of an outdoor person. The outdoor work had proven a plus for Marcy. Her trim, lean, muscular body was well prepared for the cruel expedition upon which the Brewsters were about to embark. Had the whole family known what was in store for them, they more than likely would have changed their plans.

Eventually, the girls' parents, Alisha and Stewart Brewster, returned. They carried various items with them needed for the long, weary days of travel that still lay ahead. Alisha carried a bulky basket full of goodies almost to the point of overflowing. Stewart toted many tools and implements that would be required of all the survivors that made it through the hard and torturous trip. Alisha busied herself in putting away the cache of food and goods while Stewart ventured with the girls back to the general store and supply house, and there they bought more needed items.

With kind eyes that spoke his love, Pa Brewster tapped Beth on the nose ever so lightly and told her to go get some candy. At first, Beth was reluctant to do so. But, as she approached her sister, Marcy nodded her head approvingly. Beth shyly asked the proprietor for some peppermint sticks and some gum drops. They then collected their order and proceeded toward the wagon. Immediately, everyone joined in and helped put away the meager personal belongings and the cache of goods. All of their worldly possessions now fit tightly inside the wagon. The family had been forced to sell what they could before they left Minnesota to travel to Missouri for the wagon train.

A glorious daybreak came peeping slowly into the wagon with a quiet stillness. Marcy's mind and body felt fatigued and faint. She had only slept for a short while, and then the little rest she had wasn't peaceful or very restful at all. She also knew that if she was to have any breakfast she must shake off her tiredness and get out of bed quickly.

She called Beth and began her usual morning preparations. Beth sat up and stretched but didn't seem to be in any grand hurry about getting ready for breakfast. Inwardly, she seethed knowing that again this morning she'd have to eat another tasteless cold meal of leftovers. Oh, how she'd love to have a plate of hot flapjacks with the rich taste of fresh maple syrup on them and the little pieces of crispy fried ham to go with them. She also missed the fresh milk they got every day from their cow. She decided quickly that a cold breakfast would be better than nothing at all. Her growling stomach also seconded her decision that any food, hot or cold, sounded good at this point. Beth soon found out that the only hot taste to the palate was some fresh coffee her father had made earlier when he arose. Pa Brewster had made only a small fire for a pot of coffee and then left the pot sitting near the hot coals. There was really no time to cook and clean up pots and pans before leaving, but the coffee pot could always be thrown in and departure made quickly.

Marcy was excited to some extent. She had determined to make the best of this new adventure. Why should one stay in a single place all of their life? There were things to see and do and new sights to behold. It would be good to seek fresh new beginnings. Marcy barely had time to grab a cold biscuit, some leftover meat, and coffee before she heard the familiar gruff voice of the wagon master. "Hurry up! Line those wagons up and stretch out! No time to waste." So everyone began to move swiftly and diligently as ordered.

Those who had made small fires doused them and finished harnessing their horses, mules, or oxen. In about ten minutes' time, the wagons began to rattle and roll in their assigned places. Every family member had a different description as to how they felt. It appeared that no emotion—fear, question, dread, joy, or even doubt—was the same for each individual.

The night before they left Independence, Missouri, the wagon master, Joshua McHenry, and the wagon scout, Tyler Clark, had gathered everyone together. All listened to a foreboding lecture from Joshua. Anyone who had even a twinge or entertained a doubt about going west was sure after this harsh speech to clearly make up his or her mind quickly. Joshua had taken several trains across, and his lectures to the groups were always the same. He never painted a pretty picture for anyone. He tried his level best to paint the truest and most honest picture he possibly could. He wanted no one to get the mistaken idea that the passage west was an effortless and uncomplicated road, but in fact just the opposite. The passengers, wide-eyed and all ears, assembled in a tight knit circle.

Joshua started his dialogue by saying, "Everyone who has signed the roster to go to Oregon or California has their own reasons and dreams for doing so. Let us hope that your dreams, reasons, and ambitions for this treacherous trip are worth the hardships and sufferings

MARLENE WISE

you'll go through to reach your destination. But let me be first to tell you that not all of you who start this weary pilgrimage will complete it." There was nothing but a hushed silence as they all stood and listened to Joshua.

"You will be confronted with all sorts of dilemmas and problems. Some of you will be buried along the way. You'll see old and new graves. You'll gaze upon the bleached bones of animals all along the way that could not make it for one reason or another. To list only a few of the things you must put up with, you'll have to fight against the taunting elements of wind, rain, storms, and sometimes hail and the angry, vengeful flooding rivers and streams. There will be short water rations, no water, poisoned water, dried-up water holes, and so forth. There will be food shortages, sicknesses like cholera, grippe, pneumonia, dysentery, and only God knows what other diseases we shall face that will wring the very life out of those too weak to fight back.

"Food, water, and wood will forever be scarce. There will be Indian attacks, people who will go loco, poisonous snakes, stupid accidents, and weariness from walking in the heat. And as a reminder, you will walk most of the time! The only ones allowed to ride in the wagons will be the elderly, the young children, the sick, or the driver of the wagon. Tempers will flare at times, and there will be stupid, insignificant fights; other conflicts will end in death. When a man has a great thirst and that thirst cannot be quenched to satisfy him, he may do strange things even to those he loves, even to his own family and friends without so much as a thought to the animal he has become."

MARCY

He paused at this time as though reflecting upon the words he had just uttered and then asked, "Does anyone have any questions or comments to make at this time?" All stood silently as if frozen to the ground. One could hear the breathing of the person next to him. Joshua motioned for Tyler and asked him to speak.

Tyler introduced himself and said, "All that you've heard is true. I cannot draw or sketch in your wondering minds a more perfect picture of how things will be for you than what Joshua has already stated. Everyone will soon be a witness to some of the incidents spoken of here today. Now is the time for anyone to back out if you feel you can't endure or handle the things that were discussed a few moments ago. After we start and are on our way, no one will have the skills needed to leave the wagon train and return by themselves, as it is too dangerous. Is that understood by all?

"We are going to Oregon! The only wagons to leave the trail will be the seven wagons going on to California. They will not depart from us until after the South Pass crossing and just before we reach Fort Hall. Those wagons are aware that they will then be on their own at that point. Mr. Charlton has traveled this route before, so he will assume the responsibility for the seven wagons and the passengers traveling with him. Now, if there are no questions, I bid you goodnight. We shall be promptly ready to leave at daybreak and possibly make at least fifteen or more miles. There will be only two planned rest stops each day, one at noon and the other in the late evening when we stop for the night."

Everyone bid Joshua and Tyler goodnight and left the circle to go to their own wagons and prepare for the next day's travel. Everyone knew that the break of dawn would come early. Some would sleep well, and others would not, as they would toss and turn thinking about what Joshua had warned them of and how he had seemed to speak so harshly.

UNFORTUNATE DISASTERS

The Brewsters' wagon was in the middle of a long fleet of jostling and rolling temporary homes. In front of them, all they could see was a line of white, gleaming canvas tops. In the distance, it appeared like the white sails of ships moving across the dry land.

In the beginning, everyone looked fresh and clean, as though they were going into town on a Saturday to buy supplies for the week. The livestock proved sturdy and ready for the long haul. It was realized that before long all of these scenes of freshness and newness would soon melt like the snow into weary, worn, dirty, tired, and tattered travelers. Walking fifteen miles a day was sure to induce a great weariness in both man and beast.

Just as Joshua had stated, even some of the beasts of burden would have to be mercifully shot and left along the trail. Some livestock would be completely consumed with exhaustion, some would break their legs, disturbed snakes would poison others, some would bolt and run away during storms, and others would die of thirst and heat. Any loss would be tragic for their owners, and for this reason, extra animals had to be herded along with the wagons. They were tended to by the single men who traveled alone or those who Joshua assigned to ride along with the herds as part of their work and responsibility.

The sun had risen in its brilliant and vivid hues of yellows and oranges and quickly became bright and hot. The ladies put on their hats and bonnets to shade their fair faces and necks. Long sleeves felt hot and sticky, but it afforded protection for their arms from the grueling hours in direct sun and wind. Marcy withstood the hot, dry elements much better than Beth. She often sighed deeply and stopped to rub her burning face on the sleeve of her dress. The bonnet she wore was distasteful to her, as she would much rather have the wind blowing through her silky hair. She greatly disliked the intense heat, smelly sweat, filtering dust, and scorching winds. She reminded Marcy often how she felt like a suffocating fish out of water.

"Oh!" She moaned in her heart and wished desperately that she was in the big woods of Minnesota. She envisioned the cool streams and clear, beautiful blue lakes. Memory began to recall the times she had run through the morning cool of the damp forest. She had picked lovely flowers down by the cool, crisp stream. Their snug cabin had been built in an enchanted forest clearing. Perhaps these would be the only living memories that would give her strength to stumble on day after day. She had only to close her eyes to recall these wonderful, refreshing memories.

Marcy stared blankly ahead wondering what new life

and strange adventures lay in her future. She only wished that when she laid her tired body down that night she could awaken to the place her father wished her to be. Marcy was quite anxious to build their new home and their new life and start afresh and anew.

The afternoon was silent and quiet except for the creaking and rolling of the wagon wheels against the hardened soil. Soon the quietness was shattered by horses rearing and snorting acting as though they were afraid of something. A wagon several spaces ahead wildly pulled out of line to the left. As Marcy walked close to their wagon, her mind was engaged in many thoughts of their future home and what life would be like in a new land. Suddenly her private thoughts were shattered by a commotion of shouts, horses neighing loudly, and screams coming from a nearby wagon. She recognized the voice of her friend Liza. She was shouting and trying to control her rearing horses. They were straining to be free of their confinement. Plunging out of line order and across an uncharted route was the only thing they could do. They struggled to untangle and free themselves of their tedious load, that they might run like the wind and have freedom from their quivering hearts, but to no avail; the wagon only followed them keeping them from their escape.

They were terribly spooked and couldn't hear any orders Liza yelled to them. They had become highly uncontrollable, and Liza didn't understand why they had all of a sudden become so crazy, giving her the fright of her life. They had always been very tame and good horses. One of the young men, Abe, saw what was happening; riding swiftly, he caught the reins and stopped them. Marcy had stopped in her tracks when she saw the wagon bolt out of line. She gasped and like a streak of lightning ran past the rolling wagons, across the rocky terrain and the brushy areas, and climbed upon Liza's wagon with little thought to her own safety. Out of breath, she called out to her friend, "Liza, Liza, are you all right?" But Liza had been thrown backwards into the wagon and had injured her arm. She had a good-sized lump the size of an egg on her forehead and several cuts and scratches. Tyler rode to the area where the wagon train had been halted.

A dark-haired woman was standing on her wagon seat and screaming loudly, "Snake! Snake! A huge rattler." Tyler was too close to the wagons to fire his pistol with safety, so he grabbed his gleaming bowie knife and, with uncanny speed and precision, threw it and hit the snake. How accurate! He had pierced the snake right between the eyes. It was a huge, ugly rattlesnake over four feet long. Tyler carefully retrieved his bloody knife and cut off the snake's head and kicked him aside into the brush and weeds. Tyler stood for a few seconds and watched the headless snake twist and squirm as though it were still alive.

"That one won't harm anyone again, but I'm very sure there are others around. They like to sun themselves in the daytime, so keep awake and watch your step," he said to those within hearing distance. "Pass the word to the others to keep their eyes open." He cast a glance at the lone wagon sitting some distance off the trail, mounted quickly, and rode over to the solitary wagon. He asked Abe, the young man, to take Liza over to Mrs. Colson's wagon for medical aid and treatment and then return.

Abe and Marcy carefully helped Liza from her wagon and started over to find the Colson wagon. Liza leaned upon Marcy for a bit of steadiness. Marcy sighed and said, "I am so glad your injuries weren't any worse. I will come by and visit you every day until you are well enough to travel by yourself. If you wish, I'm sure Father would let me drive your wagon for you for a few days."

"Thanks, Marcy, but Tyler said it would be taken care of. Your family needs you to help them, especially young Beth. I'll be okay with friends like you, Marcy," she said with a smile even though her whole body ached.

Tyler cautiously slid down from the saddle and began to examine the horses. The horse on the left seemed fine, but apprehensive. The heavy black on the right held its front leg slightly elevated, and its flesh shook and trembled greatly as if in pain. Tyler promptly spied the problem. The unseen disturbed rattler had struck the upper inside leg of the horse. The puncture wounds were large, and blood had already dried around it. Tyler knew with deep regret what had to be done; nevertheless, he always hated this kind of situation when he was forced to shoot a good horse. But in reality, he knew it was the only sensible solution, as nothing could be done to save the poor beast from its inevitable death, and a slow death at that. It was more humane to shoot the poor horse than to leave it to suffer a long, horrible, and excruciating death.

Abe brought another horse from the remuda for a

replacement and hitched him up with the other horses. As was promised, a new driver was assigned to Liza's wagon, and soon it was on its way back to be placed in line with the others.

Everyone heard the loud shot from Tyler's rifle. It only took a few moments for word to spread quickly as to what had taken place. Marcy understood the horrible situation all too well, and she flinched when the shot rang out. Even in the heat, her skin had gooseflesh, and she suddenly felt like she was very cold. She remembered in the big woods when the wolves had severely injured her little red calf.

Realizing it could not live, Pa Brewster had the duty of being merciful to a dying beloved pet calf. Marcy had said she would do it, but her father would not hear of such a thing. He knew how much little Bud had meant to Marcy, so he had carried out the dreaded duty and had felt the pain in every step he took toward the moaning little calf. It was a difficult choice, but he would never have allowed his own daughter to have done such a thing unless he would have been flat on his back and there had been no other way to take care of the problem the wolves had caused them.

The noon stop had been made hours ago, and everyone's stomach was telling them it was about time for another stop. Everyone was looking forward to the bidding rest, food, and bath time in the evening. Tyler soon rode back a ways and passed word that they would make camp soon. A nice place had been scouted and found with plenty of grazing for the livestock. They were just as happy to have a time to stop as the travelers, as they were thirsty, hot, and hungry too. There was a small stream nearby so all could have plenty of fresh water and fill their barrels again. It had been days since everyone could bathe freely and had had plenty of water for their needs. The children were most delighted to see the nice, clear, cool stream. The ladies could do laundry and spread the clothes over the bushes to dry before the early morning. Tyler had cautioned the families with small children to watch them closely and supervise any play near or in the water while the adults worked.

The Buckners had three children. The Andersons had two that were middle-aged, and the Abbotts had only one child. The families were all traveling close together, so the children often played happily when the wagons stopped for the day. The children were always drawn to Paul Abbott, as he had brought along his little friend, Dobie, the brindle dog. Beth watched the five children of various sizes and ages following young Paulie around. They were drawn to Paulie because of his brindle dog. They liked to pet and play with him whenever they got the chance. Dobie was usually kept on a short rope and tied to the back of the wagon. It was Paulie's job to feed and water his dog. Paulie was five years old, but he always thought himself older.

Beth had petted Dobie on earlier occasions when she had realized a dog was traveling along with the Abbotts. Beth began to talk with the children and was again taking the opportunity to pet Dobie and just be a little girl. She forgot all about helping Marcy and why they were at the stream. But Marcy didn't say anything to her because it pleased her to see Beth being involved with the children and having a good time. Right away Beth took to Paulie, and before long they were all in the soft grassy area away from the water and playing with Dobie. Beth would throw a stick and tell Dobie to go get it. Dobie would make them all happy by obeying her commands.

Marcy finished the wash by herself and told Beth she would go spread the clothes out to dry. "Play for a little while longer and then come to supper."

Darkness soon began to hover in on the wagons and close the daylight out. Paulie had eaten his supper and played for a short while until he became very tired from the day's long activities. He soon crawled under his favorite quilt and invited Dobie to come rest beside him. But Dobie began to whine and lick Paulie's face. Paulie then remembered he had not given Dobie anything to eat or any fresh water. As Paulie came out from under the wagon, he tied Dobie to a long rope and said, "I'll be right back." He looked around but didn't see his parents.

He carried a bucket to the nearby stream to get fresh water for his dog. As he did so, he noticed the water seemed to be running faster than it had earlier in the day. He sat down and watched as the dancing leaves and bobbing sticks floated gaily by. In the distance, he heard the roaring of thunder and saw lightning flashing and displaying its forked lights above the yonder hills. He decided he had better hurry and return to the wagon. He stretched out to dip the bucket into the water, but suddenly, he lost his grip on the bucket and it fell into the water. It began to bob up and down in the water like a fishing cork. Paulie sucked in his breath as he repeatedly cried, "Oh no!"

He waded out a little way to try to grab it, but it was moving away too quickly. Soon Paulie came to the realization that he was in much deeper water and the current was moving steadily and swiftly. He fought hard to keep his small curly head above the churning dark water. The ugly churning water thrashed him back and forth just as it had done the bucket he had dipped into the water. He felt like a fallen log being carried against his will. Then abruptly, large drops of rain began to fall, and the troubled water seemed to rise higher and higher. Paulie was reaching for anything to hold on to so the angry water would stop beating him back and forth. Eventually, his tiny hand caught hold of some branches along the side of the bank causing him to clutch them tightly and hang on for all his life. He screamed, cried, and shouted with all his might, but apparently no one could hear because of the storm and booming thunder.

Everyone had run for shelter when the rain started. Mrs. Abbott had run for the wagon for protection from the rain and to be with Paulie. She had not found him there, so she supposed he was with his friends. Dobie was tied with his rope as usual and under the back of the wagon. He began to bark and pace back and forth. Mrs. Abbott hushed him saying that the storm would soon go away. But Dobie continued to bark incessantly and look in the direction of the nearby stream where he had last seen Paulie.

MARLENE WISE

Paulie was still hanging on for his life knowing that if he let go the water would only carry him farther and farther downstream and probably drown him. Even though he hung onto the branches, the water whipped him back and forth, and it seemed to Paulie that the water was very vexed at him for some reason. He felt the branches were strong enough to hold him, so he fought like a wildcat trying to get some footing even though he was only a small little boy, and he seemed even smaller when he was completely soaking wet. He ultimately felt the bank and began to viciously scratch and feel for anything solid that might hold him long enough to allow him to crawl upon the bank out of the enraged dark waters. A big current of water seemed to give him the desperate needed push. Finally he was able to feel solid ground.

Clutching the branches with one shaking hand, he flung himself with the remaining strength left in his little body as hard as he could toward the bank. He finally felt solid but wet grassy ground, and he quickly began to crawl to safer and higher ground away from the stream. Frightened and scared witless, he ran for a short distance, and then his weak, achy, and cold legs buckled under him. He spied a large tree with low hanging limbs that looked like arms reaching out to him, and he gladly crawled under their welcome to him. He was tremendously cold, wet, muddy, and frightened. Then he remembered his dad telling him that if he was ever lost to stay where he was so he could be found. It became dark, and he couldn't remember which way the wagons had settled for the night. All he could do was sit in the heavy pelting rain and hope he was soon missed. After some time, the rain stopped. But by then, everyone would already be bedded down for the night.

When Mr. Abbott returned, Mrs. Abbott sent him to look for Paulie. He came back saying that no one had seen him since early evening after supper. In the meantime, Dobie had chewed through his rope and began his own search for his master. He sniffed down by the stream and back and forth on the bank of the water's edge. Dobie's sharp ears perked when he heard the distraught voice of Paulie. The stream was somewhat calmer now, and Dobie swam across with little trouble and then began to sniff and scratch and search the other side for his master.

Frightened and alone in the dark woods and shivering from the cold, Paulie began to cry. He huddled in a cold wet ball trying to make himself warmer. Dobie honed in on the crying and before long was headed in the right direction. Paulie pulled a dead branch over him and finally fell into a fitful sleep from sheer exhaustion. The next memory Paulie had was that of a wet warm tongue licking him in the face and hearing the whine of his own faithful Dobie. Even though his fur was soaking wet, he felt warm to Paulie. Now, he could be comforted by his best friend while they waited to be rescued. Both dog and boy curled up under the branch and went off to sleep.

Meanwhile, back at the wagons, Joshua was telling everyone that they must go back to their wagons. "Any tracks will be gone by morning if everyone roams around in the dark," he warned them. Paulie's parents were not satisfied, so Joshua said he would send only Tyler and Mr. Abbott to look around.

Earlier Mr. Abbott had spoken with the children and Beth about Paulie, but they had all gone their separate ways to supper and had not seen him since that time. By now, Mr. Abbott told Beth and Marcy, "Paulie is definitely missing, as he could not be found in camp anywhere."

Beth was beside herself with worry and wanted Marcy to do something to help him. "Beth, you heard what Joshua said about too many searchers messing up the tracks." But to relieve the anxiety that pierced Beth through and through, Marcy and her father went to Joshua and offered their help and services if needed. Marcy's father even offered to loan them Striker as a fresh mount for the search. The two men thanked them for their offer and started out on their search with no time for delay. Pa Brewster, feeling there was no more he could do, returned to his wagon.

Marcy understood what Joshua was saying, but Beth did not. "Beth, we need to go stay with Mrs. Abbott and see if there is anything we can do for her. She surely must be worried sick about Paulie. Go tell Mother where we will be so she won't be worried about us." Beth said she would.

As Marcy left the stream and started to walk to the Abbott wagon, Beth told her, "I am worried about Paulie being all alone or hurt and what has happened to his beloved dog, Dobie. Marcy, how can anyone rest or sleep until they know that Paulie and Dobie are all right, that they are safe and warm at home again?"

Marcy tried to comfort Beth the best she could while trying to keep a positive attitude. But Marcy's own mind raced back to the beginning of their trip when Joshua, the wagon master, had given his straightforward speech to all of them. She remembered his words so clearly: "You will be confronted with all sorts of dilemmas and problems. Some of you will be buried along the way, and some will see old and new graves. There will be stupid accidents and…" Marcy grabbed her head and tried to stop the thoughts that seemed to fill her mind. "Oh, not now, not now, mind."

"Mrs. Abbott, we're sure Paulie will be found. The men will find him. Tyler is a very good tracker. We must be positive and think good thoughts." She clasped Mrs. Abbott's hand and then bowed her head and prayed for peace and that Paulie would be found alive and well. Marcy asked God to give them strength in this time of need and to still the thoughts of fear that tried to overtake their minds.

The searchers stopped and spoke with Mr. Becker before crossing the stream. He relayed to them that just about the time the rain started, he saw the boy's dog going off in the direction toward the stream, and he seemed to be looking for a place to cross. "I supposed he was hunting," he stated.

The two men rode to the stream, crossed, and headed downstream. They searched for sometime and continually called to Paulie but never heard an answer. Then as they were about ready to go back and wait until morning, they heard the distant barking of the little dog. They wheeled around and quickly headed toward the sound of the dog.

The barking seemed loud and then muffled making

it hard to distinguish where the sound was coming from. Some wolves on their nightly prowl had found the stranded pair. They circled and stood awaiting their chance to jump their prey. Paulie retreated further under the branch. But brave Dobie went out to do battle to protect his master even though he was no match for the large ravenous wolves. Paulie could see that the huge silver wolf on the left was closing in. He had to do something, so he forcefully pushed back the wet branches and grabbed a long, big, knotted stick. He jumped out flailing the stick and screaming with all of his might until his voice hurt when he yelled, "Go away! Go away!" The noise temporarily startled the wolves, and they retreated for a short distance. Paulie's trembling knees fell to the wet soggy ground, and his arms wrapped tightly around Dobie's neck.

Only a minute later, he thought he heard the far away sound of his father's voice. "Paulie! Paulie! Where are you?" Someone was yelling. Dobie heard the voice too, and he began to wag his tail and bark excitedly. He whined wanting to go to Paulie's father. However, he would not leave his master alone and unprotected from the wolves. Paulie soon spotted two dark figures on horses and knew that he had been found.

As Dobie ran to meet them, Paulie cried out, "Father! There are wolves! Help me!" Tyler and John both pulled their pistols and shot simultaneously into the air. In disappointing defeat, the three large hungry wolves, hearing the gunshots and knowing what man could do to them, rapidly sprang away and fled into the cool darkness

MARCY

of the night leaving their meal behind for another day. Paulie and his dog were loaded onto the horses, and they traveled back towards camp.

Paulie was so grateful his father had found him that he snuggled up close to his father and didn't move until they reached the stream back at camp. As the horses entered the stream to cross, Marcy and Beth heard them. Marcy cried out, "The men have returned; we can hear them."

The three ladies left the wagon and ran toward the stream where the men had crossed over, and sure enough, they saw a beautiful sight. The two men had their precious load on board. Beth could hardly contain herself. She was so happy. Mrs. Abbott ran, reached up, and took Paulie off the horse. She lifted him down and held him tightly. "Oh, Paulie, we are so glad they found you." Marcy and Beth both hugged Paulie and told him how happy they were that he was safe and sound.

Beth reached up toward Tyler and took Dobie. Dobie was wiggling and barking wanting to be free. But Beth carried him all the way to the Abbotts' wagon. As soon as she put him down, he began to jump up and down and bark. He must have been showing his gratitude.

After all was quiet, Marcy told Paulie, "From now on when we stop to make camp, Beth can come help water and feed Dobie. You should never go to the stream by yourself unless someone is with you. Well, it is getting late and we must return to our wagon."

Mrs. Abbott gave each of the girls a big hug. "Marcy, thank you for your prayers and strong faith. You helped me realize that faith will get us through many things when we don't know what else to do."

Mrs. Abbott was so thrilled to have Paulie back safe and sound that she cried herself to sleep. Paulie could have drowned or died from the exposure to the cold water. Dobie had searched and found him in time and kept him warm until help had arrived. It was the dog's barking that had caused the men to locate him just as they were ready to give up their search.

Paulie refused to go to sleep until he knew that Dobie had been well fed. Paulie's father took a piece of meat left from their supper and a biscuit and broke them into little pieces and put them into Dobie's pan. Dobie wagged his tail with gratefulness, went to the dish without coaxing, and ate his supper. Afterwards he went over and laid himself down next to Paulie on his warm blanket. Dobie twisted around and around trying to get in a comfortable position. After Paulie's father had told both of them goodnight, Paulie lifted the edge of his blanket and motioned for Dobie to crawl in with him. Dobie didn't refuse the considerate offer at all, but he gladly slithered under the covers and snuggled up to his master happy and content to be in a dry warm place. Paulie placed his grateful arm around Dobie, and both fell into a tranquil sleep glad to be safe and sound in their own wagon again. Paulie had made a solemn promise to his parents to never go near the water again unless he had someone with him to assist him with his chores.

SNAKE EYES

Marcy's family had envisioned going to Oregon for many months. But the glowing campfire talks had been having a strange effect on Pa Brewster. He was beginning to like the idea of leaving the trail after the south pass and traveling with the seven wagons to sunny California. Mr. Abraham Charlton seemed to have a great deal of influence on Pa Brewster and Alisha. He had been over the trail before and gone to California with others in the past. His memories and tales were great lively fireside stories, but Marcy put no more stock in them than just that—tall tales of Abraham. She wished that her father would not be so gullible and believe all of the wild tales Abraham told, especially about the shiny gold and rich fertile lands. He told how it was there just for the taking of it. He repeated it over and over that one just had to work the land and live on it for a year, then one didn't even need to pay for it. Or you could become a prospector and find your riches in the gold of California.

Pa Brewster began to believe the stories Abraham

told. He spoke often to his family about making the travel changes to California. Alisha didn't really say much about the changes. All she desired was to get to their destination before the harsh winter set in. As a faithful wife and mother, she tried to make all of her family happy. But she realized Marcy and Beth were not in favor of making the change to travel to California.

When her mother would speak to Marcy about not liking her father's thoughts of this change, Marcy could not really give her a straight answer. It was a strange feeling that she had in the pit of her stomach. She really didn't know if Abraham could be trusted. Had he really traveled this way before? If he had and it was so wonderful in California with so much rich land and gold, then why was he here on another wagon train heading for California again? Marcy had tried to talk with her father on several occasions and tell him that she didn't approve of the plans to pull away from the wagons. She also relayed to her father that Beth had friends on the wagon train and to leave would separate her from them causing her great disappointment and pain.

Marcy, in a last attempt to sway her father, said, "Don't you think that only a few wagons traveling by themselves would be an open invitation to Indians or others who might want to bring harm? What if one of the wagons breaks down or loses a wheel? Will Abraham be willing to stop and help that family, or will he have to leave them on their own in order to make time before the first snows?" Marcy's belief was that there was more safety in numbers than only a few unsure travelers following a man who said he had gone this way before.

But her father's reply was, "Joshua would not allow this to take place if he didn't have confidence in Abraham and believe it to be okay." Marcy realized she was not making any progress in changing her father's mind. She decided to leave it alone for now and perhaps try again later when he had more time to think about what she was saying.

Marcy and Beth loathed the sight of the short little friend of Abraham Charlton. His name was Raney McBride. He had dark wavy hair, somber beady eyes, and a black, crooked mustache. He was very brusque and curt when he didn't get his way. She could tell he came from the east somewhere because he wore a fancy, well-tailored suit that by now was well tattered. He carried a gold watch in his pocket that he was always flaunting. Joshua told him he had seen men killed for less gold than that of his fancy timepiece. He politely asked him to put the watch away and not be flashing it around until he reached his destination. "A watch will do you no good out here. We use the rising and setting of the sun for our timepiece so everyone has the same time," he stated.

Marcy was quite uncomfortable and ill at ease around Raney, as he would impolitely stare at her until she looked at him and then he'd give her a wicked smile. He was constantly trying to talk to her, to start up a conversation with her about anything. He followed her like a shadow whenever he could, especially when he noted Marcy's father was not in close range. Beth detested him so much that she always referred to him as old "Snake Eyes." When Raney spoke to Beth, he would always say in a sarcastic tone, "Little Miss Beth." She would reply that only her family and loved ones called her Beth. "If you wish to speak to me, you should call me Elizabeth," she advised him angrily.

His reply was a very cold, "My! My! Now aren't we testy today? You better learn to like me, as one day when we leave Joshua's train you may need my protection and assistance," he warned her. Raney turned on his heel to leave, and then, removing his hat, he looked at Beth and said, "Elizabeth, may I speak to your sister?"

Beth in her fury turned and quickly said, "No! Snake Eyes. She isn't here!"

He abruptly and furiously placed his hat back on his head. "Look, young lady!" he said caustically. "If you were my daughter, I'd give you the thrashing of your life!" As he lifted his hand in midair, he pointed his long bony finger at Beth and shook it with hate at her and declared, "Young lady, you need to have a civil tongue in your mouth and not be so rude to your elders."

Pa Brewster stepped out from behind the wagon. "Well, Raney… Mr. McBride, she isn't your daughter. So I wouldn't worry about it if I were you," he stated calmly. Marcy came from behind the wagon and put her long, tanned arm around Beth. Beth's father looked at her tenderly and said softly, "Daughter, I do believe you spoke a bit harshly."

She turned slightly so Raney could hear her and said, "My apology, Mr. McBride. I am sorry."

"Your apology is accepted. You can call me Raney, as Mr. McBride sounds a little too formal for me."

Beth said no more. She stood close to Marcy and glared with anger at Raney as he took leave of their presence feeling that he had won the battle this time. "Don't let it worry you, Beth. I can fend for myself. I don't trust Raney McBride either. He seems like a troublemaker, and his eyes look as if they are full of mischievousness and evil. I'm going to ask Father if I can wear the revolver he bought me and taught me how to use. I know Mother thinks young ladies shouldn't be toting guns, but I think Father will understand the situation."

In a matter of minutes, Marcy approached her father and had a talk with him. She discussed her never-ending fears and her uneasy perceptions about Raney. Her father had already felt some of the same disturbing uneasiness that Marcy had so vividly expressed from her heart about Raney and his peculiar actions. He agreed reluctantly to her idea, but he did understand the situation all too well. "This is only one more reason to think twice about leaving the wagon train and going on the California shortcut, Father. Raney seems like an unpredictable and even mean person. Are you sure he can be trusted and help Abraham make wise decisions on our journey? Why put ourselves in his way by going to California on the same wagon train with him?" Marcy spoke her thoughts and fears to her father. He also had some of the same concerns, but they evidently weren't as strong as Marcy's because there was no change in any plans.

After weeks of travel, they would soon reach Fort Kearny, which would indeed be a blessing for all. Some definitely needed to make some serious wagon repairs and pick up a few depleted supplies if any were available. The days had passed by quickly, and they reached the fort with few problems. Those who needed medical attention, dental care, or fresh supplies would be able to obtain all of these things. The livestock would be inspected and thoroughly checked over and receive a much-needed and earned rest from their travels.

Soldiers had brought in fresh meat, and the colonel had invited everyone for a fiesta and a night of dancing and music. Joshua said, "Okay, we'll spend the rest of today and tonight at the fort." Everyone dressed up in the best they had to wear. This would be a night of well-deserved fun and celebration and a wonderful break from the tedious burden of walking for many miles in a day's time.

Marcy took out her lovely green dress with small white flowers and a lace collar. Beth wore a beautiful yellow dress with little pale-colored buttons and a yellow ribbon in her hair. This was the nicest and loveliest dress she had ever owned. Her mother had made it for her with loving care, and until tonight she had only worn the dress on two other special events. But this occasion seemed very special to Beth, and with anticipation, she could hardly wait to hear the banjo, violin, guitar, and harmonica music waft through the air and see dancing partners taking their places. The clapping and toe-tapping seemed to indicate that everyone was having a good time.

Marcy spotted a young handsome soldier standing across the room smiling at her, and she reciprocated with a gentle and happy smile. Beth looked at the young man and then at Marcy questioningly.

"Well, are you going to dance with him or not?" she inquired.

"Beth, hush! He'll hear you! I would dance with him if he asked me," she said innocently. The young soldier was trying to make his way across the room to Marcy just as Raney brusquely appeared in front of her. As Raney approached Marcy, he asked her to dance with him. The young soldier had suddenly stopped and stepped to the side out of the way but within hearing distance of the two girls and Raney.

"Marcy, my dear, may I have this dance?" he asked. He knew many staring eyes were upon him, so he bowed to her from the waist and flashed a huge, toothy smile at her. Beth moved closer and hung on to Marcy's arm like a small child who was suddenly afraid. Snake Eyes turned to Beth in a leering way and said, "Of course, I shall save the second dance just for you."

Marcy, terribly annoyed at his brazen and discourteous display, said, "No! I don't wish to dance with you!" Marcy had said it loud enough that several people had heard and now watched them even more intently.

In a hushed voice and embarrassed by her rejection, Raney said in a growling throaty tone, "I really wish you would reconsider, ma'am, because there is something we need to discuss." He placed his rough and dirty hand on her arm and tried to pull her a little closer to him. Marcy quickly moved backwards as if he had burned her arm. "I am free to dance with whomever I choose, and it is certainly not going to be you!"

She could not stand the ugly sight of him and his

beady dishonest eyes. All Raney could do was stand with flared nostrils and a crimson face filled with anger and hate for how Marcy had treated him in front of all these witnesses.

The young soldier saw it was time to step in, and he courteously asked the girls if they would like some refreshments. "Oh yes, that would be fine," they both stated. As they started across to the table, Marcy glanced back at the childlike pouting and sulking Raney.

The young soldier asked, "Is everything all right? Is that man making a pest of himself and bothering you?"

But before Marcy could even form an answer on her quivering lips, Beth spoke sharply and quickly. "Yes, he won't leave us alone."

Marcy tenderly placed her hand on Beth's shoulder. "It's okay, Beth. Don't ruin a good party because of the likes of this rude and callous man. We'll be just fine," she told the young soldier.

"Allow me to properly introduce myself. I am Private Emory Sikes," he said, smiling. After refreshments and a time of welcome conversation, he did ask Marcy to dance with him, and then he asked Beth also.

He was a smooth, wonderful dancer, very good and light on his feet. Marcy caught the glaring beady eyes of Raney out of the corner of her eye as she whirled around and around on the dance floor. She could feel that he was rudely staring at her again and that he was livid. His raw contempt and horrible anger made no sense to her. She didn't really know him very well, and she had no idea why he was so furious with her. Marcy didn't feel that it had all that much to do with the rejection of not dancing with him. She felt it had to do something with another idea of his. He had been a strange fellow ever since he had joined the wagon train. She had noticed at previous times that he had seemed to have a hateful and frightening disposition toward her even in very small unimportant and insignificant things that shouldn't have made any difference.

It was getting late, and Emory walked them back to their dark, lonely wagon. Just as they neared the wagons, they noticed a dark form coming from the inside of their wagon. Someone said in an almost inaudible voice, "Pardon me, the wrong wagon." The person, whoever it was, hurried off into the cover of darkness. Private Emory ran immediately and looked around, but he didn't see a soul, not even a shadow around anywhere. Whoever it was had purposely disappeared as though they had not wanted to be detected. Marcy shivered as if she had a sudden chill. The person had been short and resembled Raney in several ways. He had tried to disguise his normal voice so as not to be recognized, for surely he didn't know what else to do because of the sudden appearance of Marcy and Beth. He had almost been caught in the shady act of whatever he was up to. She knew in her heart that it was definitely Raney. But why? What did he want? Was he a common thief? Was he trying to frighten her for some reason?

Emory lit a lamp and looked around several wagons and places that someone might hide. Only a few personal things had been disturbed, but nothing seemed to be missing. Others later complained to Joshua that someone had pillaged through their personal belongings too but had not taken anything of value that they were aware of at the present time. Marcy clammed up and would say no more hoping not to frighten Beth unnecessarily. She could see no reason to upset Beth without any real proof.

Joshua asked Colonel Bicker to have some of the soldiers on duty through the night and watch for anything unusual. Joshua shouted, "There is one thing I won't put up with on my wagon train, and that's a thief. Anyone caught stealing, whether large or small things, will be dealt with in an extreme measure."

Twilight came, stealing across the land bright and early. Every wagon was hitched by first good light. Joshua mounted his silent big black horse with great haste and then flapped his worn old hat across his leg and shouted, "Let's move out! Get them stretched out! Stretch them out!"

Marcy, Beth, and Pa Brewster were prepared for another long, hard day. Alisha would drive the wagon again today. When she did drive, her husband sometimes walked and sometimes rode his friend Striker. This beautiful horse had been saved from death or maiming by Pa Brewster in Minnesota. The man who had owned the horse was going to shoot him in a fit of anger. He was somewhat mean to animals if they didn't respond to him properly or the way he thought they should. When they responded incorrectly, he would then commence to beat them viciously with a black snake whip or hit them with his rifle or even shoot them on sight if his anger was uncontrolled.

It seemed to be on one of these days when his anger was out of control that Pa Brewster had courageously stepped in and defended the horse from any harm. It had all happened so quickly as Pa Brewster stood and watched the man nearby the corral trying to train and break this beautiful broad-chested, half-wild, chestnut horse. When the horse was mistreated badly, he would rear up and strike with his front feet in self-defense. On this particular day, he had been greatly mistreated, and the horse, in self-defense of the wicked black whip, reared and struck the man across his left shoulder, injuring him. The man, in great anger and in severe pain, ran and grabbed his rifle with intentions of killing the horse out of revenge. At this moment, Pa Brewster felt he had to step in, and he did. He purchased the horse after much squabbling and arguing with the man and brought him home. He decided to call the horse Striker after the incident he had witnessed when he saw the horse strike out in self-defense.

Pa Brewster respected the horse and worked with him every day until he became as gentle as a baby kitten and just as loving. He had long race-horse legs and was quite a fast runner. Several people had offered to buy Striker, but Pa Brewster would never consider selling him because they were now partners till death separated them. He felt that Striker knew he had been delivered out of the hands of a devil and a very mean man who would have eventually injured, maimed, or killed him.

MARLENE WISE

Beth walked with her father, and Marcy strolled along beside the wagon by herself. She was far away in thought and did not hear Raney walk up beside her. "Good morning, my fair lady. Or are we trying to be a man today? I see you've strapped a gun on," he said, chuckling under his breath.

Without even looking his way, she said in a cold matter-of-fact voice, "I can't always predict when I might wish to shoot a snake right between the eyes." Raney smirked and jested about her "big" gun. Marcy stopped abruptly with no warning and suddenly looked at him with great contempt and anger. "Look, Mr. McBride, I know how to effectively use this gun because my father taught me to shoot when I was younger than Beth. Everything I take aim at, I hit. Now, I don't know or care what your silly game is, but I'm not intimidated. Do you understand me?" she said very hatefully.

Marcy then laid her hand over the handle of her holstered gun and said in a rather testy voice, "If I ever catch you snooping around our wagon again, I'll shoot you on sight, if my father doesn't do it first. I've nothing else to discuss with you, now or ever! Now clear away from me and my family! You are not welcome near this wagon or any of us. Do you understand this, or do I need to say it again with a little more force behind it?" Raney's face had the appearance of strong hate. His only desire at the time was to find a place to go hide as everyone curiously stared at him as they passed by.

He finally came out of his shocked daze and realized that he was absorbing the dust from the continuing

46

MARCY

wagons. It riled him greatly to know that a seventeen-year-old girl had adamantly put him in his place and had severely admonished him about his actions. He began to walk slowly toward Mr. Charlton's wagon. Raney was muttering words to himself. "Wait and I'll teach that hateful little girl a good lesson she won't ever forget. She'll be forever sorry that she humiliated me like that in front of all my friends. I'll make her pay for this outburst if it's the last thing I do. No one treats me like she has treated me and gets away with a grand display like this. Not even an apology can mend her vicious ways and take back the cruel words she has spoken to me. She has embarrassed me in front of all of my friends, and she won't do it to me again!"

UNNECESSARY DEATHS

The month of June was bringing the wagon train closer to the South Platte River. The heat was beginning to bother both people and livestock. Tempers were now fiery and short, and people were becoming too edgy over little differences and unimportant things. The livestock showed their temperament by balking, butting, and trying to run away. Arguments could be started very easily over the least little incident or accident or a foolish word spoken out of turn. There never seemed to be enough fresh water for everyday use for everyone. All had to willingly be rationed or forced to ration themselves. Everyone was always cautioned to be saving the water and not use it needlessly.

The sun beat down on the passengers and animals alike for ten hours a day. The days were always very long, dusty, dirty, and hot. Clothing became sweat-soaked, and then the dust and dirt dried on the wetness and created a stiff scratchiness against the skin. Legs cramped from the long miles that had to be walked each day. Wheels came

MARCY

off the weakened axles and had to be repaired. Animals died from exhaustion and thirst or sickness and had to be mercifully shot and left along the way. It seemed like an overwhelming and never-ending chain of challenges and troubles.

As they neared the South Platte River, wagons began to slow down almost to a halt. Normally the wagons raced when the animals smelled fresh water. People casually looked to the right as they passed by, and their eyes beheld a scene they didn't wish to see. There were burned remains of supplies, clothing, trunks, and ruined wagons. Some personal articles and clothing had been partially burned and strewn all over the ground. Off to one side, they could not help but view a row of fresh graves with wooden crosses for markers. The graves had not lost their newness and were not very old. This had happened within the last few months or so. Necks stretched back and forth trying to catch a glimpse of Tyler so they could inquire as to what had taken place at this secluded spot along the way; however, Tyler was nowhere to be seen, as he was out scouting for the wagon train.

Joshua beckoned to Travis and Dave to come quickly. "Go back there and see what in the world is slowing everyone down. Tell them to keep moving at a normal pace and stop dragging behind. This is a perfect place for an Indian attack, as they can already see, and we haven't heard from Tyler in several hours," he said sternly. So the men rode quickly and wildly swinging their hats back and forth.

"Joshua's command is to stop moving so slowly. He

49

doesn't know for sure, but there may be Indians around close," the men said. The word *Indian* was like a magic potion, and it did the trick. The wagons picked up their slowness and certainly moved speedily onward. Shortly, a rider appeared coming in fast from the southwest. As he drew near to the wagons, they could make out that it was Tyler. He stated that he had picked up signs of Indians, a Cheyenne party, not too far from here. The wagon train that left Council Bluff on the Mormon Trail had been ambushed several weeks ago. The dead had been recently buried by an army patrol and any survivors taken to Fort Laramie. But Tyler feared they might strike again, as they had now had time to regroup. The party of Cheyenne he had spotted had been a good distance away, but he could tell there appeared to be at least twenty or twenty-five. Joshua and Tyler decided for the good of all, they would not slow down but continue on hard and fast and cross the river quickly before dark.

Suddenly, a deathly silence fell over the long and winding train, and it was very evident by appearances that no one wanted to lag behind or be the last one in line. A burst of energy had been shot into each one because their footsteps were quickened as though they had just begun a fresh new day. The intimidating word *Indian* had had its effect on them. Tyler had quickly scouted with two other men and found a less dangerous crossing or what they assumed to be a good and safe crossing. The Platte was swollen with heavy rains from upstream a few days ago. They must hurry on and get across with all speed and safety. It would be better to have the river behind them than in front of them in case of an attack because trying to cross in a hurry without checking out the banks and water depths could only spell out great and terrible mishaps for all concerned during an attack. Tyler gave Mel, Travis, and Henry orders about where to take the wagons as soon as they crossed.

"Begin to circle them and prepare as though an attack was imminent," he ordered.

The movement of the wagons across the river was going smoothly. But Bill and Harriet Marsh felt it was taking entirely too long and that it was too slow and tedious. Consequently, their patience was now wearing somewhat thin, so they pulled their wagon out of their assigned line order and proceeded to try to cross in a different place without ropes as guides. Joshua yelled for them to get back in line and wait their turn.

"It's too dangerous to cross down there!" he screamed. Tyler was trying to cross over to stop them, but it was too late. Others had decided to follow them and had intended to do the same as the Marshes. Suddenly, the Marshes' wagon was jerked around in a swift current of the water. The horses struggled for balance and steadiness but were swept into soft sand and couldn't move. Every time they attempted to move, the horses went deeper into the watery grave. The burdened-down horses proceeded to try to free themselves only to find they were pushing themselves farther and farther down into the quagmire of sand and soft mud.

Tyler shouted for the Marshes to jump to safety and abandon the wagon. Mr. Marsh immediately obeyed and jumped when Tyler said to do so. But his wife was frozen with fear and would not move nor jump. As she stood up on the seat of the wagon and held on tightly, she looked about with fear and begged for someone to help her.

Marcy was tying a rope around her waist and preparing to enter the water. Her father ran to her and asked, "What are you doing?"

"If someone will hold the rope for me, I can swim out to help Mrs. Marsh."

"No, Marcy, the water is too strong for you. I can't allow you to do this."

"But I have to, Father. I am a good swimmer, and with the rope, I know I can do it. I just need a little help." Before Marcy could persuade her father to help her, the horses in their fright and nervousness gave one last jerk trying to free themselves but to no avail. The sudden jerk had caused Mrs. Marsh to topple down between the horses, and she was caught in the harnesses and reins, frightening the poor horses even more. Soon the flailing, frightened horses and Harriet Marsh's screams were heard no more. Bill Marsh had been trapped under the wagon trying to save his beloved wife. Both husband and wife met their death in a watery grave of the South Platte River.

Marcy crumpled to the ground with a moan as tears streamed down her cheeks. She felt so helpless and even angry that she had not been able to save their friends. She felt sick to her stomach and weak in the knees. As Pa Brewster put his arms around her, she looked into his face and said, "I will never forget the cry of Mrs. Marsh asking someone to help her. It will always remain in my mind forever and forever. I can't believe that someone couldn't have helped and saved them."

"Marcy, this is why Joshua and Tyler spent a lot of time in trying to find a good crossing. They know there are places like this in the rivers, and they always try their best to keep everyone safe. If only the Marshes would have listened, they would probably still be alive. You cannot blame yourself for their disobedience and wanting to rush the crossing. Your father is proud of you for wanting to help in this situation. I hope you can forgive me for holding you back and not letting you do so. I was not willing for you to gamble with your life in such dire circumstances."

As disbelieving onlookers watched, they slowly and sadly turned their wagons and returned to the line to cross in a safer manner. Everyone made it safely across except for the Marshes. The chilling fright of an Indian attack had caused needless disobedience on the Marshes' part. The wagons were finally all circled tightly together. Some animals were inside the guarded circle, and some were picketed close outside with guards on careful watch all through the night. It had been a harrowing day, and everyone just wanted to relieve their minds of all that had happened, especially the drowning of some of their friends. But they knew that was not going to be done so easily. Everyone had realized after they were well into the water there was really no help that anyone could have afforded them because of the sand and mire.

They hadn't heard from Joshua as of yet; nevertheless,

they continued their work and chores as before with little thought as to what they were doing. Joshua and Tyler had both given lectures to the new travelers before they had left Missouri. They had been warned in no uncertain terms to do just as they were told. Joshua, at that time before leaving, had given his speech and spoken a little testily, but he had meant to do so and leave a lasting impression upon all of them.

He now cleared his throat and stated harshly, "Today's accident need not have happened. From now on, all orders are to be obeyed and carried out fully as given. He who chooses not to heed the rules and decisions of my command will suffer the consequences. My orders are the law on this wagon train! Is that clear in all of your minds?" He turned and nodded to Tyler and then crossed over to the supply wagon. With much weariness, he leaned against the wagon with a cup of lukewarm boiled coffee in his worn old cup of many travels and slowly sipped the tepid drink.

Tyler slowly arose from the camp stool he was sitting on and walked carefully out to the middle of the circle. He took off his hat and mopped his forehead with the sleeve of his shirt. "I don't think we have too much to worry about right now. If the Indians attack, it will be early dawn. They are quite superstitious about starting fights in the middle of the night. However, they have no qualms about stealing horses at night. Those who are on first duty, keep awake! Don't smoke! An Indian can spot a tiny little light far off in the darkness." He warned them with intensity hoping they wouldn't need a second warning or admonition.

Joshua ventured over again and announced that it had been a trying day for all of them and that Mr. and Mrs. Marsh would be buried the next day before they left. A somber sadness like a heavy fog seemed to envelop the camp as each went to their own wagon. Close friends of the Marshes dreaded for the light of day to appear as they knew this would bring a final separation forever. Their friends would have to be left here in this uninviting lonely place without a name. Their graves would be viewed by others who passed by at a later date just as they had looked at unmarked nameless graves along their journey today.

Mrs. Chapman told Marcy that she must write down in her journal what had taken place so as to never forget. She described the place and how it looked and the feelings of all the travelers. She wrote what had caused the accident and then described how they would have to leave their good friends, the Marshes, in this lonely, desolate place. She wrote how one brave girl named Marcy had begged her father to let her go out with a rope to try to save poor Mrs. Marsh. But her father in his wise decision had not allowed her to do so. Mrs. Chapman hoped the records she kept would be useful to relatives and friends of the Marshes and others that had lost their lives along the way.

Mrs. Chapman felt the same as Marcy when she had cried and felt so helpless. She realized that nearly everyone had the same emotions and feelings about the accident. Marcy knew Mrs. Chapman liked to keep records and details of all the happenings along the trail for future use, but this was one memory that Marcy wanted to forget, especially the sound of Mrs. Marsh's frightened voice and the picture in her mind of Mrs. Marsh falling into her watery grave.

Sleep was beginning to take hold of Mrs. Chapman after this long, trying, weary, and sad day. She placed her well-worn journal back into the tin box that she carried it in and blew out the lamp. She never realized when she had fallen off into the deep sleep that finally captured her weary mind until the calm morning light came sneaking into the end of the wagon. She then realized that this day would be the last and final day to say good-bye to her good friends the Marshes. She would think of them and remember them every day. They were the best of friends with her and her husband, Will, and with the Brewsters. They would miss the Marshes jostling wagon in front of them. Marcy's wagon would now replace the Marshes in the long line of wagons and be in front of the Chapmans. But they knew it would never be the same as traveling with the Marshes.

After the horrible incident, Marcy had reminded Mrs. Chapman about Joshua's lecture to them before they had started the journey. "There will be stupid accidents, and all sorts of things will happen on our journey before we reach our destination. Not all will make it to the new land that you are starting out for; some will be buried along the way."

Oh, how Joshua's words seemed to echo the truth at this time. Marcy was glad that somebody else kept records of deaths, births, accidents, places of burials, and the travels and happenings along the way. Marcy knew that all had to take the good and the bad. But many times she only wished to forget the bad things and proceed on with their travels. Of course, Marcy knew Mrs. Chapman was doing a service for many who would later have questions about their loved ones and those who did not make it through.

MORNING SILENCE BROKEN

Marcy was combing Beth's hair and starting to braid it just as the sun came up. Her father and mother had already been up for some time now. It was not unusual for them to get up just as daylight was beginning to be birthed for the new day. It was a very serene, calm, and peaceful morning. Marcy was enjoying the coolness, since she knew as the day went on it would become hot and almost unbearable again. But all of this morning quiet soon came to a screeching halt as Marcy's thoughts were broken by a thundering of hooves and the most blood-curdling screams to ever pierce the stillness of a brand-new morning.

Arrows, some tipped with fire, began to fly toward the circled wagons. Loud shots rang out, and bullets whizzed close by their wagon, a little too close for comfort. Marcy pushed Beth down on the floor in a narrow place not large enough for her to really hide in. "Stay down, Beth!" she screamed as she threw a blanket down over her head. Marcy grabbed her pistol and peeped out the back of the drawn canvas. Everybody was behind some sort of barrel or covering for protection from the flying bullets and the whizzing arrows. Some had been rudely awakened and barely had time to grab for their clothes. Others had to take aim from the inside of their wagons.

Marcy saw her first savage Indian with a drawn bow and a flaming arrow of fire on the end of it. He aimed and was ready to shoot it into a nearby neighbor's wagon when she realized it was the Hollisters and that she had to help them. She raised her pistol, took careful aim, and then pulled the hammer back and fired. The Indian jerked violently and fell from his horse, hitting the hard ground with a dull thud. It seemed then like the Indians came one after another for a long period of time. She knew that wagons were on fire and burning and others were already smoldering; however, she had no time to observe closely and identify those who had been hit by fire, bullet, or arrow. She kept working diligently with her pistol until suddenly the Indians seemed to just disappear from her sight. They had taken a real beating this time. Nevertheless, Tyler knew only too well that they would leave for now, go and count their losses, and then regroup and hit them again while they were down and trying to salvage their items of worth.

In the meantime, they hurriedly counted their losses. There were eight wounded and seven dead. They waited nervously for hours, but the Indians never came back. Tyler thought they might have gone for more reinforcements. Everyone paid close attention to their surroundings and watched across the land where the unexpected attack had first originated. Hours and hours tortuously and distressfully passed by, but the Indians never returned or were seen again. They surely must have gone for more reinforcements. The nervous sitting and waiting was not a good sign for the wagon train.

Tyler said they should prepare to leave and travel as fast as possible. He didn't think they should linger around any longer, especially when Fort Laramie was not too far away. Joshua posted riders on either side of the wagons and riders behind. Everyone knew exactly what to do in case of another attack. Tyler reminded them to keep their rifles and pistols loaded at all times. "We're going to go ahead as though nothing has happened even though we all know better. Everyone needs to think and be calm before they act. Foolish actions have sometimes cost a lot of lives simply because fear got the best of a person and they reacted to that fright in the wrong way. If we see Indians, we will not shoot unless they are attacking and shooting at us first. We have already lost a number of our people to various accidents and now the attack. Everyone knows what to do in case we are attacked again. Hopefully, we can make it to Fort Laramie before another attack."

"Stretch out! Keep them moving!"

As they began to advance, nervous eyes flitted here and there, always on guard and watching every little move, hearing every noise as though it were amplified many times over. The horses and mules even seemed to sense a foreboding atmosphere surrounding them, and their steps were nervous and quick. Tyler rode ahead with

MARCY

two other men constantly watching their surroundings and the horizons ahead of them for even the slightest movement or possible warning sign of any trouble. It proved to be an eerie and unsettling ride, as the Indians seemed to have disappeared off the face of the earth.

Two days away from the fort, it seemed as if hell's gates had opened up again. Piercing screams, chilling shouts ringing, and bullets whizzing close by heads caused frightened travelers to scurry about to form a circle, a circle which everyone prayed would lend a degree of protection for them. The Indians came fast now, formed in a group of about thirty or thirty-five of them this time. They brought a bigger group hoping to inflict more pain, death, and misery on the wagon train. Again, it was going to be hard to keep all eyes watching in all the directions they were coming from, as they seemed to be sweeping in from the north, the south, the east, and the west and making a large circle around the wagons.

Hearing the horrible cries of the Indians, Pa Brewster yelled at the girls, "Beth, Marcy, into the wagon and quickly!" Marcy manned a rifle this time and proved to be a very good shot. Alisha was beside her husband as he was crouched down under the back of the wagon. Alisha loaded the pistols and rifles for him as quickly as her shaking hands could retrieve the bullets from the ammo box. Beth was horrified, and again she wept openly and sobbed aloud with great frustration and fright. She crouched down in the small space of floor as best she could as her slender body trembled. Marcy could pay no attention to Beth at this critical point. She was perched on a box close to the opening of the canvas and firing her rifle as fast as she could.

Beth heard a creaking movement on the wagon seat. She cautiously raised her head from beneath the blanket Marcy had placed over her head and peered toward the seat of the wagon. Her heart beat wildly as her eyes envisioned a wild, painted Indian with a large knife held tightly in his hand. Beth, near the point of fainting, found enough strength to scream, "Oh, Marcy! Marcy!" She turned just in time to see the Indian and fired twice. He fell backward and onto the ground right next to the wagon. Beth's face had turned a ghostly white, and she was sobbing so hard she could hardly speak or control her voice. "I want to go home, Marcy! I want to go home! I hate this place." She wailed and cried out in distress and pain.

The wagons had been pinned down for over an hour. Several had been wounded and hurt, and they didn't know how much longer they could stand, especially if the Indians regrouped and came at them again with more flaming arrows to burn wagons and possessions. Fires had been started; some had been quickly extinguished, but others had not been so fortunate as to quickly put out their fire and had suffered more damage. The fires had taken their toll on several wagons and families. They had great loss and were visibly shaken and distraught.

Suddenly, Beth stopped crying and became very quiet. She tilted her head toward the opening of the canvas. "Listen, Marcy. I hear a strange noise." The Indians began to move away from them in all directions very rapidly.

They could see dust flying from the far northwest. They could hear the beautiful faint sound of a bugle floating over the wind. They knew help and salvation of safety were now just minutes away. They began to help the injured and check their losses once again just as they had done earlier in the previous attack. Thank God, only one had died, a young boy by the name of Andrew Walls. Several had been hurt from minor to major injuries, and those with the most severe injuries would need to be tended to first.

The blue-uniformed soldiers arrived at last. They had been on patrol when they spotted the smoke of the wagons and heard the firing of rifles. The sergeant stated, "We have been chasing this particular band of renegade Cheyenne for over six months. They follow the lead of one called Blue Feather, who has created serious problems even in his own tribe. He is not well liked or even tolerated by very many. We'll give you an escort into Fort Laramie and any immediate assistance that we can provide for you." Needless to say, the help from the soldiers was most welcome, but the most-appreciated sight anyone had beheld in these long, hard days was the grounds of the fort. Joshua declared they would have to spend at least one or maybe two days to inventory their supplies, repair the damages, and care for those injured.

Joshua had only discovered as they neared the fort that Mrs. Hensen had been wounded rather badly. She had lost a great and dangerous amount of blood. A bullet had ricocheted and hit her in the right rib cage. The bullet had done its damage to her and was now lodged in

MARLENE WISE

her deeply, causing her to bleed profusely. Her husband had never realized that she had been injured, as he was too preoccupied in trying to save their lives and their belongings. In the midst of battle, he had not even heard the deep moan of his wife. She had leaned against the wagon wheel for support and continued to reload his rifle for him until the loud shooting had stopped. Then she gave a deep moan again and grabbed her chest as she leaned forward and passed out from the burning and excruciating pain.

When she next opened her eyes, a well-worn brown-faced soldier with white wavy hair called Dr. Holiday was at her bedside. He had removed the bullet and bandaged her severe wound. He feared for her life, as she had lost so much blood before he had even been able to operate on her, and then she had lost more during the surgery. The surgery had taken a long time because it was a difficult procedure to perform under such extreme conditions. Mrs. Hensen slept fitfully through the night, and by morning, she had a high fever and was delirious. She kept calling for her husband. "Ben? Ben?" she would mumble. She also kept mumbling something about Bible and Ben being left alone.

The doctor had left Mary Henson's bedside to go restock his medical bag and obtain some new bandages. While in the next room speaking with Ben about her condition, they heard a big thud. It sounded like a chair falling over and hitting the floor. Both men quickly ran to the room and found Mary on the floor holding on to the overturned chair.

MARCY

Ben knelt down by her, crying softly, "No, Mary! No! You must stay in bed now!" As he picked her up and started back to the bed, he nodded his head at the doctor and said in a trembling voice, "She is really bleeding profusely again, Doctor."

Mary tried to speak in slow, anguishing breaths. "Ben … Ben … you must go … go … on now. I will … not … not be ab … able to go." She reached out her small, thin, shaking hand to him, and he kissed it ever so gently.

"Mary, you need to rest," he said tenderly.

"Oh, Ben." Mary formed her lips to say something, but she labored even more now to just breathe evenly. Her breath came in short, labored gasps, causing a look of twisted pain upon her sweet, innocent face. She paused as though trying to muster more strength and breathe one more time so she could speak her peace. Then suddenly, with great determination, she spoke these broken words to her husband. "I love you, Ben. God keep you always." He heard only a faint sigh and then observed a look of peace on her sweet face. She struggled no more for those last breaths but lay in perfect quietness and the stillness of death.

Dr. Holiday stepped closer to Mary and placed his fingers on her neck and then on her wrist. His sad, tired eyes beheld Mr. Hensen as he slowly shook his head no. He placed his large weary old hands on Ben's shaking shoulders and said as tenderly as possible, "Ben, she's gone. She's gone to her eternal rest. She has no more pain now and has gone to see her creator. I'm sorry that I could not have been of more assistance. I did all that I knew to do for her."

Ben knelt by the bed and held Mary close to him for a few minutes, weeping quietly in great sadness. Through teary eyes, he gently whispered in her ear, "It will never be the same without you, Mary. My dream has been shattered, but I must go on. There is no place to go but forward. I would rather die myself than leave you in this wild and remote country that took your life. Oh, Mary, I shall miss you. You were my sunshine; indeed you were." He stepped back and slowly pulled the sheet over her, seeing her lovely face for the last time. "Dr. Holiday," he inquired softly, "will you tell Joshua of Mary's passing, please? I wish to be by myself for a little while."

"Yes, I will do so, Ben," answered Dr. Holiday somberly, wishing that he could somehow make the pain a little easier for Ben.

Pa Brewster was with Joshua when Dr. Holiday came to bear the news of Mary's passing. Pa Brewster shook his head and said, "So many friends seem to be passing on before they reach their destination. Alisha and the girls will be sorry to hear of her passing."

When Pa Brewster came in for lunch, he told his family about Mary. Marcy was very sorrowful. Marcy had been helping Mary make herself a new gingham dress. Marcy's eyes were much better than Mary's, and she could make the tiny stitches much better. Often when they stopped for short periods of time or in the late evenings, Marcy would make her way to Mary and Ben's wagon and sew for a while. The dress was almost finished except for the hem. The last time they had stopped, Marcy told Mary she would take the dress and finish it as soon as possible. Knowing Mary would have to be buried tomorrow, Marcy decided to finish the dress so Mary could be buried in it. Marcy held the dress close to her when she had finished it almost as if she were hugging Mary. She rubbed over the smooth blue gingham and thought how pretty Mary would have looked in it with her bright blue eyes. She somberly took it over to the ladies who would be preparing Mary's body for burial. The ladies thanked Marcy, and she left feeling blue and depressed.

Eight men were chosen for burial detail. The hard black earth must be opened up and prepared to receive two friends, Andrew and Mary. The graves would need to be dug deep, and the bodies would be rolled in gray army blankets. As soon as the earth hugged their bodies with the mounds of freshly dug dirt, the train would be forced to move on, leaving their loved ones to the final resting place chosen for them. Andrew and Mary had unwillingly and prematurely claimed this small plot of earth as their very own before they could reach the rich valleys of California or Oregon.

After Mary's passing, Ben had disappeared into the quiet of his own wagon and stayed until he had completed a piece of work that was especially for his sweet Mary. The next day when it was time for the burial, Ben walked slowly to the grave. He carried with him a large bundle wrapped in an old blanket. Curious eyes sadly focused on him as he took his place beside the head of the grave.

MARLENE WISE

Throughout the ceremony, Ben wept quietly and hugged the bundle close to him. When the ceremony was over, he knelt on the hard ground and began to lovingly unwrap the curious and mysterious lump in his hands. He gently lifted out two boards made in the form of a square. They had been smoothed down and carefully carved with names, dates, and inscriptions. In the corner of Mary's board, he had carved a little cross. It read, "Mary Jane Hensen, 1825–1862, died in Indian attack. My sunshine. My love." On the young boy's marker, he had carved another cross but placed it in the middle. It simply read, "Andrew Walls, 1847–1862, Indian attack, a brave fighter to the end." The soldiers were amazed at this work. The carvings were unusually well done and beautiful for this rugged country. Ben had retrieved a wooden plank from his own wagon to make the markers. Most usually, markers out here were only two rough and uneven sticks placed in the shape of a cross or a rock with names crudely imprinted on them. Ben Hensen was a wood carver and mighty handy with his tools. He felt as though he was leaving a little piece of himself if Mary could have a carved marker placed on her grave.

After the markers were placed, everyone just stood for a moment and stared at the grave.

Then, in a quivering voice, Marcy began to sing Rock of Ages. One after another soon chimed in. Marcy chose this song because Mary used to sing it around the wagon when she worked or traveled.

It was difficult and trying to get everybody started moving again. Burying the dead always took a toll on

MARCY

everyone's spirits. For several days gloom hovered over them quite thickly. But Joshua had to lay aside all thoughts and move toward the South Pass immediately. No one wanted to linger too long and not make South Pass before the snow and cold weather, or they might have more friends to bury and leave behind.

The continuing journey led them into a valley along the side of the North Platte River. They would eventually have to cross the river in order to get to South Pass. The weather had turned miserable with a heavy soaking rain, making it hard to see at times. While the train slowly went up in elevation, the cooler winds were starting to chill everyone. They plodded on through cold rain and thick black mud in very rough and hard terrain. They all must go forward no matter how difficult or how hard the trek would be on them if they wished to reach their destination of dreams and hopes for a new future.

RANEY'S DISCORD

Marcy suggested that Beth get inside the wagon and ride for a while because her small-framed body was completely soaked. She shivered and shook with the cold wind beating upon her tired and weary body. This was quite a change from the hot broiling sun beating down upon their heads and the sweat running down their cheeks. Pa Brewster had taken over the driving of the wagon, as the terrain was becoming a little rougher and harder to handle the mules and the loaded wagon. He had traded places with Alisha and helped her upon gentle old Striker. Alisha was not afraid of Striker even though she had heard the stories of the times when he had reared up in anger and lashed out at some people. Alisha was certainly not the horseman that Pa Brewster or Marcy was, but she got along as she let Striker do his job and lead the way. He walked gallantly along beside the mules and horses as though he were keeping in step with them. The big, sturdy, and large-boned mules didn't seem to mind plodding in the cool rain.

It was August, and they had previously suffered their days of torturous heat and searing hot winds. The rain created other problems for them while they pulled their heavy load, but not that of the unbearable heat. The heavy rain began to let up some and fall as a gentle light rain, so Tyler wisely decided it would be best to camp about two miles from the river in case of flooding. At daylight he could find the best possible crossing that would afford all as much safety as possible. Joshua chose a place where a small stream ran into the river and there was room enough for all the wagons in the surrounding area. They circled the wagons and prepared for the evening that was about to engulf them like the gray fog that rose from the lakes back home in Minnesota. Tyler had taken what daylight was left and scouted as much as he dared before dark fell. When he returned, he was wet, cold, and hungry; however, he arranged a private conference with Joshua to fill him in on what he had observed and his thoughts of the trail farther on down for a few miles.

Tyler, shaking his head, stated, "It doesn't look good, Joshua. The river is swollen and irritated, and the banks have washed out in several places. The normal crossing doesn't look appealing either. If I read my weather right, we're in for more rain for a couple of days." He sighed heavily. Joshua dashed his half cup of lukewarm coffee across the ground in disgust.

"It's too big a risk for everyone to try to go across in these conditions," muttered Joshua. "We'll lose lives, not to mention wagons, stock, and precious supplies that we can't afford to lose," he snapped as he kicked at the wagon wheel.

MARLENE WISE

Tyler shifted nervously from one foot to the other as though this was helping his thought process. "There may be another way, but it would take a day to get set up; perhaps it could be a little shorter time if we had a lot of help," he suggested. They got some fresh hot coffee and food and went into Joshua's wagon. As they drank their coffee, Tyler told him about a scout named Adam Bryce who had been in a similar predicament. "His way out was to build a large log raft to cross the river. Men pulled the raft with ropes from either side of the bank," he stated. "It appears that this may be our only rational hope now. We'll call a meeting this evening and inform the people of what has to be done, and we'll also choose our workers." He sighed with great tiredness and weariness in his voice.

After discussing the situation and being told why they had to go this route, all seemed to be in agreement. When Joshua and Tyler asked for volunteers, only one man stepped forward to say his piece and protest. "Surely," complained Raney McBride, "there must be a crossing somewhere. Look at all the time we would waste, time which we cannot spare. We shouldn't be forced to do such a thing. Why don't you just admit that after the other river crossing, you're afraid? You promised to get us through, but now you're going back on your word!" Surprise filled both the faces of Marcy and Beth because it was old Snake Eyes who had stepped forward. Why would he even try to defy Joshua? "Tyler, I scouted about by myself today, and it didn't look that bad to me. You know, some of us have deadlines to meet, and we can't

MARCY

waste precious time with your little games. You hired on to take us through; now how about doing your job?" he asked very sarcastically and with a tinge of bitterness in his voice.

Joshua threw his cup on the ground and stomped over in front of Raney. "Oh really, Raney? How many trains have you taken across rivers, flooded rivers? I'll answer for you. None! It's my responsibility to get people, stock, and supplies over safely. I'm the wagon master, and what I say goes. You will follow all rules just like everyone else," he said in Raney's angry red face.

Raney shifted his weight and looked around at the crowd of people gathered. "Well, I know there are others who feel as I do. So speak up! Do you want to sit here till the water is so high that we are trapped? Then we can't reach South Pass in time. We're all going to lose our lives over a fear of a little water," he said, as though needling Tyler. "Who is standing with me?" Finally, after a long silent pause, Mr. Charlton, Mr. Pence, and the Baron family stepped out and stood by Raney.

Joshua knew the longer Raney talked the more he would win over. Joshua stepped over and in a very testy and disgusted voice said, "I want everyone to go over to their own wagon and get some sleep. Tomorrow you will be thinking more rationally."

Indignantly, Raney walked over to Joshua with his hands on his hips. "Charlton and I are pulling our wagons out of line and crossing over now! There's still time to travel at least another hour, and I think we should avail ourselves of this time. We certainly don't have to listen to the likes of a—"

But before he could finish his sentence, Tyler had swung around and struck him, hitting him on the right side of his jaw. Raney, losing his balance from the punch, spun half around and hit the ground with a thud. Tyler retorted sharply, "Go to your wagon and sleep on your stupid idea!" Raney pulled himself up to his knees and brushed the dirt from his shirt. His eyes glared like that of a wild animal, and he ground his teeth in anger. Suddenly, with a shaking hand, he pulled his gun from its holster and aimed at Tyler's back.

Marcy stepped from the shadow of a wagon and screamed, "No, Raney!" As she did, she shot at Raney and nicked him just across his left shoulder. Raney's gun fell from his hand and hit the ground as Tyler whirled around like a rattlesnake with his gun drawn and ready to fire. Raney groveled in the dirt trying to retrieve his fallen gun, but Tyler had rapidly kicked the gun away from his reach.

"It would be just like you to shoot a man in the back," he snapped at him. Hearing the gunshot, the others came running to see what had happened. The commotion and loud talk had also brought Joshua over to the scene, and he was furious.

"Take him to the brig in the back of the supply wagon. Maybe a day or two will cool him off and do him some good," offered Joshua. As Tyler and Jeb dragged Raney off to the wagon, they paused, and Tyler thanked Marcy for what she had done.

Raney curled his pouting lip and snarled, "I might have known it would be you. Lucky for me that you're such a poor shot." Marcy flinched as a stream of anger riveted through every bone in her body.

"No, Raney. I could have shot you through the heart! I was only being kind to a coward who likes to shoot people in the back."

As Tyler dragged him on, he looked back and shouted, "You'll be sorry, missy, for sticking your nose where it doesn't belong!"

Jeb stopped and twisted Raney's arm a wee bit and exclaimed, "Raney, shut up, or we may take what you just said as a threat against Miss Marcy. How would you like to spend a long time in the brig? I know your sort, Raney. You are perpetually hunting for trouble, consistently in with the wrong fellows, and always on the wrong side. Someday you'll get killed for your pig-headedness and cocky ways. Now come on, or do we have to drag you all the way to the wagon?"

"Wait! Don't I get some medical attention first? Or had you forgotten that little snip just shot me?" he testily inquired. Tyler reached up, grabbed his shirt, and ripped it open.

"Why are you so worried, Raney? It's just a puny nick," he stated flatly. "Jeb, I'll watch him, and you go ask Beams, the cook, to bring something to put on this 'vicious' wound," he said with a slight chuckle. Jeb sauntered down to the cook's wagon and found him already in sleep land. He thought he'd permit him to take his rest, as he had to rise earlier than everyone else. So, he stirred and poked around looking for the medicine box. A metal pan fell, clanking and shattering the stillness of night. Old Beams flew out from under the wagon with his rifle in hand ready to defend his cook wagon.

He pointed it at Jeb and hollered, "What are you doing in my cook wagon?"

Jeb quickly identified himself. "Beams! It's me…Jeb!"

"Well, what do you want poking around at this time of night? A feller could get a belly full of lead!" he sleepily exclaimed. Jeb explained the situation to him. "Oh, that fella, uh? Well, never did like him anyway. His beady eyes tell me a whole lot," he muttered. "Wait here!" He went to a miniature wooden box and took out some cloth. He poured some liquid in a cup and said, "Here, take this. Pour it over the wound and use this as a bandage."

Jeb smelled the cup and looked at his old friend Beams. "This smells like a shot of—"

"Shh!" he warned. "Now go on, and don't you be sipping any of that stuff. It's medicinal use only."

"This smells too good for the likes of him, but I'm sure he won't get any infection if this is used," said Jeb.

"Scat! Now go on! I have to rise and soar even before the birds," grumbled old Beams. Jeb returned with the "medicine." He ambled around behind Raney, pulled his shirt back, and poured the "liquid" medicine on the nicked skin. Raney howled like a bear with a thorn in his behind and tried to wriggle free.

"Here!" snapped Jeb. "This cloth is for a bandage to put over that 'big, gaping wound' to keep out the dirt, and perhaps it won't get infected," he stated in a jesting way.

Tyler and Jeb locked Raney in the wagon brig and

then started for their own wagons. Tyler laughed and said, "I wonder what he would do if he was really wounded?"

"He may be before this trip is over if he doesn't have a change of attitude," declared Jeb sourly.

Tyler agreed and stated, "It only takes one person like him to bust up a wagon train and cause real problems."

DEFIANT RIVERS AND PASSES

Marcy had been awake well before dawn. Turning restlessly in her bed, she decided to get up. Her mind began to think about the river crossing. She remembered another crossing that hadn't had a very happy ending. Marcy said a prayer that all would go well today and no lives would be lost. She dressed and went out to saddle Striker. Marcy wanted to go see how the river looked this morning, as yesterday it was a frightening sight to behold.

Marcy stopped by Liza's wagon to check on her. Liza was up making biscuits and coffee. Liza invited Marcy to stay a while and have breakfast with her. But Marcy declined the invitation and said, "Maybe another morning sometime soon." Full light had already opened up the new day, so Marcy headed Striker toward the river. She soon came in view of the river but kept her distance because she knew how cantankerous and deceiving a swollen river could be. Again as she sat upon Striker and watched the rolling river go by, she asked God for strength and endurance for the men who would have a difficult job in cutting, trimming, and hauling enough logs and timber for such a big task. She then wheeled Striker around and headed toward her own wagon. She knew her mother would probably have breakfast ready and her father would be with the men making plans for cutting lumber.

As she passed by the wagons on her way back, she smelled the familiar aroma of biscuits, bacon, gravy, coffee, flapjacks, or corn dodgers. Her stomach began to growl with a great hunger, so she hurried on thinking about her own breakfast.

Beth woke to the sound of men's voices, the rattling noise of saws, hammers, and tools being taken from the wagons. The men gathered around the wagon master to find out their assigned duties. Joshua chose six men as captains of six groups, and then each captain was to choose helpers and start on their project to aid the building of a raft large enough to carry a wagon across the river. Trees had to be cut, trimmed, and hauled into place. The raft had to be put together, ropes collected, and small logs had to be found and then cut for the sides to haul across the livestock a few at a time. If all performed well together, they could start across today. The men toiled feverishly all morning long and soon had enough trimmed logs to be hauled and drug down by mule and oxen to attach them together.

The men were fatigued and utterly exhausted. The tedious work had caused them to have an unquenchable thirst. It made them irritable and touchy as already several

79

MARLENE WISE

arguments and fights had taken place before the work was finished. But finally, when the last rope was put in place and the raft was ready for use, it was almost noon, and the men were more than ready to eat the meals the ladies had prepared for them.

Joshua said for everyone to eat and prepare themselves to move on. "In short time, we'll send the first wagon across," he said. The tired, starving men had great appetites, and they cherished the few precious moments that they would be afforded to sit and rest and eat their meal in peace. So it was, after about an hour's rest, the men heard the announcement. "Let's go! Make sure everything is fastened down and put inside of the wagons. Each family will go with their own wagon and be responsible for their own belongings."

Marcy quickly began to help gather items and assist in making ready their wagon. She needed to be with Beth inside the wagon when the raft went across, as Beth was quite nervous about this unknown expedition over the churning waters. When all was about ready and the wagons loaded, Tyler gathered the travelers together and said to them, "The difficult part is yet to come, as we need at least eight volunteers to go across to the other side to secure the ropes and help tow the raft. Well, that's part of my job. So I'm man number one; now we need seven more strong, able-bodied men. We will not choose for you because this must be your decision and yours alone. As you all know, the crossing is dangerous on a horse and even more so on foot when the water is so high."

The silence seemed to grow louder than any noise

80

MARCY

they had heard along the trail. Worried faces cast looks of doubt and uncertainty at each other. Eventually, in the back of the crowd, one man raised his hand and said, "I'll go." He was a large heavy-boned man with broad shoulders and large hands. He was called Big Jake by his friends and family. His towering stature told the whole story how he came by his name. Jake seemed to break the quiet cycle as four others quickly volunteered their services too. Nevertheless, while others arranged their wagons for the crossing, the six men and two stragglers who took their time in deciding to go crossed the river two at a time. As the first two started across, they tied a length of rope to themselves. The ropes were to serve two purposes. First, it would be a very safe way to save lives should the horses lose footing and fall into the swift running river. Second, if they reached the other side successfully, the rope would be used to pull the raft across while ropes from the other bank kept the raft from going downstream.

Midway across the river, Danner noticed a movement in the water but thought it to be just some debris floating by. At the instant he realized it was alive, so did his horse. The moving object heading toward the horse and rider was a long snake thrashing about and looking for some solid ground. More than likely, he had been washed off a log upstream by the swift current. Danner's horse spooked and began to try to rear up in the water and distance itself from the snake. The horse continued to thrash about until he had knocked Danner into the water. The poor frightened horse turned abruptly and started downstream

81

MARLENE WISE

in great confusion while all the time fighting the current for sure and solid footing. Big Jake ran along the bank and threw a rope over the horse's head and began to pull him toward the bank. As Jake pulled harder and harder, the terror-stricken horse began to fight even harder not understanding what was happening to him. While Jake worked to save the horse, others were pulling on Danner's rope to save and rescue him. Luckily, both man and beast were rescued from the cold water without harm, only a case of severe fright. Not far away, Tyler drew his pistol and shot the snake that by this time had made it to the debris-covered bank. Tyler had no intentions of a repeat performance when the others started across because it was now time for the first wagon to be rolled carefully up on the raft.

Small smooth logs were placed through all the wheels to keep them from rolling off the raft. It was a long and tedious chore, but it had to be done for the safety of all. Pa Brewster decided their wagon would go across second, and they pulled out of line and prepared to do so. Many were nervous and very apprehensive about the crossing in this manner. Alisha, Beth, and Marcy sat in the back of the wagon, and Pa Brewster sat on the front seat.

As the raft started across, the ride was not as pleasant as was expected. It jerked and bobbed back and forth along with the waves that snipped viciously at the raft. Marcy could not believe it—she was becoming a little sick at her stomach. Her head ached, and she didn't feel well at all. Suddenly she felt the raft hit the bank on the other side, and her stomach seemed to push up nearly into her throat. As soon as she could, she scrambled down off the wagon and headed for a place with lots of little bushes and violently threw up. Marcy felt a little weak but was glad to feel solid ground under her feet. This had never happened to her before, so she was a little embarrassed. She only hoped that everyone else was too busy to take notice of what had just happened.

The men were hollering to grab the ropes. The crossing was at a very wide place in the river, and it took time to navigate properly and safely. In no time, they were rolling the wagon off the raft and preparing to pull it back across for the next readied wagon. All of the wagons were all safely taken across to solid ground. It took nearly all day for all of the wagons to be ferried across the river.

Marcy sighed a breath of relief at having this crossing behind them. She hoped there would be no more incidents like this for everyone to go through. However, she knew there would probably be other things they would have to go through that were just as frightening before they reached their destination. After the crossing, the Brewsters re-hitched their wagon and made their way to the campsite that Tyler and his men had chosen for the safety of all concerned. Shortly thereafter, dusk began to settle upon the wagons before the final family cleared the river. Camp would have to be made a couple of miles farther from the river to ensure safety for all. Everyone was impatiently awaiting nightfall when rest for weary bodies would finally come.

However, to the dismay of all, a gloomy and dismal morning was ushered in with looming gray and black

MARLENE WISE

clouds hanging overhead like laundry on the lines. Before the day was over, they would find themselves trudging along in the rain and mud again. An occasional march in the rain and black sticky mud was not really such a bitter pill to deal with, as happenings of bygone days proved that other things could be more painful and annoying than a little rain, even though at times it was a great nuisance. They were gaining ground now, and hopefully before long, they would reach the destined South Pass, which would prove a challenge. South Pass was high up in the Rocky Mountains where it had been known to snow early and cover the pass with a white carpet for all to trudge upon. However, August still lingered on with very hot days and bone-chilling cold nights. Hopefully, snow wouldn't fall too early this year before the trip could be completed. There would be many other afflictions and trials to endure, so they didn't need the hardship of extreme cold and snow to battle and deal with for themselves or the livestock.

Marcy reflected about Joshua's warning concerning Arapaho country to the north of them, Ute country to the south, and Cheyenne to the north-northeast made everyone a bit edgy. No one wished to tangle with warring savage Indians again. "So, let me remind you, you may see hunting parties on either side of us. We don't fire at them unless we are being attacked first. Not every Indian you see is out for blood and scalps. If anyone provokes anything in this pass without a good reason, we could all be annihilated. Keep your weapons at hand's length just in case they're needed. Oh, Tyler, it's probably necessary to go find Raney and make sure he understands my orders. He consistently likes to disagree with what I say."

"Now that you mention it, I haven't seen Raney since we entered South Pass. He's made himself scarce since we let him out of the brig."

"Has anyone seen Raney around?" Joshua asked.

Mr. Charlton spoke first. "He was up around daybreak, loaded his horse with some supplies, and quietly rode off due north. I figured he was doing some more of his own 'scouting' again."

Marcy spoke up and said, "I was up around daybreak riding down to the river. I did not see Raney anywhere at this time of day; neither did I see his horse."

Joshua and Tyler looked up as they heard a group of angry people talking with loud and upset voices. "Well, I say it was him! He's a big thief! He's the only one gone, isn't he?" asked portly Mr. Cage.

"But we don't know for sure," replied Alice Bradey.

Mrs. Maggie retorted in her high-pitched voice, "I do, Mrs. Bradey. He's been strange since he joined up with us in Independence."

"Hey! Break it up! What's all the argument and commotion? We have work to do!" declared Joshua in a fit of disgust and annoyance.

"It's that Raney fellow. Joshua, I don't think he's coming back to join us anytime soon. He stole supplies and some personal articles out of several wagons. I think he intends to travel on without us," commented Mr. Cage indignantly.

"Okay! Everybody who had things stolen, make me a

MARLENE WISE

list and bring it to me. There's nothing we can do about Raney now," said Joshua. He shook his finger at them and sighed. "And listen to me, if anyone gets the same stupid idea that Raney had, I would strongly suggest some serious thought about your intentions. Raney doesn't have a prayer out there alone. All possible odds are against him to reach his destination alive. There's a lot more strength in numbers than being out there all alone. All I can say is may God be merciful to his soul if he's captured by any of those Indians out there, especially the Cheyenne. He could hardly bear the nick that Marcy put on his shoulder a while back. It is too horrible to think about the torture he may have to face alone."

The pass showed them just how cantankerous it could be. Wagon wheels came off, axles broke, the weary livestock stumbled over the heavy loads that they bore, and one mule stepped into a hole and broke his leg. He had to be mercifully shot immediately and removed from the pathway. Each time Marcy heard a shot that took the life of an animal, she cringed, and gooseflesh always ran over her body as though she was cold. Nevertheless, she knew there was no other way to handle this. Knowing it had to be done to alleviate any suffering did little to console her. A mule or any animal could not be left to suffer in pain. They certainly could not walk on a broken leg over the rough terrain that lay ahead. So, someone had to do the kind and decent thing even when they really didn't want to. Life had to be cut short for a few who had so faithfully labored to bring the travelers thus far.

Ropes had to be tied on the back of the wagons to ease

MARCY

them down the steep slopes so they didn't go down too fast and too wild to control. The ropes frayed and broke on the Jades' wagon, relieving all the pressure of speed from the wagon, and it began to rumble too fast down the slope. The horses, in utter panic, broke loose and ran one way leaving the wagon to tumble wildly in the opposite direction, smashing against rocks and crevices. It landed at the bottom of a ravine, crushed and upside down. Screams and cries of those remaining in the wagon could be heard from worried onlookers as the wagon bounded and careened over brushy and rocky terrain until it came to a halt at the bottom of the ravine.

The Hollisters had seen Mrs. Jade tumble out with her child wrapped in a quilt. She flew out of the wagon and hit the ground and lay very still, not moving at all. The frightened child began crying desperately and trying to move about, so they knew there was some life from the horrible accident. Mr. Jade had jumped to the left and landed in brush and piles of rocks. Tyler strained and squinted his eyes trying to see any movement, but he greatly feared the scene they would find when they reached the bottom of the ravine. Cautiously, Tyler and Joshua made their way down the steep slope, which protruded with sharp rocks and uneven terrain making it hard to find good footing. They quickened their steps as much as possible in order to reach Mrs. Jade first. Upon pulling the blanket back, they both gave a sigh of relief when they found that the two-year-old girl was not harmed too much but was more in shock from the hard fall. On the outside, they could only see scratches

MARLENE WISE

and bumps but didn't know how she fared from probable internal injuries. Mrs. Jade was turned over as gently and as easily as the men could feasibly do, but in doing so, she winced in great pain and suffering as her right arm and leg were broken. Her face and body were bloodied with cuts and bruises.

Joshua checked out Mr. Jade and found that he was breathing but knocked unconscious. At present, things didn't look too good for him, but at least he was alive, and he might have a fighting chance. The family was transferred to waiting wagons that had already passed down the slope in safety. The little girl of the Jades, Julie, was put in the care of Mrs. Hardy. Joshua had set bones many times, but he always cringed and dreaded the thought of setting a woman's bones. But regardless, he always felt the pain as if it were his own and grimaced as he did what had to be done. Several people helped to hold Mrs. Jade down while he set her leg and arm. She screamed with anguish and tried to writhe free of the hands holding her down and of the horrible pain penetrating the bones of her body.

Marcy stood next to her mother at the top of the hill with her arms wrapped tightly around her mother's shoulders. Marcy hated to hear the screams of another person's pain knowing she could do nothing to help or cause the pain to go away. Marcy finally relaxed her tense body when she heard the voice of Mrs. Jade stop crying and moaning. Mercifully, she had collapsed and passed out when she could stand the fierce pain no longer. Joshua mixed some laudanum from the medicinal box and told Amy Finley, "Give her some when she comes to, as she'll be in great and severe pain. As we travel, if she is experiencing more anguish and discomfort, give her some more. But keep watch over her." He advised, "We don't want to overdo it." Her husband, Bill Jade, was cleaned up and placed in the wagon with his wife until he regained consciousness. Amy stayed with both of her patients and caringly nursed them. If Bill lived, it would be a miracle from a greater power from on high, the Almighty himself.

After much hard and strenuous climbing, Joshua presented himself to the others at the rim of the slope. Out of breath, he said, "I know this has been a shock for all of us. We've done all that we could for Jades." One lady questioned as to what had happened to the Jades because not everyone could see to the bottom of the steep incline. Joshua spoke truthfully as he related the details, and then he tried gently to remind everyone that they must move on even though a great tragedy had befallen them. "The days are shorter now, and we must make every day count in our favor," he advised them. "Please, move the next wagon into place and tie on all new ropes," he uttered strongly. He asked each one to thoroughly check the wagon and the ropes before attaching them. "Make sure you've done everything to be as safe as you can possibly be."

With nothing more to say, every person on top of the slope stood in silent cold fear staring off in the direction of the accident. No one budged; their gazes could not be taken from the battered and broken wagon that lay

MARLENE WISE

in shambles at the bottom of the ravine. Some shivered at the thought that this could have been their family in this situation and their loved ones who had been hurt and had bones broken. With these thoughts in mind, no one desired to be first after such a horrible accident. "We must move forward because there is no other way over the mountains, and it is too far to go around. Winter would be upon us before we could reach our destination. We surely don't want to be caught in a deadly blizzard with cold freezing temperatures. Neither the livestock nor any of us could survive a winter storm in this pass. We do not have enough supplies, so we must not remain in this place too long. It is onward or die here," Joshua said sternly.

"What is it going to be? Tell me!" he asked them. Tyler and Jeb came riding up extremely exhausted.

"What's the delay?" inquired Tyler, almost out of breath. He glanced at Joshua and then realized what the problem was. "Has anyone paid any attention to the low hanging dark clouds to the far north?" As he wheeled his horse around to start downwards, he turned slightly and slowly in the saddle and strongly suggested that everyone get started as quickly as possible and try to put the horrible past behind them.

Knowing that Tyler spoke the truth, Abe Miller spoke up and said, "Our wagon will go next!" He quickly darted about making ready to go. But Sarah, his wife, ran and grabbed Abe roughly by the arm.

"No, Abe!" she wailed. "We're not going! We have to think of the children!"

MARCY

"Sarah! That's what I'm doing. I am thinking of the children," he rebuked her sharply.

"No, you're not! I won't go! I won't go!" she yelled like a crazy wild woman as she beat the chest of her husband. "We'll all die trying such a foolish thing. Why can't we go around? There has to be a better route for us!"

"Sarah! Sarah!" her husband said while shaking her back and forth. "If there was a better way, surely Joshua would know about it." He sighed with disgust. Sarah crumpled to the ground like an old rag doll and began to weep loudly and travail at her dire situation.

"Oh!" she moaned. "I wish we had never come! I hate this land! I hate this land with all my heart!"

Marcy and Alisha came over and put their arms around Sarah. "Sarah, it will be okay," Marcy said soothingly. "Look, we're going down now. If we make it down all right, you follow behind us. I know you can do this, Sarah. It is hard, but you must be brave now for your children and husband." With nothing more they could say to Sarah to reassure her, the Brewsters' wagon went down next with no problems.

Abe went to the edge of the slope and declared loudly, "Come on, Sarah! We can do it! We can!" Everything was made ready, and Sarah unwillingly got into the wagon with help from her husband. She refused to look out or even move. She sat on the floor of the wagon and held her children to her bosom tightly. Her frightened eyes were closed so tightly that it caused her head to throb and ache painfully. It seemed an eternity going down the bumpy grade.

MARLENE WISE

The jostling, swaying wagon suddenly smoothed out and came to level ground with no mishaps. Sarah had not yet realized that they had safely made it down the slope. Abe turned on the seat toward Sarah and bellowed out, "Sarah! Sarah! We made it down without incident." But still, Sarah in her high state of fear was not able to yet comprehend what had just taken place. The children began to stir, and she grabbed at them. "Don't move, children!" she commanded as she swatted at them. Then it dawned on her, only after she opened her eyes wide enough to really see, that they had stopped moving. She listened intently and heard no motion, no creaking of wheels, no movement at all.

Marcy was climbing up on the front seat of the wagon. "Sarah, you made it! You're alive and well," she chattered. Marcy was completely bubbling over with great joy. Sarah's body seemed to go limp, and she bowed her head and wept, relieving her body of all the pent-up nervous tensions and emotions. Sarah was finally able to get out of the wagon and look up and watch as those who had been lined up behind them came down the mountain and made it just fine with the exception of one broken wheel and a balking mule that seemed to have a taste of Sarah's fright and fear. The best news of the day was when Marcy passed the word that Mr. Jade had regained consciousness and was going to be all right in a few days. Marcy reminded his friends he would have to take it easy for a while and others would have to help with his family's chores for a few days until he was fully recovered and could do for himself and his family. Of course, Mrs.

MARCY

Jade's recovery would take much longer than his, but at least the family had survived the harrowing incident on the slope. Time would heal their wounds and the horrible memory of that day, and they would be together to see their dreams come true if no other unfortunate accident befell them.

STRANGE PREMONITIONS

Several weeks of travel brought the train to a route that would lead to Fort Bridger. But Mr. Charlton decided it to be better to travel on between Soda Springs and Fort Hall and take the California trail from this point. There would be some mountain range and some desert later on down the trail, but he thought this better and a much wiser decision.

The latter part of August still brought hot and intense days of agony to all travelers. By mid-October the train should roll into Oregon territory, the dream that so many had faithfully hung on to. Hopefully the worst part of the trek was behind. But even Joshua knew all sorts of dilemmas and trials, whether small or major, could present themselves yet, without much notice. Nevertheless, many knew that whatever happened, they must press onward, and when they reached the area between Soda Springs and Fort Hall, they would depart from their new, dear friends. After months of travel, they came to the cutoff where company would part, perhaps never to see one another again in this lifetime. The seven wagons, plus the Brewsters, made eight that lined up to proceed to travel the southwest trail.

Joshua had a strong talk with Mr. Charlton about being a good leader, a good wagon master, and the burden of responsibility upon his shoulders that he alone must bear. After his lecture and words of advice, he bid them goodbye and Godspeed. There were Mr. Charlton; Reverend and Mrs. Payton; the Trevor family; the Wilsons, an older couple; the Burks, who were newlyweds; two middle-aged single men seeking for gold; a proprietor and his older son; and then the Brewster family wagon. The others watched as the small wagon train of eight stretched out and began their journey not knowing or even dreaming of what a horrifying passage they would make.

The dusty creaking and groaning wagon wheels only rolled about ten miles that day due to the late start at Soda Springs. The wagons circled in a small protected area of low mountains and hills. Marcy could not put her finger on the ill feeling and uneasiness she had in the pit of her stomach. She had experienced feelings like this in times past, usually just before something had evolved that had not been expected. She had never given any strong thought to premonitions, but she could simply not shake the frightening feeling that all was not well. It made her a little irritable and uneasy. At times she felt the hair rise on the back of her neck, and she felt that she must always be watching over her shoulder all the time.

Marcy didn't have time to give in to these strange feelings and sensations; she had a sad and sulky sister

MARLENE WISE

to help take care of and no time to be thinking of premonitions or to dwell on strange happenings. Beth had begged and pleaded with her father to remain with the other wagons, and so needless to say, she was not in the best of moods at this time. She was the only one of the family who had not really wanted to leave their home in Minnesota when they had hitched up to go and left for Missouri last spring. Marcy felt it an unwise decision to discuss her inner feelings with Beth because her sister was in a foul mood and not thinking clearly.

As darkness fell heavier and heavier, campfires were put out, and everyone readied themselves for a good night's sleep. Mr. Trevor and Mr. Wilson inquired of Mr. Charlton if someone should stand guard as they had done with the big train. He was reminded that Joshua had spoken about Paiutes that roamed in this part of the country. No one had heard of any problems with them lately, but it never hurt to be on the safe side. "Okay, you two stand guard for two hours, then we'll exchange with two other men," he ordered.

Even with guards on duty, Marcy could not relax and go to sleep. Nervously, she arose and stood just outside the wagon staring off into the darkness of night. As her eyes finally adjusted to the darkness, they were pulled like a magnet to a small yellow-red glow of a campfire behind them in the distant hills they had just come through. As she stood on tiptoe and strained to see better, thoughts ran through her mind that someone at the last minute had decided to come along with them and had not yet caught up. But perhaps it was Indians sitting by a fire and discussing an attack on these few wagons. A little wind suddenly stirred and blew dust gently around, swirling it into her face, causing her to turn her head and blink her eyes. When she raised her head again and peered off into the darkness in the same direction, she could no longer see anything but vast total darkness. She then began to doubt that she had seen anything at all. Maybe she was just exhausted and had only thought she'd seen a glow of a fire. She then realized that she was extremely tired from the day's activities, and she wearily went to her bed and lay down. Soon sleep became the master of her mind and overtook all her vivid thoughts and active imaginations, and she fitfully fell asleep. It seemed as if she had just gone to bed, but old man dawn was already knocking with a hardy good morning and bringing a glimpse of bright sunny light to her sleepy, tired eyes.

Morning work and chores were completed, the heavy wagons were hitched and made ready, and they slowly clattered on their way. After days of hard travel, they came to the crossing to turn to the California trail. "This trail will lead us straight into California territory," said Charlton excitedly. The mountains were refreshing and beautiful and somewhat cooler. The day went without even a slight incident. That evening after all had unhitched and done their chores, the reverend read some scriptures and prayed, and then all went their separate ways to their own wagons. But as Marcy slowly walked back to their camp, she again noticed a small glow as if there were a campfire in the distance. The hair seemed to prickle on her neck, and she felt that strange uneasiness in the pit of

MARLENE WISE

her stomach once again. Surely if anyone was following and trying to catch up, they could have done so by now.

They had camped close to a wooded stream almost hidden in the mix of trees and brush. They had taken on fresh water, washed clothes, watered the livestock, and cooked supper. Marcy had told Beth that when all necessary work was done they would go bathe and wash their hair in the stream below. The sun was still up but would be setting before too long. On their way to the secluded stream and the tall grasses, Marcy stopped suddenly. Just for a quick instant, a flash of bright light caught her eyes. "Beth, go on down and find us a good spot, and I'll be down in just a minute," said Marcy, almost in a whisper. Without question, Beth ventured on down to the water's edge and carried her soap and towel with her. She placed her small dainty hand in the quiet cool water and swirled it back and forth. The water felt so good that Beth had forgotten about waiting for Marcy.

Meanwhile, Marcy stood perfectly quiet in the tall wavy grasses almost like one of the rigid trees nearby. She focused her eyes on a clump of trees and brush back in the area they had just come from. She saw a bright flash and then another. Her eyes then followed another flash of light from a small group of mountains not very far from the origin of the first streak of light. There was no way it could be lightning because there were absolutely no clouds or signs of storms. She wondered if it might be an army patrol sending signals about Indian movements or other military procedures of some sort. She had seen no signs earlier or while traveling and walking beside the wagon. There were no hoof prints or tracks to even support this idea that raced around and around in her head.

As Beth and Marcy returned from their bath into the clearing, they spied two men with a mirror. Beth laughed out loud, and immediately upon hearing the girls, the tall one swiftly placed the mirror in his pocket and disappeared. Again, Beth laughed and said, "And some men say women are vain!" They both agreed that it might do the two fellas some good to look in the mirror and see their unshaved and dirty faces.

"A good shave and bath would do wonders for both of them," whispered Marcy. But Marcy knew that the mirror didn't have any purpose for them except as a tool for signals. Of course, she hadn't yet figured it all out. Why was it necessary for them to send any kind of a signal, and who were they signaling and for what? For now, she must let Beth believe that it was just what she thought it was. She had no desire to further upset her sister in any way. Marcy later made some excuse for leaving the wagon and went to find her father so she could unburden her heart and soul to him about the strange things that had taken place and her sightings these past few days. He agreed with her that this was a serious thing to be involved in and promised that he would explain the situation to Mr. Charlton and see what his ideas were about the incident. Her father warned Marcy that they should all keep their eyes open and be on guard at all times until they could figure out just what was really going on.

Marcy was tense and anxious and eagerly awaited

MARLENE WISE

the dawning of morning light. She could hardly wait to get started and leave this place of uneasiness they were in now. She bid her father and mother goodnight and returned to the wagon and to Beth. She brushed her sister's hair and helped her prepare for bed. The girls whispered and talked until Beth finally lay in a hushed and quiet sleep like a little innocent baby. Marcy leaned over and smiled at her. "Goodnight, my sister. I love you," she whispered in a soft voice. Marcy lay thinking of all the things she needed to attend to come morning light. She had promised her father that she and Beth would water the horse and mules while her father and Mr. Charlton took a look around. She had also volunteered to help her mother braid her long, freshly washed hair. Soon the dancing pictures in her mind faded away, and the tired worn-out body and mind of this tough seventeen-year-old girl finally slipped into a deep sleep. Marcy was so tired and keyed up from the day's events that she hardly moved all night.

She awoke feeling a little more refreshed and ready to line things up and move out. Perhaps in her mind, she felt that if they quickly moved on they would leave all the uneasiness and worry behind them. As promised, she quickly combed and braided her mother's beautiful long hair. Alisha thanked her and disappeared to start some breakfast, as Pa Brewster had already made a nice hot campfire. Marcy shook Beth's shoulder and told her to rise and shine. She always kept her promises or nearly died trying to keep them. She believed that it was better never to make a vow or promise than to make it and then break it. Marcy had promised her father that she and her sister would water and care for the animals while her father tended to other important duties and details. Beth stumbled out of bed and dressed hurriedly.

"Okay, let's go. Boy! I'm sure hungry this morning," Beth said, stretching her arms over her head.

"The food does smell delicious, doesn't it?" Marcy asked. Marcy smiled at Beth as she tousled the front of her sister's hair. "We'll hurry and be back in no time," she declared. The girls went to the picket and took Striker and the mules down to the stream. They tied them to some low-hanging branches that were easy to reach so the animals could drink and eat their fill before they had to leave. The two girls sat down patiently not far away and waited for the livestock to get their fill. Beth threw little rocks into the water and watched the ripple effect of the tiny stones making large circles. They sat for some time talking just like they used to do when they had more time in their home that they had left so far away. Hesitantly, Marcy splashed some of the cool water on her face and smoothed her hair. She told her sister that she hated to leave this nice clear stream of water and the quiet beauty that surrounded it. It had not always been easy to find clear cool streams of water during their travels. Sometimes the water had not been safe to drink or had been so low it was murky and uninviting. Beth followed suit and also splashed water on her face and sipped water from her hand. "We need to get Striker and the mules and head back to camp now because Mother probably has breakfast waiting for us and is wondering where we are."

WHITE MEN RENEGADES

Beth was stunned to hear the beating sound of horses' hooves coming in so close. Marcy picked up her ears too, as she had heard the sound about the same time as Beth. "Now, who could that be way out here?" asked Marcy.

Beth replied, "Oh, Marcy, it's probably some of those nice soldiers. Let's go see!"

Marcy said cautiously, "Beth, bring Striker, and I'll bring the mules." They walked quietly downstream and tied them to some small trees. Marcy motioned for Beth to walk very quietly and not make any noise. "If this is the army, then we'll soon know, but I don't think it is." As Marcy and Beth came from the stream a second time, Marcy walked in the lead. By this time, the riders had reached the wagons, but one rider was alone and coming in slowly from a distance. Marcy could tell quickly enough by their looks that they were not soldiers or friendly men.

She heard one of them say, "Toss your valuables in this sack and be quick about it."

Marcy in a flash promptly ducked in the bushes and pulled Beth down beside her. She hoped they had not been seen, but quickly Marcy looked at Beth and signaled with her fingers to her mouth. "Shh, shh, Beth. Don't move at all because we've got real trouble on our hands," she whispered as lightly as possible. Some of the men looted the wagons and took personal possessions along with food items and whatever they deemed as valuable or desired to have as their own.

The two single men from the wagon train came from behind the wagons and said, "Matt, we did just like you said to do."

"Where's Raney? I don't see him here, and he swore that he would be, as that was the plan we had set," he said bitterly.

The taller man of the two, Broyle, spoke up and said that Raney had left the train before South Pass and no one had seen him since. "We don't know which way he went or where he is at present. He's been gone for several days now," he stated hotly in both men's defense of themselves, as they knew Matt had a bad temper.

Marcy said in the softest whisper she could, "So this is what they're up to, and Raney was in on it all the time. I should have finished him off, as it would have been better for all of us." Marcy grimaced with great disgust.

The lone rider finally reigned in and came up close to the wagons. "Why, hello, Matt. I began to wonder if you were close enough to read my signals," stated Raney.

"Come on, we've work to do. Horace, bring the wagon around and load our winter supplies and cache of goods," ordered Matt.

Raney got off his horse and took a few steps closer to Matt. He raised his voice so Matt could hear above the commotion. "Remember our deal, Matt? Now make sure that I get all that's coming to me," he said with a look of pure greed on his face.

As Matt turned to walk away from Raney, he turned slightly and said with contempt, "You'll get it, Raney, real soon." He smirked as he continued to walk away. Matt had walked up about two wagon lengths when he suddenly whirled and whipped his pistol out of its holster and shot Raney before he could hardly blink an eye. Raney had seen it coming but hadn't moved quickly enough, so he turned and the bullet hit him in the side. He grabbed his wounded side and crumpled to the ground in great pain. He finally ceased to move about but lay quiet as though dead. "Move it now; get this stuff loaded," yelled Matt. "Okay, boys, now get rid of everyone! This time, I mean all, everyone. I don't want to leave any witnesses around to tell stories about us. I don't want someone giving out information to the army on us." He swore very hatefully.

The shooting and slaughter began, and Beth, hidden in the grass, grabbed her head with her hands and started to gasp and cry out, but Marcy quickly cupped a hand over her mouth to silence her and pushed her head down so she couldn't see. She knew there was nothing they could do but try to save themselves. The girls heard Matt say, "Remember, men, this is supposed to look like an Indian attack."

A couple of the wagons were set on fire; some feathers were thrown around as well as a few beads. Two of the men wore some moccasins and made tracks all around trying to make the scene look more authentic. The final thing done to try to give their dastardly deeds authenticity was to shoot some arrows into two of the already dead victims and a few into the wagons.

It was plain that Horace and Broyle were getting very nervous, which probably meant this was the first for them in this type of cruelty. "Let's go and get away from here before an army patrol happens to spot the fire and smoke," said Horace on edge. Tearfully, Marcy watched the thieves take the two miners and their wagon and head off for the lower mountains in the northeast direction. They left at breakneck speed never looking back, only wanting to get away from their horrible deeds. Neither Marcy nor Beth moved or spoke for what seemed an eternity.

Marcy finally said, "We have to get close to the wagons and see if anyone is alive." Beth was frozen to the ground, her hands clutched the grass and twigs tightly, and she would not move. She lay on the cool ground as though completely paralyzed from head to foot. Marcy told her to wait right there and she would be right back. She carefully crawled over the rocks and brush. She looked first one way and then the other to make sure that no one was around. She had seen them leave, but she chose to be on the safe side. The outlaws had vanished with their load of stolen goods and had killed all the people who could identify them. Marcy didn't think they would return, but they could. She figured they would not want to be found anywhere near the scene of destruction

MARLENE WISE

and death. After some minutes, she found the courage to finally run to their wagon. Her sweet mother lay dead next to the fire with her apron covering her face as though she had tried to hide or shield herself from the attack. She found her father next with two bullets in his chest. He was clutching his chest and just barely breathing, but not for long. In less than five minutes after she had found him, he too had passed on. He had only been able to speak a few words, to which Marcy was a witness.

"I love you girls very much. Take care of Beth," he said in broken sounds. The temptation to sit beside her parents and mourn and cry was great, but she knew she could not afford herself even a little time of grief. There would have to be another time for this. She could not find anyone alive until she came to the Reverend and Mrs. Payton. The reverend was wounded in the leg, and Mrs. Payton only had a shoulder wound. They miraculously escaped by falling down and feigning death. As Marcy came around the last wagon, Raney lay on the ground moaning.

"Help me! Help me!" he begged.

Marcy scowled at him with great scorn. "You helped kill my parents, and now we are orphans. I can't tell you how much I hate you. Even the sight of you makes me sick. There is nothing I can do for you, Raney," she stated with disgust.

"Then shoot me! My gun is over there somewhere, and my rifle is on my horse. I dropped my pistol when Matt shot me," he said as he writhed in pain.

"Oh, how I would love to do just that, but you're

106

not even worth a bullet, Raney," Marcy retorted through clinched teeth. As Marcy turned she heard the click of a hammer of a pistol. Beth stood behind her shaking vehemently.

"I'm going to kill him. He helped killed my father and mother, didn't he?"

"Beth! No! Give me the gun! You can't shoot him even though we know he deserves it. Please, hand me the pistol! Beth, if you fire the gun, those men may return. You heard what they said about witnesses, didn't you?"

Beth suddenly released the grip on the revolver and looked up hopelessly at Marcy and then slowly dropped the gun. "I hate him for what he's done to us," she whispered with contempt.

Marcy nodded her head in agreement. "I feel the same as you, Beth. Believe me, I do feel the same." At the moment, she felt no compassion for him, nor any other feeling but pure hate. In intense pain, Raney rolled over on his side and asked Marcy for a drink of water and then gave a throaty gurgle from his dry, parched throat. He gave one last roll back over on his back and seemed to go limp, then he lay very still and motionless. Marcy stood still for a moment not hearing Raney's ragged breathing but only heard her own breathing coming from spurts of fear, hate, and pain. The thought ran through her mind that Raney had died from his own evil plotting of wickedness and deceit.

As Marcy turned to attend to more important things that had to be done promptly, she suddenly felt a sense of relief. No longer would she be burdened down with the

MARLENE WISE

decision of what to do with Raney. His death had already
saved her from the misery of having to deal with him
at a later date. She had others to consider and decisions
to make quickly before the bandits decided to return for
some unknown reason.

Marcy knew that they must hurry; it was only her
and Beth and the Paytons now. The Paytons were both
injured, so it was really more like being by herself again.
Beth was in a state of shock and was not thinking too
well. Marcy had no time for shock, tears, or grief, not
even for a short while. Knowing full well that they could
not stay long at this site, Marcy knew again that she must
take charge and set things in order. The wagons that had
been set on fire were now dying out, but smoke could still
be seen for a distance, she was sure. Even so, the Paytons
volunteered to do whatever they could to help deal with
their wounds as best they could. Marcy asked them to
look into the wagons that were left and get anything that
hadn't been looted or that was left behind in their rush.
"Get supplies, food, guns, ammunition, anything that will
help us survive or prove to be useful," she shouted.

Marcy suddenly turned and held her aching head
between her two shaking hands. It dawned upon her
what had to be done, and all of a sudden it seemed an
overwhelming task, almost too much for this seventeen-
year-old girl. The dead had to be buried right away.
They couldn't be left here, or wild animals would tear
the remains of their loved ones and scatter the bones all
over the place. Marcy could not let this happen to their
parents and to their friends. So as soon as usable items

were salvaged and gathered and shovels could be found, grave digging began.

The reverend suggested they place two or more people in each grave knowing that it was the only sensible and logical action to take since time was of the essence and they were not in any physical shape to dig so many graves. As soon as they marked off the amount of graves needed to be dug, Marcy started at one end and the reverend at the other end. The reverend was a good worker, but he needed to rest often because of his leg wound. They all had blisters on their hands due to the hard work of using shovels in the hardened ground. But finally all of the dead were placed in the holes and buried. Marcy had kept a close watch while working, fearful that the thieving men would return again. She straightened her aching back and rubbed the sweat from her brow as she declared to the others that they must hurry on and get away from this place only if it was a short distance. Before they turned their backs and left their loved ones sleeping deep within the brown earth, they gathered around, and the reverend said a prayer over them. Crude sticks shaped as crosses marked the graves of those who had so violently been taken away from them. As a final act of love, Marcy took her blue hair ribbon that her mother had given to her and tied it around the cross on her parents' grave. Their hearts were heavy and saddened that they had to leave their parents in this lonely and forgotten place.

Beth sat in the back of the wagon peering out as the tears rolled copiously down her whitened cheeks. She watched until she could no longer see even a glimpse of the graves or the burned wagons. Beth spent much of her time weeping softly to herself and displaying a face of great sadness as they rolled along in the wagon trying to determine what they should do and where to go. Hours passed by that she hardly said a word, not even to her beloved sister, Marcy.

On the morning of the second day, Marcy spotted a lone rider with a pack mule. The man paused and watched their wagon for a spell. He then tied his mule to some little trees and brush and began to ride out toward them. After a while, when the rider was in shouting distance, Marcy abruptly stopped the wagon and asked Beth to hand her the rifle. Slowly, Beth did as she was asked, but she did not comprehend the reason for all of this.

The Paytons' wagon pulled up beside the girls. "Reverend, get a pistol just in case," Marcy commanded him nervously.

"But, Marcy, I'm a man of the cloth. I don't use guns," he stammered.

His wife scrambled back behind the seat of the wagon and thrust a gun over to her husband and said, "Remember yesterday? These girls and I need your help. You've got to help protect us."

Marcy stood up in the wagon, bracing her body against the seat. "That's far enough! Stop right there!" she warned him. The man could see the rifle aimed in his direction, and he halted immediately. He inquired where they were going. He asked if they were from the burning wagons. Marcy replied, "Well, what if we are? What do you want?"

"I mean you no harm," he called to her. "May I come in so I can talk with you?"

"Okay," she said hesitantly. "But keep your hands where we can see them. There are two guns aimed at you." After a while, Marcy was convinced that he was all that he had claimed to be. He had come from Fort Hall with his winter supplies, which he had ordered through the wagon train. He knew Joshua very well and claimed they were good friends. So Marcy quickly decided that any friend of Joshua's could surely be trusted.

The stranger told them he lived up in the mountains a little ways. He had not freely chosen this as a place to live, but it had been thrust upon him without his consent in the beginning. However, in a time of trial, he had come to love his home and this area, and the rich land had been good to him. He trapped, hunted, fished, and raised a good garden for a few vegetables. So far, he had enjoyed the quiet life and its surroundings. It took a lot of talking, but he finally convinced them to come with him to his cabin. He lectured them on how dangerous the trail could be for two lone wagons. He defined the hardships that could still come their way. "September is almost upon us now. It is possible for us to have snow at any time. I'm afraid you would never make it into California alive," he said. "You also have two wounded, and they need to have medical attention and rest to gather back their strength."

Marcy shivered, however, not from the cold, but from knowing that what she was hearing was the plain truth, spoken by a stranger. She knew the other lives depended

MARLENE WISE

upon her and her strength. Marcy's mind was cleared of her thoughts again, and she heard the man's voice saying, "You may have to winter here and then go to Fort Hall next summer. It is your only chance of survival."

The word *survival, survival, survival* kept running through Marcy's head, and finally Marcy took all things into account and consideration quickly. Her eyes wandered over to Reverend Payton as though to say, "Please, help me! What shall we do?"

The reverend leaned out of his wagon. "Yes, my dear, I believe this is a miracle of God. This seems to be our only solution to the horrible predicament that we have found ourselves in. This door has been opened, and we must all walk through and hope for the best. Besides, I doubt that we could find our way to California now by ourselves. There is no one to lead the way going through the desert, and it would be very difficult for us with no leader who had not crossed before." Marcy, knowing the reverend had spoken the truth and that he was being very logical, then eagerly turned the wagons with their possessions and began to follow a man named Clint Brody.

Marcy could not believe that they were going to any kind of a home way out here. This was the furthest thing from her mind at the present. She just wanted to get to California and get settled in someplace to call home and take care of Beth. But also it felt good to have someone else share the burden that she had been under. At times, Marcy felt she stood on the brink of complete and utter physical exhaustion and a strong case of overwhelming mental fatigue. At times, she just wanted to close her mind and not think. This long journey would never be forgotten because somehow everything from the littlest to the biggest incident seemed as if it was burned into their memories with a hot branding iron, forever to stay buried in their minds. Even if Marcy lived to a ripe old age, all she needed to do was close her eyes, and the memories and pictures, both bad and good, would roll and churn within her memory as though they had just taken place.

This journey had been horribly hard. Marcy missed her parents greatly, especially her father, probably because they had been so close to each other. She cherished all her fond memories and good times she had had with him. But she was finding his death even harder to accept. She had not had time afforded her to weep openly for her family and friends. In a strange sort of way, Marcy almost felt a twinge of jealousy because Beth had so openly displayed her tears and seemed to have the time that she did not to grieve for her parents.

However, Marcy realized that Beth was only a little girl of twelve years of age who had given up a lot of childhood this past year as they had moved and traveled a lot. In recollection of many things, Beth had always appeared to be much more fragile than her sister. It was much harder for her to deal with serious problems than it was for Marcy. Fitting into new places was easier for Marcy than for Beth. So, in reality, Marcy was not really jealous, but she felt her great sorrow and could not seem to find the proper time to just release it as Beth had done.

Beth cried a lot because she missed her parents so dearly, and now she was far removed from her parents' place of burial. She was afraid that she would forget them, what they looked like, and even how their voices sounded as time rolled by. She yearned for the soft touch of her mother's hand and the gentle sound of her father's voice. She had lost her whole life when her parents had been so cruelly taken from her. But memories, her blessed and marvelous memories of her parents, the good times back in Minnesota, no one could ever take them away. She could call upon those memories and pictures in her mind whenever she wanted to. It would be the good ones that would cause her strength to soar and her spirit to lift her above the gloom and darkness, causing her to plod on seeking her place in this life. Even though her parents were not alive, there would be days that she would draw from the strength of both of them by things she remembered. Even now she could hear her father saying to her to be strong, help her sister, never forget her dreams, and be kind and honest to those who were down and out, and to keep her faith in God and his provision. She could almost hear the sweet voice of her mother too as she spoke so softly to her and said, "I love you, Beth. You are such a joy to me." Beth hoped that she would never forget that sweet voice.

STRANGER IN THE DISTANCE

Clint Brody chatted with them as they nervously headed toward his home up in the wooded area straight ahead of them. He rode beside the wagon and asked Marcy a lot of questions. He occasionally raised his eyes and scanned the low mountains directly behind them. Clint sensed that someone, perhaps even the robbers, might be following them. He took careful note of Beth, who had hardly spoken since he had ridden up to the wagon. Beth sat quiet and motionless next to Marcy. Clint tried to converse with her, but Beth spoke as few words as possible without eye contact or any kind of emotion.

The wagons began a slow climb up a small incline until they entered a small group of beautiful low mountains; their eyes were refreshed by stands of lodge pole pines, spruce, firs, and junipers. There were lush green grasses and shrubs of all sizes mingled with gorgeous displays of colorful flowers all along the way. They displayed hues of red, pink, white, and yellow. There hung in the air a feeling of peacefulness and a calming effect on each one. Finally, hidden back in a thick stand of tall pine and spruce, sat a sturdy cabin.

Clint stopped and pointed ahead. "Well, this is home." As they pulled up, their eyes caught a breathtaking view, and they were captivated and utterly amazed. Plenty of wood had been cut and stacked close to the lean-to making ready for cold winter weather. Marcy noticed that behind the cabin was a good-sized corral and a long, sturdy barn that looked as if it could weather any winter storm and provide warm shelter for all of the livestock.

Marcy and the Paytons anxiously scrambled down, but Beth remained seated in the wagon in an unseeing daze still as if in shock. Marcy's eyes glanced to and fro until she gazed to the east of the cabin. Slowly she began to walk toward a square, fenced-in area. When she reached the fence, she stood upon tiptoe and peered inside. There were two large crosses and one small one. Marcy could then read the inscriptions, which read, "Joseph Brody," "Anna Brody," and "Annabelle Brody." She felt a little shiver as she turned and caught Clint looking at her a little uneasily. He had his hat in his hand, twisting its rim around and around in his long fingers.

He spoke softly, almost in a whisper. "It's a long story, and I'll tell you about it later. Right now we need to get settled, as darkness comes early in the mountains," he said. They emptied the wagons of their small amount of contents and placed everything inside the cabin. For the first time, Marcy noticed the raised floor of the wagon. She pried up some of the boards and found that her father had wisely placed his valuables and some money in hiding in this guarded area for safety. Her mother had also placed some of her own secret items in the hidden compartment. It was her treasure of gifts and goods that she had purchased in Independence. Marcy placed everything in a blanket and rolled it with her own personal items that she was able to salvage from the burning wagons and the thieves.

Strangely, Clint asked Marcy if he might borrow one of the wagons early the next morning. He said he needed to make a little trip and would be gone about one full day and probably return on the second day. Marcy's quizzical eyes rose to Clint's face, and she desperately wanted to ask why but did not.

"Sure. You can use ours," she said softly.

"Thank you. Oh, by the way, there may be a visitor come by, but he's a friend of mine. His name is Hank O'Dell, and he traps and hunts higher up in the mountains for our supply of fresh meats. When he comes by, please give him this note," he instructed.

Marcy stretched out her long thin hand and took the folded note and placed it in her pocket. She replied, "Yes, I will do this for you."

Clint was packed and ready to go before first daylight. He had stayed the night in the barn with the horses so he could leave without disturbing anyone, so no one had heard the wagon rattle out of the yard. He had placed two coffins in the back of the wagon that had originally been built shortly after he and Hank had arrived. One was for Hank, but he had survived against all odds, and the other was for Clint just in case Hank had to bury him. Clint knew the horrible heartache of leaving family members buried out in a lonely forgotten spot. He intended to do the same thing for the Brewster girls that he had done for himself and Hank. He would dig up the bodies out of the fresh shallow graves, place them in the boxes, and rebury them in the fenced-in area beside his own parents and sister who had faced the same disaster as the Brewsters. He had always felt better because he knew they were close by, at least until his grieving period was over. He knew that someday he would probably have to leave them and move on to new things and new places. But for now, he could always attend to the graves as should be done.

Clint knew from Marcy's description and where he had seen the burning wagons, about where they were buried. He ventured across unknown trails that others knew little about, and it cut his travel time in half. He reached the graves and found the blue ribbon still tied to the cross gently blowing in the wind. He removed the blue ribbon, slipped it into his pocket, and started to dig in the shallow grave. Just as he thought, it didn't take him long to recover the bodies, as they had not been buried as deep as they could have been due to the hard ground. He placed the Brewsters in their coffins and made ready to start back. But before doing so, he threw more dirt on the remaining five graves and took some time to put rocks on top of the dirt. It was hard, hot, and sweaty work; however, he felt he was doing the only decent thing he could. So with speed, on the morning of the second day, he returned. He pulled the wagon as close to the little family cemetery as he possibly could.

MARCY

Hank had indeed come by as usual and following Clint's request had dug two fresh graves as Clint had specified. Hank then rode back out and met Clint on the trail with the loaded wagon on his return trip, and they rode in together. As they pulled up close to the gate, both men somberly dismounted from the wagon. They carried the coffins over to the freshly dug graves. With the use of ropes, they began to lower down the boxes gradually and with great reverence.

The door to the cabin opened, and Reverend Payton came out with quick quiet steps of reverence. He somberly went over and leaned on the fence looking down upon the coffins. "Who are you burying so early today?" he questioned.

Clint looked at the reverend solemnly and then back to Hank. Clint's lips moved slowly as he answered, "It's the Brewsters, Reverend. I thought they would have a more decent burial here. The girls could take proper care of the graves if they were closer to them. Even when your parents are dead, it's most soothing to know that they had a decent burial and they're still close by. I think the trauma Beth has been through will be eased some when she realizes that her parents are here. It will give her something to do in caring for the graves and putting flowers on them occasionally."

The reverend slowly bowed his head and said, "Well, son, that was a mighty noble thing to do, and I'm sure the girls will appreciate your kindness. But why would you be driven to risk going back to do this for Marcy and Beth? You didn't know the Brewsters, did you?"

119

MARLENE WISE

"No. But two years ago…" He paused as though reflecting back on those years. "Hank and I were the only survivors of a massacre. It was not renegade Indians though; it was renegade whites, thieves pure and simple. The army never found them, and I can't help but strongly wonder if it's not the same men holed up around here somewhere that have repeated their evil deeds again with Marcy's family and others. If they had stolen ample supplies, it would be feasible to live out the winter months here. I have had less, and I've made it okay. I had to make the same decisions as you and Marcy had to make a few days ago. The only difference, we were two men, and Hank was seriously wounded. It was almost the exact same time of year, and winter preparations had to be made and shelter found. The thieves had taken almost all of our food supply and goods and left us for dead too."

A choked-up voice spoke up from behind the reverend. The men's heads all turned to see Marcy standing there with tears in her eyes and sadness engulfing her entire being. "I'm sorry, Clint. I know now that you can feel our deepest anger and hurt," she said with her head bowed low. The coffins had been lowered and were nearly in place. Marcy turned to the reverend and asked if they could have a service and prayer for her parents this morning.

"Sure we can, Marcy. We'll gather back here in an hour or so," he declared. Marcy said she should go prepare Beth for the news of the ceremony. She turned and walked away as quietly as a kitten knowing that she must muster all of her courage, as she had a strange sort of surprise for Beth. When she entered the cabin, she found Beth sitting on a knotty wooden stool combing her long brown silky hair.

"Beth, I have something to tell you," she said. She knelt down by Beth and removed the comb from her hands. She placed her long arms around Beth's quivering shoulders.

"Oh, Marcy, I hope it isn't bad news again! Has something awful happened?"

"No," said Marcy as she squeezed Beth's shoulders. "Beth, remember a few days ago when we had to bury Mother and Father in the shallow graves out on the trail?" Beth looked at Marcy with a startled look on her face, but she never answered. "Well, Mother and Father are here at the little burial plot outside," she said as tenderly and gently as she could.

"What? How can that be, Marcy?" she asked in a disbelieving whisper. "Oh, Marcy, what kind of cruel and mean trick is this?" Marcy's fingers immediately shot up to Beth's lips. "Now, now, shh, shh, Beth. It is true what I've just said because Clint and his friend Hank have brought them here for a decent burial, a Christian burial. We must go prepare for a better and more respectable burial for them. Reverend Payton is going to have a more fitting ceremony for them than what we were able to do in such great hurry. Then they can take on their eternal rest. We'll be better able to care for the graves at least for a while until it is time for us to leave here. I know that you want Mother and Father to have a decent burial and have some Christian words spoken over them."

The coffins were completely lowered into the graves

MARLENE WISE

and half buried, so the ceremony could start at any time the reverend wished. By the time all six had gathered at the site, the graves had all been filled in with freshly dug dirt. Beth stood frozen in a spot next to the foot of the grave and wished to move no closer even though Marcy nudged her trying to move her a little closer to the head of the plot.

Beth stiffly leaned over to her sister and said, "What if Clint didn't even go to the graves and these are only empty coffins?"

"But he did, Beth. I know that he did," answered Marcy with confidence in her voice.

Clint had overheard Beth's hushed words of doubt and disbelief; nevertheless, he completely understood her feelings and thoughts, so he didn't feel bad. He had even surmised that this might be a question that came especially from Beth, so he was prepared. He calmly began to fish down into the pocket of his vest and retrieved a somewhat frayed blue ribbon. Quietly he reached over and handed it to Marcy without a word or gesture. Wide-eyed, she immediately recognized it and sighed deeply as she gazed over at Beth. As Beth's eyes watched the ribbon clutched in her sister's hand sway gently in the breeze, she knew in her heart that Clint had done just as he had told them he had. Silently, Clint moved a little closer to Beth until his tall-built frame stood next to her, making her seem so fragile and small.

"I know it hurts, and I don't blame you for the feelings of mistrust you have. If it will ease your pain and suspicions, I can tell you that your mother wore a green dress with little pink flowers and your father wore a blue plaid shirt. They were each one wrapped in a gray blanket," he volunteered. It was then that Beth knew for sure that there could be no doubt, and a warm sense of relief swept over her whole being. For a minute she thought she was going to simply faint and fall on the ground in front of everyone. It was then that she felt strange warm arms around her small quivering shoulders. She had a strange sensation that it was Pa Brewster, her father, but knew all along that it was Clint Brody. She gently leaned her head over on him and began to cry out all of her frustrations and days of grief as though she had not cried any before today.

Marcy cried for the first time since her parents' death. She wept openly and allowed the hot tears to cleanse her soul of the strained emotions and anger that she felt so deep within her. She felt days ago that she would like to cry, but she had not had the time or the place to release her feelings. She had denied herself even that little luxury, as so many had come to depend upon her, and she had made promises which had to be kept. Realizing that this was her time to express her grief, she leaned heavily upon Mrs. Payton and sobbed uncontrollably and unashamedly.

After some time, Reverend Payton stepped to the head of the grave and began the rites of a Christian burial. He even said words for Clint's family. All six of them seemed to draw a lot of strength from each other from this strange mixture of bold strength, love, complete understanding, grief, and outright anger added with sorrow and finality that seemed to entwine their lives together like that of a strong rope. Afterward, they all filed out of the small gate one by one and ambled toward the cabin.

Beth's attention was immediately drawn off the path to the cabin and into the wooded area a short distance away. She turned and almost glided down the flower-strewn path. She had spied various patches of brilliant-colored flowers and seemed to be drawn to them like bees to honey. Her soft small hands darted out and gently picked a varied hue of red, white, yellow, and pink flowers. After picking a large handful, she silently headed back to the graves and began to divide the large bouquet, placing some on each grave. Suddenly, she felt somewhat better and returned to the company of the others with a faint smile upon her pale face. Marcy felt from that moment on Beth would be in a much needed healing process. Marcy's heart melted and went out to her sister because of all the problems, hardships, death, and sadness that she had experienced in this short span of her life. She longed for Beth to have some happiness and joy, which seemed to have been long taken from her.

A WINTER HAVEN

Clint let the Paytons and the girls stay in the cabin, and he bunked in the barn for the time being. At breakfast the next morning, Clint said that he had been thinking about their situation. He felt that they should try with all speed to build another small cabin and enlarge the corral and the barn before the cold winter storms, winds, and blowing snows came in upon them.

He had planted what seed he had in a big place just south of the cabin. He had saved seed from his plantings of last year's crop so that he would have vegetables again this year. Marcy was sure that their seed had been left intact in their wagon in the little wooden box that her father had made to transport them in. The thieves surely didn't want to have to plant and work for their food. It was easier for them to just steal what food they needed to survive, and more than likely they didn't stay in one place long enough for the grass to grow under their feet.

Clint told Marcy that the army had told Joshua about the Indian attacks. The army, thinking this was

MARLENE WISE

true, always had troops out on patrol to find these renegades. Joshua had spoken to Abraham before they left the train to be aware of Indians and attacks coming from the least expected places. Joshua reminded all the travelers that anywhere they traveled, they stood a chance of facing danger of all sorts, and Indians were only one of the dangers. Clint knew that when the wagon train came through, they sometimes would trade or sell any extra supplies they might have. Clint always made a trip into the fort sometime in September to obtain any extra supplies that might be available. He could not wait much later than the end of September to get prepared for the cold winter months, as snowstorms could be expected anytime after this. Sometimes light snows fell before the month of September and then quickly disappeared but nearly always came again in the latter part of September or first part of October.

Clint had made friends with the Indians, and they would often trade and barter with him for needed items. He had also saved the life of Silver Moon's son the first year they were there. The Indians had never forgotten his kindness, and they never seemed to bother him, Hank, or any of their livestock. This statement piqued their interest, and finally Marcy asked Clint, "How did you save the little Indian boy's life?"

"Well, the story goes like this. One cold day while out hunting, I paused at the top of a deep ravine thinking there was a deer just ahead. Hearing a whimpering and moaning sound coming from the bottom of the ravine, I got off my horse and walked as close to the edge as

MARCY

possible. Looking down into the snow-covered brush and weeds of the hollow below me, I could make out the size and shape of a child. So to be sure, I ran to the lower end of the ravine and cautiously crawled down until I was at the very bottom. A short distance away, I found this little child, an Indian boy, about eight years old, injured, and he could barely move. Quickly checking him over as best I could in the cold and snow, he was found to have cuts and bruises and a broken leg. At the time, Hank and I being new to the area, we had no idea where the Indian camp was located or which direction the boy had come from. Not knowing what else to do, I took the little boy home with me and doctored his cuts and bruises and then set his leg. He stayed with me at the cabin for two or three days. I figured his family must be worried sick with fear and was wondering where he was by now and what had happened to him. I got Hank to help me, and we made a travois for him to lie on, and the boy guided us in the general direction of his tribe. His family was grateful to us for our concern and the medical care of the boy because he could have easily died out there alone.

"We've never, not even once, had any type of problems with the Indians here. Occasionally, they would bring by gifts of food, furs, blankets, or deerskin clothes, for which we were very grateful. During that first year, we would probably have frozen to death if it had not been for the gifts that they so generously bestowed upon us. Nonetheless, the Indians were aware of these marauding bandits and how they'd tried to pin their evil works on them. We've lived in close proximity and peace all this

MARLENE WISE

time, able to get along and help each other. They know you all have faced the same thieves and are in the same situation that we were in two years ago. They also know that you're friends of ours, so they won't bother or harm you, but more than likely will offer any help they can give to you. Sometimes, when there is a medical problem that the medicine doctor can't seem to cure, they will bring the sick one to me.

"My father, Joseph, was a doctor, and my mother was a nurse, and I also studied to be a doctor. We were going to California to set up a medical practice and had planned that I would assist my parents in their work until I was well established. I would then go on farther in northern California territory or perhaps on to Oregon. But before we could realize our dream, our wagon was set on fire by the same thugs that attacked your wagons, I'm sure. But between Hank, who was wounded, and I, we put out the fire and saved the medical books, doctor's bag, and a few supplies. On very cold snowy winter nights, I usually sit by the fire and read in my medical books so as not to forget needed information. I am also able to order medical supplies from the fort when they order theirs," he explained to them.

It was agreed upon to build another cabin, so the work started immediately. They had decided to add another room to the first cabin for Marcy and Beth; however, there would not be much time to work before bad weather, so they would have to work quickly. As the three men worked hard cutting the logs and building, the women worked in the garden and prepared the food.

Clint also showed the women where to cut loads of tall willowy grass for the livestock. The barn needed to be well stocked with food for the animals for the coming winter. This was also important for Marcy because she wanted to make sure Striker had sufficient food for a long winter. Clint had come by some corn seed, so he had planted a lot of it. Some of this would be dried and stored for the animals when they needed another source of food besides the willowy grass that was to be cut. Clint and Hank had worked hard that first year just to survive the winter in the mountains. The Indians had taught them some ways of survival, and some they learned by trial and error. But nevertheless, they had proved themselves and had done well. They liked this life so well that they decided to stay up here in the mountains instead of traveling back to Fort Hall and waiting for a wagon train. They had no idea how long they would want to stay in this place, but it was home now, and they felt comfortable here.

Hank came in early one morning to help with the work. "Say, Clint, I talked with Silver Moon and Black Wolf yesterday, and their prediction is that the weather will turn cold and snow will be here by the first moon of the new month. They're usually always right, you know," said Hank.

"If so," replied Clint, "the first week of October, we'll have our first snowstorm. Perhaps we should hurry and add on rooms to this cabin instead of trying to complete a new one. We can build more next spring if needed. Okay, let's take out the end window, cut the logs for a door, and add to this part of the cabin. One room for the girls and one for the reverend and his wife. We'll take the small room at the back for me and you when you're here. You should consider moving down here off the higher mountains until spring, Hank. This may be a horrible winter, and it's not good to be off by yourself for so long."

Marcy asked what she and Beth could do that would be the most helpful. Clint motioned toward the wagons and said, "Do you and Beth think you could unload those two wagons and remove the canvas covers off each one of them and store them in the barn? The other things you will know what to do with." Marcy looked in the wagon Clint had borrowed a few days back and realized Clint had picked up some more items from the plundered wagons that had been overlooked previously. He had found a couple of wheels, canvas off the spoiled wagons, some damaged reins and harnesses, and other items that he knew could be used as possible survival aids and pitched them into the wagon or the empty barrels attached to either side of the wagon along with the coffins in the back. He had only limited space, so he chose wisely what was needed and what he could afford weight-wise to bring back with him.

Marcy and Beth were completely surprised at what Clint had brought back besides the coffins. He was very courageous and brave, very thoughtful indeed! He was bent on survival for Hank and himself, and now he had four added people to think about. He had not asked to become responsible for all of them but did what he knew had to be done.

MARCY

Marcy was angered to think that these beasts of men could do such to their fellow countrymen. They valued no life but their own, and this was shown by their evil actions as they burned, looted, killed, and stole from trains crossing into California possibly three or more times. The army was searching desperately trying to find them but had little success. The mountains and hills had too many places where thieves could hide for long periods of time and not be found. They had followed the trail so far, and then rain or wind had erased many of the tracks and made what was left hard to see and read, making it almost impossible to follow.

Clint had requested that the ladies lay out some of the canvas to be measured for some mattresses. Marcy and Mrs. Payton sewed two large pieces to be filled with soft grass, sawdust, leaves, and soft pine needles. After a lot of hard work, the rooms were added on to the main cabin where the two rooms on the far end were divided with thick, newly cut logs. Wooden pins were placed in some of the logs for hanging clothes. Hank traded a few of the wagon items to the Indians for some heavy fur hangings to be used as a door to each room. The blankets and sheeting were divided equally, and the large fur blankets brought as gifts by the Indians would be warm and toasty for the girls and the Paytons in the coldest of winter.

Now that the rooms were finished, Clint moved his things into the smaller room. The new rooms had a fresh scent of newly cut wood, which made a pleasant smell when one entered. Beth liked the fresh smell of the newly

131

MARLENE WISE

cut logs, as it reminded her of home. The spaces between the logs had been fully chinked by the girls and Mrs. Payton. At least, everyone would have shelter from the cold winds and the blowing snow, which would soon fall. Even the animals would fare better than before, as the corral was lengthened so the livestock could better graze and move around on days they could be outside. In short time, they would be shut up in the dark barn, as there were only two windows up high, but not much light came through on dark dreary days. Pieces of canvas had been rubbed with oil and stretched over the windows for light in both the barn and cabin. The cabin had windows with pieces of leather for hinges that were made like doors so the windows would close over the canvas when nighttime descended or when the wind blew cold. The extra wagons were moved down to one end of the barn and placed in a sturdy lean-to. They were filled with tall grass for the livestock food and at the same time would be preserved for any springtime trips. Clint had cut a good supply of wood and also trimmed a lot of extra logs that could be quickly cut later if needed. Just like the previous year, he had tried to think ahead and make them as ready as possible for their survival. They had already passed the first part, as they had survived the gruesome attack. The bandits had meant not to leave anyone alive who could possibly identify them or cause them any problems or grief in later days to come.

Beth and Marcy went to the garden plot and picked part of the readied vegetables. They were dried a few days and then placed in layers of sawdust, pine needles, grass,

MARCY

and leaves so they would not freeze. Fresh water was carried daily from the spring, and the water barrels were kept full all the time. The water trough for the livestock was also kept full and ready.

UNIDENTIFIED BOOT PRINTS

Several times Clint and Reverend Payton had noticed strange boot prints down by the corral and close to the barn door. At times, it really looked as though someone had made a special attempt to do away with them by trying to brush them away with a branch or a piece of bush. Neither of the men had mentioned this to anyone else, especially to Marcy. She had a very special fondness of Striker, and something like this could only make her have undue worry about her horse and his welfare. Clint had never seen a woman so close and loving to a horse as she was. He had no intentions of unduly upsetting her with some story that he could not explain to her.

This morning he had found tracks again going into the barn, and this time he was positive that a couple of old blankets and some livestock food was missing, especially some corn and an old saddle from Hank and Clint's wagon trek. He had mentioned this to Hank but had asked that he not say anything to the ladies about this for the time being. They had already been through more trials and tests than most girls their age or for that fact even more than most mature adults had ever experienced.

A beautiful morning crept in across the land with a new quiet and peacefulness about it. However, sometimes there was stillness just before the big storm broke. Marcy and Mrs. Payton, the reverend's wife, prepared to cook breakfast while Clint and Hank went to check on the livestock. As they stepped outside, they were met with a damp chill that ran up and down their spines, and their bodies soon became a mass of gooseflesh from the coldness. Everything was covered with a massive cloth of glistening and sparkling frost that made the ground appear to be shimmering and shining brightly. There was not one place his eyes beheld that did not appear to be an array of diamonds cast across the land, on the trees, the corral, and the cabin. Consequently, not one place was exempt from the frost unless it was under something or inside where it couldn't be touched. The first hoarfrost had silently crept across the land while all had slept snugly in their warm beds. This was a sure sign that the first winter storms would not be far behind this silent omen.

Last year when the first frost had come, it had been only days when a thick snowfall had arrived just afterwards. It had dumped about four inches of pure whiteness all over the face of the sedate mountain leaving its pretty green and rainbow of floral colors softly hidden from man's or beast's view. It had framed the cabin and the corral like a giant painting. But Clint found out later that this storm was as tame and tender as a soft white kitten because the following storms were much more intense and powerful.

The bitter temperatures dropped maddeningly low, and brisk winds from the low black clouds blew with an angry fury. At times the cabin was half covered with its angry whiteness, and the corral fence could not be seen at all. It was necessary to tie a rope from the front door to the barn door so one would not get lost while going back and forth. The burial plot was completely covered from end to end with a thick white blanket. It made one think that those who were buried there were tucked into a nice warm place of their own and covered with a beautiful blanket all snug in their rest. One never knew; the snow could last for days or even weeks at a time.

Returning to the warmth of the homey cabin, Clint announced that the first frost had arrived. Marcy stated that they must go out today and gather the last of the squash and pumpkins. Beth asked Marcy if she might go look for some remaining flowers for their parents' graves.

"Sure, Beth, but don't wander off too far," she stated. With excitement, right after breakfast, Beth did the dishes and swept the floor. She grabbed her cape and ran out to gather the last of the fading and probably wilting and droopy flowers. A small patch was found just down the hill a ways, and Beth picked all she could carry in her arms. Although the first frost had done some damage to them, they were still pretty to Beth. She spent a little longer than usual at the graves today, until finally she was pleased with the flower arrangements on all of the graves, and she arose from the cold ground and said in a low voice, "I'll bring more on another day. I miss you so very much."

Beth turned and ran from the burial plot eager to help Marcy gather in the squash and pumpkins. As soon as their baskets were full, they carried them into the cabin to dry a little before packing them into the barrels of sawdust and leaves. They returned and were finishing their harvesting of the crops when Beth asked Marcy why they had not come and gathered the crop when it was sunny and not so cold. Marcy replied that if they left the squash and pumpkins until after the first frost, it would toughen the skins and they would preserve and endure the cold winter months much better.

A crisp "Good morning, ladies" came from among the trees just a short distance away from the garden area. They looked up and spied Hank on his horse leading his mule loaded down with supplies and a fresh-killed mule deer. "Guess I'm moving in to stay out the winter with you all. It gets mighty lonesome up high all by myself, and I figure I can hunt from here as well as up there. Locked up my cabin tight till spring peeks through again," he relayed. "I don't have to worry about it though because there's no one around here but us and the Indians, and an Indian would never live in a cabin. They prefer their warm, snug teepees in the place of cabins like ours. I've been in a teepee when it's snowy and cold, and they're all right I guess, warm and homey. But for myself, I like my home settled and attached to the ground," he stated jovially.

"Good morning, Hank. Had breakfast yet? There's some breakfast and fresh hot coffee," Clint said.

"I don't mind if I do. It sure does smell good."

He licked his lips and rubbed his stomach like he was starved.

The girls completed their job and headed inside. They warmed themselves and drank some hot coffee with Hank. As Marcy began to unload the basket, she asked Beth if she had brought the knife in that they were using to cut the stems of the squash and pumpkins.

"Oh, I must have left it on the tree stump near the garden," she replied. "I'll go get it." Beth pranced back out to the stump to retrieve the knife, but it was not there. She looked around on the ground and in the leaves, but no knife. *Surely,* she told herself, *it must be in the basket, and Marcy just overlooked it.* As she turned to go back to the cabin, she heard the distinct crackle of breaking sticks and twigs. It sounded like someone had walked across the sticks in the quiet of the morning, and the noise seemed louder than usual.

The hair stood up on the back of her neck, and she had the uneasy feeling in the pit of her stomach that someone was watching her or spying on her. She looked around a bit but did not see anything unusual or see anyone around, and there was now no movement at all. She again slowly looked at the stump where she thought the knife had been, and it was definitely not there. But this time she noticed something she had not seen before. There were small boot prints all around the stump and in the garden area. They led off into the direction where she had picked the flowers around the trees. Her eyes slowly followed the prints from the stump across to the wooded area. As she lifted her head, she saw an area of brushy bushes and spruce trees, and she could have sworn that somebody had ducked down behind them. Shivers ran up and down her spine, and all that Beth could think of then was to get away and back to the cabin for safety. She ran as fast as her legs would carry her until she reached the door. Her heart was beating wildly like it was going to jump right out of her chest. She quickly darted inside the door, closed it, and stood rigidly against it as though something was about to overtake her.

Her pale face and rapid breathing brought all conversation to a halt. Mrs. Payton was moving rapidly toward Beth with outstretched arms and saying, "Well, Beth dear, what is it? Looks like you've seen a ghost. You are so pale and out of breath. What's wrong, dear?"

"Marcy," Beth said still breathlessly, "the knife was gone! It was not on the stump or in the garden anywhere! It was not where we left it!"

"Now, Beth, that's nothing to be so upset about; more than likely, it will show up somewhere, I'm sure," consoled Marcy.

"It's not the knife that I'm concerned about, Marcy. There were some boot prints all around the stump and in the garden. I thought I saw someone duck behind the bushes and spruce trees. The tracks led off in the very same direction yonder where I picked the flowers this morning. It was like someone was watching me, but I couldn't see them. It was just a spooky feeling that I had come over me."

"Beth, you must remember that there are three men around here and they all wear boots, so any one of them could have made those tracks."

Then Hank spoke up and said, "Well, more than likely it was a mule deer nosing around to see what had happened to his friend that I shot this morning. Besides, there's no one out here this time of year but us and a few Indians who didn't go south for the winter."

Beth sighed. "I guess I'm just being silly; it probably was a mule deer or an animal," she said, suddenly embarrassed that she had acted as she had.

Clint returned from the barn and bid everyone a cheery good morning. He helped Hank unload the packed mule and his personal belongings. They then dressed the deer, chopped wood, and finished their chores. As they worked together, Hank relayed the story Beth had revealed to them earlier about the boot prints. He had purposely not said anything as he again didn't want to cause any undue worry. He knew how women had a tendency to worry about things like this. Clint told Hank that they needed to keep their eyes and ears open at all times. They would of course need to speak with the reverend, as he was with the women most of the time. He didn't do much of the hunting or going away to the Indian camp like the two of them did.

Two days passed. Beth still had not found the knife, and it continued to worry her a great deal. But she said no more about it to Marcy or even discussed her concern with Mrs. Payton. As everyone seated themselves around the table for the noon meal, heads lifted just as the reverend started to say grace. The snorting and stamping of horses' hooves could be clearly heard not far from their door. Clint pushed himself away from the table, walked across the room, opened the door, and peered out cautiously. He was immediately greeted by Silver Moon, his brother Black Wolf, Dancing Star, and one other Indian who waited a distance off the path. Dancing Star held little Brave Wind close to her wrapped snugly in a silver coyote skin.

Dancing Star asked Clint if he could give her son some medicine and make him well again so he could run and play with the other children. Clint asked what was wrong with the child, and Dancing Star replied, "The heat and fire of the evil spirits have long tormented him for three moons." She carefully extended the wrapped bundle to Clint and said they would return in three moons to take him home again if he was well. "You will make my Brave Wind well again, won't you?" she begged. Clint could see the deep concern in the mother's eyes. He had no idea what the problem might be, and of course, all he could do was say that he would try his very best to make him well so he could run and play with the other children again. He hoped deep within his heart that they had not waited too long to bring him for medical attention. Hopefully, Dancing Star would again one day soon hear her child laughing and playing with others.

Clint bid the Indians good-bye and carried little Brave Wind into the cabin. He laid him on a blanket close to the hearth of the fire and asked Marcy to watch over him until he returned. So she knelt down beside the boy and patted his arm and head while speaking to him in a soft reassuring tone. However, she doubted that he understood what she was saying in words, but every child

MARLENE WISE

knew the touch of love and reassurance. Meanwhile, Clint had gone to his room to retrieve his medical bag and look through his assortment of medicines. He returned with his medical bag, some instruments, little bottles, and medicines wrapped in papers.

He listened to the boy's heart and his breathing with one of the instruments and then dug down in the bag and pulled out a little round box full of strong-smelling powders. He handed it to Marcy and asked that she place about two teaspoons of it in a cup and make a paste out of it with some warm water. He took out a roll of bandages and tore off a piece of the cloth. He quickly unwrapped the boy from the silver coyote skin and removed his shirt and sponged him off. He dried the boy and put his clothes back on him. "Bring the powder paste now, Marcy, please," he beckoned. He then spread the thick paste over a new cloth and laid it on the small boy's chest. He put the deerskin shirt back on him and covered him very lightly. Beth inquired of Clint how long it would take for the boy to get well with this treatment. "I really don't know, but if he's no better by morning, I'll have to try something else," he admitted with concern.

Clint sat by the boy's side all night giving him sips of cool sugared water and checking to see if the fever was down. By light of morning he was doing a little better, but Clint repeated this same thing for two days, and on the third day he gave him a spoonful of elixir. The boy's fever broke the third night, and he sweated profusely. He was given plenty of sugar water to drink all night and the next day. He was soon able to sit up by himself and eat a

142

small amount of breakfast, so it looked as if he would be all right and recover.

The evening of the third day, the Indians returned to find Brave Wind doing much better, as the evil fire was gone and he was well. Clint gave his mother, Dancing Star, instructions to follow on how to keep Brave Wind well. A smile spread across her smooth brown face as she reached into her warm fur robe and pulled out a bag and handed it to Clint. She thanked him and said, "May the Great Spirit look upon you with kindness always." Smiling, Clint went back into the cabin and stood close to the fire. He opened the bag slowly as everyone gathered around with much curiosity and anticipation. He took out a pair of beautiful knee-length moccasin boots with intricate bead work, burned designs, feathers, and rawhide ties. There was a star that represented Dancing Star, a symbol of wind for Brave Wind, a sign for friendship, and the initials C.B. at the top of the boot. Clint was utterly surprised at the work and the time that had been put into making these. It was one of his most cherished gifts from the Indians. Marcy was amazed at the confidence and trust the Indians seem to have in Clint. They seemed to be a generous people and really wanted to live in peace. She hoped to get to know them as well as Clint and Hank. Marcy was happy Clint had been able to help Brave Wind overcome his fever and sickness.

Clint had learned some Indian language, and they understood some English. So, using both, and sign language too, he had managed to have conversation with them. In the conversation, sometimes broken, they had mentioned something to him which had greatly disturbed him. They had passed Hank's cabin a couple of days ago while deer hunting. Hank had not been there for some time, and the Indians knew this. But they related that a fire had been burning at this place, and at dark they had not seen Hank return home. They inquired of Hank and his whereabouts and were told that Hank had moved in with them about four or five days ago and that he had closed his cabin and had not returned. The Indians looked at one another somewhat astonished. Marcy noticed the look on their faces and was concerned as to what this meant. She wondered, but not verbally, who could be using Hank's cabin. She would later ask Clint if this was something they should be concerned about. Hank had brought all of his personal items down with him when he moved in, so there would be nothing for anyone to steal.

Silver Moon spread his hands toward the higher mountains and said, "Great Spirit says that an evil one and a great storm are coming. You must keep watch so no harm comes to you." He raised his right hand and bid them good-bye. He made the sign for friends as they turned their horses to leave. Again, Clint felt an unusual closeness to his Indian friends and wished deep within his heart that all whites and Indians could have the same relationship as they had with the Indians here.

SILENCE THE WITNESSES

Clint spoke to Hank about the incident at his cabin that had been relayed to him by the Indians. Again with good reason, Clint thought it not wise to discuss this in front of the women. However, Clint found it very difficult to hide or keep things from Marcy. She was a strong young woman, but at the same time she seemed so fragile and alone. Clint had found the same small boot prints that had earlier upset Beth all around the barn and corral again. He could not imagine who it could be, as Indians didn't wear boots like this. Clint felt a strange cold sensation in the pit of his stomach but didn't understand why he had this feeling all of a sudden. Hank stated that if it was someone who meant no harm, then they should show themselves and come to the cabin. It was beyond his comprehension and his imagination that anyone would be out in this cold weather with no place of shelter from the cold winds and storms. It was difficult for them to think about the strangeness of all this too, and they were supposed to be the strong protectors of the ladies.

MARLENE WISE

Marcy made her usual trip down to the corral to check on Striker as she did each day. She was glad that he had a good, warm place to be in for the long winter and would not have to suffer the cold winds and biting snows and storms. However, this morning Striker wasn't his usual self. He seemed nervous and a bit antsy and proceeded to snort and paw at the ground rolling his eyes and twitching his head back and forth. Marcy spoke to Striker in a low, soft voice and stroked his quivering side. Soon he began to settle down when he recognized her voice and felt her touch. The first thing Marcy noticed was Striker's saddle over close to the door, which was not the proper place that it was kept. She wondered why this was so and if Clint was going to ride Striker and let him exercise a bit. As her eyes darted back and forth to things in the barn, her eyes finally caught the sight of blood close to the barn door. She ran over and began to check the horse for any cuts or abrasions on him and found none on him but did spy some dried blood on his right front hoof. Striker had only used his hooves in defense and kicked or cut someone when he was being beaten or abused or if someone was around him that he didn't like or trust. Striker had always trusted Clint and had never reared up at him or acted mean in any way. Marcy was very upset at her findings and fearful at what was going on.

She immediately ran to get Clint and Hank to tell them what she had found and show them the strange boot prints that were also visible just inside the barn door. As they returned to the barn, Hank and Clint went inside to have a look around. Marcy did not go in with them because she stood frozen in her tracks at what she had just seen. She saw a man running from the side of the barn and into the woods. She could not scream, as her throat seemed to be paralyzed. How could she believe what she had just seen? "No! No! This cannot be true!"

Suddenly, she felt her legs beginning to buckle beneath her as her head began to swim and swirl in dark circles. Almost as if in slow motion, she felt as if she was just melting away and going down to the ground. Clint came to the barn door just as Marcy was wilting and falling to the ground. Clint reached out and caught her. "Marcy! Marcy! What's wrong? Are you okay?" He called for Hank as he scooped up her little slender body in his arms and started for the cabin. He pushed open the door and went in with his heart thumping so hard he could hardly catch his own breath. Finally he reached Marcy's bed and laid her down as gently as possible. Mrs. Payton rushed over with Beth right behind her, and they simultaneously asked what had happened to her. Clint felt very silly that he couldn't answer them, but he replied that he had no idea.

As Clint picked her up to bring her inside, she stirred and pointed off towards the woods as best she could and said something about the rain. It didn't make any sense to him, and it wasn't raining. They let her rest for a while knowing that soon she would come around, as she had only fainted. True enough, suddenly she came to and raised herself upon one elbow trembling and shaking very hard, almost like someone having a hard chill. Her whole body was a great mass of gooseflesh, and she had a

MARLENE WISE

worried and frightened look upon her face. She lay back on the pillow and folded her arms across her chest to stop the shaking. Mrs. Payton brought her a warm blanket and covered her hoping she could stop the shakes.

Marcy leaned forward and said to those standing around her, "I need to speak with the reverend quickly." The reverend came over to the bedside, leaned down close to Marcy, and asked her what he could do for her. "Reverend, this is very important. Did you bury Raney when we buried the other bodies?" she asked pleadingly. She hoped with all of her heart that the reverend would say he had.

But the reverend wrinkled his brow as he thought for a moment. "No, I can't say that I did. I don't remember him because he was not with the others that we had laid out in the blankets. We were all in a hurry, frightened, and in a state of shock, but I don't remember him at all."

"Yes," said Marcy. "If you recall, we dug a total of six graves and had to put two people in a grave. Raney was at the back of one of the wagons rolling around on the ground and holding his side and stomach begging me to shoot him. He then gave a throaty gurgle and lay very still. I thought he had died, but he must have survived. He was nowhere around when we gathered the supplies unless everyone was too busy, in a state of confusion, shock, and disbelief to pay him any attention after we thought he was dead. Oh, he has come to silence all of us as witnesses. It has to be him; no one else looks like old Snake Eyes," she cried out in deep grief and torment. Again, she felt that heavy load upon her as it had been in past days. "I saw him running away from the side of the barn when we were down there. It was his boot prints; I know that now. He wants to get rid of us."

Clint returned from the barn again saying that he didn't see or hear anyone. Clint reminded them that if he was shot in the stomach, he couldn't have gone very far. "But he was!" said Marcy testily. "Or at least he was holding his stomach and his side and asking me to go ahead and shoot him and put him out of his misery. Of course, he could have been faking it so that Matt would not shoot him again. Thinking back, when I shot him on the wagon train and just barely nicked his shoulder, you would have thought that the bullet had ripped into his chest. Raney whined about it for days, and it had only creased the top of the skin. Beth and I and the Paytons are in danger as long as Raney is around. He wants to kill us, all of us. He wants no witnesses as to his cruel dealings with Matt and the others. He wants no one to know about the little California wagon train massacres. I see now that Raney's part of the plot was to try to get wagons that had valuables, money, or lots of goods and supplies to turn and go on the trail to California instead of staying with the main wagon train. Raney has a strong hate for both me and Beth and also for Matt and his gang that betrayed him and left him for dead. He very much detests all of us; his hate is strong enough that he would chance coming here to do us evil and do away with us. I can only believe that his deep-seated anger must have driven him and given him the will to live."

As the days passed on, Marcy and Beth could no

MARLENE WISE

longer go anywhere without Hank, Clint, or the reverend to guard them and watch over them. But Marcy decided that she could not live in fear for the rest of her life, and she strapped her revolver on her and went to the barn to see Striker. He was happy to see her, and he nuzzled his big warm nose against her arm and pushed it back and forth. She flung her slender arms around his neck and rubbed his beautiful long nose and up between his ears. She reached into her pocket and brought out a piece of folded brown paper. She poured the content into her hand and let Striker lick it. He licked her hand clean of the sugar and then looked to see if there was more in her other hand. Patting Striker's side and speaking to him in a gentle tone, she led him to the corral to graze on what little bit of grass there was to eat and to let him exercise his legs some. After giving Striker a good deal of time out, she led him back to the barn and then started back to the cabin. She had almost forgotten about what had happened in the last few days until she heard the crack of a rifle and felt a bullet whiz by her left ear. She dropped behind a pile of cut logs and looked about cautiously with her revolver drawn.

Clint came around the corner of the cabin yelling, "Stay down! Stay down! He's in that stand of trees just to the right of the barn." Clint and then Hank fired their rifles into the stand of trees trying to get Raney to move so they could see him. Raney fired twice and then fled away on what seemed to be a good riding horse. Where had he gotten the rifle and the horse? He must have hidden them away somewhere, or else he had stolen these things from the Indians.

150

"No one is allowed to go out by themselves again," said Clint in a raised voice such as Marcy had not witnessed before. "This man is desperate and will stop at nothing to get what he wants. He wants to try to kill us off one at a time when we have no protection or are not aware of his presence. We cannot afford to give him this opportunity to do so and make ourselves an easy target for him." He looked straight at Marcy when he asked, "Does everyone understand me when I say do not go out alone again?" Everyone answered yes or gave a nod of the head to imply that they did indeed understand completely.

Beth had slipped back into a state of depression and had become sullen and sulky. She often cried to go home again, but she had to realize that they had neither home nor parents to go to. Clint went to the bedroom where the heavy fur blanket hung in the doorway. "Beth, may I come in? I need to talk to you," he said softly. Her weak and frightened reply came and sounded like the voice of a little girl who had been badly frightened by a bad dream in the middle of the night.

"Yes, come in," she said in a very low whisper. He walked over to Beth, who sat on the edge of the bed twisting her brush around and around in her hands. Her eyes had a far away look and her face was drawn, and she looked as if her soul was in great torment.

"Listen to me, Beth. It is going to be okay, and we will protect you and keep you safe, but you must do just as I have asked. I know you are afraid now that Raney has seemed to appear from nowhere. But we will catch him, and he will be punished for all the evil things he

MARLENE WISE

has done to everyone. I don't want you to spend all your time worrying about the situation and about Raney and what you think he might do. But for safety's sake you must promise me that you will not go outside by yourself anymore unless one of us is with you. Will you promise me that you will do this for me?"

"Yes, Clint, I will do that because I no longer care if I go outside anymore or not. I hate this Raney for what he has done to me and Marcy and the Paytons. At the wagons, I found a gun lying on the ground and I was going to shoot him for what he did to my parents, but Marcy would not let me do it. She said the shots might bring back the murderers and thieves again if they thought someone was alive. I wish now that I had done it anyway," she said as she grimaced; her teeth and face and her slender body trembled.

Clint pulled her to him and held her tightly. "No, you really don't wish that, Beth, and Marcy was right not letting you do such a horrible thing. You would have had to live with that deed for the rest of your life, and it would not have been a nice thing to think about or forget. As long as I am here, I will protect you and Marcy and not allow anything to happen to you," he promised her as he hugged her tightly again.

By late afternoon the sky had turned dismal and dark, and the heavy shadowy clouds hung low with a look of winter harshness just waiting to hover in with a big storm. The clouds swirled and rolled in an unilluminated sky. By early evening as gray dusk approached, snow began to dance and softly flutter to the earth. At first, the flakes fell so softly that it appeared they were dancing in a ballet and softly kissing the earth with a great gentleness. But within the hour the wind had revved up and began to howl with such fierceness that one could barely hear the person next to him. The snow began to dart down heavily. It soon began to drift against the cabin and corral, several feet in some places. If Raney was out in this, he better find shelter prior to nightfall, which would soon make its appearance as the evening dusk had already settled in with the blinding snow. It soon had the eerie appearance of a very sad and gloomy day. It snowed like this for almost three days, and the livestock had to remain inside the closed barn for their own protection from the cold and from wild animals. The snow was too deep to venture out except to care for the livestock at least once a day.

Everyone was forced to stay inside due to the severity of the weather and unseen enemy. However, after three days, everyone was getting cabin fever and longing to get out and brave the winter day even for a short time. Marcy loathed the thought of being shut up for so long not even seeing the light of day or having fresh air. There had been days like this in the big woods back in Minnesota, but the family had been together then. Marcy suddenly remembered how her father had played the violin and they had sung songs, played games, and her mother had read stories to them. Her beloved parents had caused the time to pass by a little faster and made them forget the bad weather outside. It made the long days shorter and even more enjoyable for them because the whole family had participated and relished these times together. Time

MARLENE WISE

was a strange thing; it had a way of passing by without much thought of many trying things. Then other days seemed to drag on and on with too much thought and too many memories, some good ones and some very painful ones that were better to be forgotten.

Already Marcy yearned for the warmth of spring and the beauty of new life it would bring with it. But always she was grateful that Clint had found them and brought them to his home here in the mountains. She would often sit and think of where they might be now if Clint had not found them. Would they have been able to find some shelter from the winter, and would Raney already have found them and killed them? Questions like this often came to her mind, and she was eternally grateful for what had been provided for them and for the protection of Clint and Hank.

Two weeks passed. The weather had almost straightened up, for the forceful drifting snow had pretty well settled and no more had blown in. The snow wasn't as deep as it had been; it had even melted some in certain areas. On a cool crisp morning in mid-November, Black Wolf and his family came by. This did not seem to be a friendly visit as before. Silver Moon was in deep mourning because his only daughter, Dancing Star, had been shot and killed and her horse and rifle had been stolen. The thief had left her in a ravine near some spruce trees to die alone in the cold of winter. Black Wolf stated that the white eyes, their friend, had taken her life. He had stolen food, her moccasins, and a medallion he had given to her when she was a young girl. "We will hunt

154

your friend down and see that he dies slowly by the knife for the great evil he has done to us. We wish his memory to be etched with the wrong that he has done."

Clint spoke words of truth to Black Wolf about Raney and told him what kind of man he was. Clint was strong, but it now sounded almost as if he was begging when he said, "Black Wolf, please understand me, this man may be white, but he is not our friend. He has killed his own kind also. He has taken the lives of many on a small wagon train, and he now wants to kill the people who live here with me, especially the two young girls. We also are looking for him because of the evil and wrong he has done to us. He helped kill the parents of the young girls and stole all of their belongings." He hoped that Black Wolf would believe that they had nothing to do with this horrible crime Raney had committed.

Black Wolf let them know that they must kill Raney and avenge themselves for the death of Silver Moon's daughter. "When we have finished with him, you may do whatever you wish to do with him or bury him however you see fit. We do not want you to interfere with what we have to do. If this man is captured, you will still be friends with Silver Moon and his tribe. Your help, loyalty, and kindness are not taken lightly. You are like a blood brother to me, and because of this, Silver Moon will be told of this evil man and the wrong that he wishes to do to you and your friends. He must be captured and his evil works stopped. We will lay a trap for him and catch him as we do the bear or the silver coyote." Immediately they left to make plans of the capture of this evil man.

MARLENE WISE

Luckily, there was a break in the weather, and Black Wolf and eight of his braves began to search for this demented man.

Clint had no doubt Raney would be found and Indian justice meted out, or at least what the Indians felt would be true justice. The Indians knew this country far better than Raney ever did or could ever hope to know. He had no place to hide that the Indians could not find or that they didn't already know about. They knew every cave, ravine, hole, and place that man could take shelter during a storm. However, there was no doubt that Raney could elude them for a period of time, but the snow tracks would be hard to cover and even easier to find. If Raney moved about, he was sure to be found, as the Indians would search diligently for him.

Two days had passed when Silver Moon showed up in front of the cabin. The grim look on his face told them right away that Raney had been captured. There were no words that really needed to be spoken, but as Silver Moon turned his horse, he paused and then said in a flat tone, "We have found the man called Raney. Do not interfere with our justice and our customs, for it would only cause grave problems for us all." Hearing this now, everyone knew that Raney had been captured, and they cringed at the thought of justice that the Indians would mete out to him.

It was usually a slow and torturous death that any person that found themselves in this situation would want to have over and done with. They usually screamed at the top of their voice and begged for instant death. But

156

the cries and begging always fell on deaf ears when it was a matter of justice for the Indian family. They had their own ways and customs to deal with people like Raney. There was no help for him this time and nothing they could do to save his worthless hide. Marcy shivered and cringed at the thought of his severe punishment as she remembered the day she had barely nicked his shoulder in order to save Tyler's life. He had wailed and moaned like a dying man with a bullet deep inside of him. Marcy thought how he had begged her to shoot him at the burned out wagons and how she had wanted to in all of her anger but had only told him that he wasn't worth the precious bullet to do the deed. He had gasped and fell back like he was dead, making her believe that he had died at that moment, but he had not; it was only another of his tricks. She was sure now that he would probably try to feign death many times but that it would be of no help to him. In her mind, she thought, *May God have mercy upon his wicked soul.* Marcy and the others went about their work even though it was hard to concentrate and keep busy. They were relieved in one sense but felt saddened in another, for they knew Raney would suffer much unspeakable torture.

Hank had prepared a nice grave marker for Stewart and Alisha Brewster. He had carved the names and dates and other important information on the marker very carefully. The markers were taken and placed on each grave, and this somehow gave a sense of completion.

As they sat at the table, Mrs. Payton reminded them that it would be Thanksgiving before too long. "Yes," the reverend agreed, "and we surely have a lot to be thankful for."

Beth suddenly smiled at Marcy, and her eyes glistened with joy. "Marcy, have you forgotten what happens in a few days?" she asked excitedly.

"What do you mean, Beth?"

"Oh, you have forgotten. Your birthday! Marcy, your birthday!"

Marcy leaned back on her chair and sighed. "Why yes, I had forgotten, Beth. I really had," she said with a surprised look on her lovely face.

Mrs. Payton rising from the table, said, "Well now, we must celebrate, so I shall bake a cake for you and we'll have a party too."

Hank spoke up and added his bit too. "I reckon I could play to you on my old harmonica."

"Oh." Marcy sighed. "I would like that very much. You're not teasing me, are you, Hank? Do you really play the harmonica?" she asked with glee in her voice.

"Sure I can, Marcy. But just when will the big occasion be?" Marcy replied that her birthday was the week before Thanksgiving.

"It is not many days away then," Clint announced.

Hank asked Beth when her birthday was, and Beth smiled proudly and said, "In April, the most beautiful month of the whole year."

Word came by a lone brave for Clint and Hank to come get Raney's body if they wanted it. They reluctantly saddled up and took a pick and shovel and three boards off one of the old wagons and an old worn blanket. They rode with the Indian in silence to a remote area on the other side of the low hills. The Indian pointed with his rifle in a general direction and spoke his native tongue, but Clint understood most of what he had said. The Indian cast a last look in the direction of Raney's body and then headed south to the lower mountains in the direction of Outer Ridge. The Indian's face showed no emotion at all, not even a look of victory or satisfaction, joy or contentment, or even sorrow or hate. It was as though he had done his job and now he moved on to other things that needed to be done. He was simply saying that justice had been meted out and they could come do what needed to be done according to white man's customs. Clint knew this, but he did not relish what he knew he was about to behold.

With a knot in his stomach, he turned and told Hank that he could remain behind and he would attend to this by himself. However, Hank very adamantly refused the offer Clint made to him and made preparations to go with Clint. They rode on in deathly silence. Soon they came to a stand of trees and dark boulders. Off to the far right hung upside down was the body of Raney with his limbs pulled taunt. He had been scalped and had tiny deep cut marks all over his body. He had been tortured slowly and had bled to death. There would be no jokes or tricks this time. There would be no more attempts of stalking Marcy and Beth and trying to kill them. There would be no more chances of any kind for this poor misguided man who had made so many wrong choices. He surely had suffered more than one could even imagine.

MARLENE WISE

The men took the body down without further delay and immediately rolled him up in the old blanket so they wouldn't have to view him while they worked at digging a grave for him. Digging the grave with the pick and shovel took a long while, as the ground was still partially frozen in places; however, the job they had come to do was finally completed. They laid the three boards down and bound Raney's scarred and bloody body with ropes to hold it in place while they lowered the boards down into the grave. They lowered the corpse until they felt the boards touch the bottom of the grave. They then removed the ropes and began to shovel the cold dirt back into the hole. The last step was to cover the fresh pile of dirt with some rocks and boulders to prevent wild animals from digging into the grave. Two sticks were hurriedly bound together for a crude marker until something better could be done. The sticks were pushed into the fresh dirt and held in place with the rocks. No name could be put on the grave at this time, and as the men rode back in weariness, Clint wondered if Raney had any family, perhaps a wife or some children. If so, it was almost kinder to let them think he had died along the wagon train trail. No one would want to hear of all the sorrow and death that he had caused many people. Most of all, they wouldn't want to hear of the gruesome death and torture that Raney had experienced for all of his evil deeds and bad behavior. He was laid to rest and would soon be forgotten. He'd be just another person that the frontier land had taken in a horrible way. His own family would probably never know what had happened to him or how he died, only guesses.

160

The cabin never looked so good, as both men were cold, hungry, and very tired, both physically and mentally. The only pertinent information the women were told was that Raney was indeed dead at the hands of the Indians. They had sought out true justice for Dancing Star and meted out what they felt was fair punishment for Raney's thieving ways. They told the ladies that they had buried Raney themselves about five feet under the cold, uninviting ground, and he was now a prisoner of the cold, damp, dark ground where he would never bother anyone again. He could now be forgotten forevermore; only the cold grave would know that he was its prisoner.

BIRTHDAY BLIZZARD

A sweet smell filtered throughout the entire cabin. This day could not hold any surprises as far as a birthday cake was concerned. Mrs. Payton was baking a cake filled with wonderful warm spices for Marcy's birthday. She was preparing the sugar in the kettle for a nice glaze to top off her masterpiece. Everyone had eaten a good breakfast not long ago, but the heavenly smell wafted into their nostrils and made their stomachs growl as though they had not eaten for several hours. Their mouths watered for a bite of Mrs. Payton's birthday creation, but they would just have to wait until the right time for everyone to be served a luscious piece of cake. However, since the celebration would not be until evening time and right after supper, Mrs. Payton rushed around tidying up and finding all sorts of things to do because she wanted everything to be just right for Marcy. If anyone deserved to have a good time and a nice birthday, it was certainly this young lady.

Beth was only too eager to help with the all the festivities for her dear sister. She loved her sister very much, and she felt even closer to her now since their parents had been killed. Marcy had not only been a great sister to her but also like a mother to her many times. The men went outside to chop wood or to work at the barn thankful that they didn't have to remain inside and continue to smell the taunting wafts of cake baking. Marcy went to her room to mend some clothes and work on her own secrets, as the Christmas season was not too far away now.

Mrs. Payton went to her old charred trunk and took out a large piece of colored cloth. "Here, Beth, we'll use this for a pretty tablecloth," she said. Clint had told Mrs. Payton that there was a wooden box in his room and that for this special occasion she should use what was in the container. Mrs. Payton remembered this and like a little child could hardly wait to go to the room and find the wooden box that Clint spoke about. Indeed, she did find it. She pried the wooden lid off, and to her amazement she found wrapped in paper and straw a set of very old dishes. A cup and a few other pieces had been chipped and one plate had a slight crack, but all the rest were in perfect shape. They were white with little tiny flowers of gold and blue. Mrs. Payton could hardly believe her eyes, but seeing the beauty of the dishes before her, Mrs. Payton called to Beth with a sound of excitement in her voice. "Beth, help carry these dishes to the table, and please be very careful with them. I'm sure there is a story behind something as pretty as these and how they found their way out in this forsaken land," she said with curiosity.

Beth took six of the plates Mrs. Payton handed to

MARLENE WISE

her, and with great care she carried them to the table almost as if she were carrying a basket of eggs and placed them in their proper places. Beth stood gazing down at the plates as if she were in another world. Finally her hand slowly touched one of the plates, and she gently rubbed the gold rim that circled the plate. Immediately her thoughts raced back to the big woods of her forgotten home. Her mother had had a beautiful set of dishes too, and she remembered how they had used them for special days and when company had come to visit. It brought back a whole flood of memories, some very painful, but for the most part good ones about her parents.

"Hurry, Beth," called Mrs. Payton as she flitted about here and there with great speed. "Our meal is almost prepared, and I'm sure everyone will be very hungry, especially the men who have been outside working so hard and diligently." Quickly, Mrs. Payton placed a lamp close to the table for a little more added light. "Beth, if you will, go get the men, and we can start our celebration," stated Mrs. Payton. "Hurry along now, we don't want the food to get cold."

Beth started and then paused. "Oh, Mrs. Payton, before I do, I want to go put on a special dress and comb my hair," she stated.

"Okay, my dear, run along and tell Marcy to get ready also." Beth, full of delight and happiness, ran to get her pale yellow dress that she had worn that night at the fort dance. Marcy slipped into her green dress with the tiny flowers and lace collar. Both girls combed their hair and then entered the room together.

MARCY

Mrs. Payton clasped her hands tightly to her chest and sighed. "Oh, how beautiful you both look! I could be no prouder than if you were my own daughters," she boasted out loud. Beth slipped her coat on and started outside to call the men, but she met Reverend Payton, and he said he would go tell the men to come to supper. So Beth hurried back to the warmth of the fireplace to be with her sister.

It was still damp out, and the mountain's breath blew quite cold air into the room when the door was opened. It had a cool crispness when it touched Beth's face and caused her to shiver a little. Perhaps the weather was getting ready to turn and bring another winter storm soon. The door opened, and the three men came in anxiously awaiting the food they had been smelling all day. All of them took a turn at the wash basin of fresh water, and then Clint disappeared into his room as the others washed and made ready for supper. In a short while, he returned looking somewhat different than anyone had seen him look because he was wearing dark trousers with a blue shirt and a dark vest. As he entered the room, he walked over to put some more logs in the fireplace.

As he reached for a log, Marcy came to the table and set down a big bowl of hot spiced pumpkin. Clint's eyes were immediately drawn to her. He touched the log but did not pick it up or move it, and his hand rested on it as though he was trying to remember what he had utterly forgotten he was going to do. His head was swimming around and around with so many thoughts it was hard to concentrate. Never had he seen a young woman so

165

beautiful and so glowing as the one standing in front of him right now. Her auburn hair seemed to glow from the light of the lantern that she stood next to. She looked so beautiful and yet so strangely fragile and so alone. Her cheeks were rosy, and her complexion was smooth with a warm glow of happiness. This was the first time he had seen Marcy appear to be so happy and have a real smile on her face. After a few minutes, Clint realized that he must be staring at her, and he quickly grabbed a large log and put it on the fire. Mrs. Payton's voice came floating through the haze that Clint had been caught up in at that special moment.

Everyone gathered around, and Mrs. Payton sat Clint at the head of the table. Just to his right she sat Marcy and Beth, and to the left she seated herself and her husband and then Hank at the end of the table. As everyone was being seated, they all admired the table and its settings.

Clint looked around and said, "Reverend, let us all hold hands and return thanks." Each one clasped the hand of the person sitting beside them. They bowed their heads, and then the reverend began to pray. But after the reverend said amen, Clint held on to Marcy's hand for a little bit longer. "Happy birthday, Marcy. May you have many more happy ones." Then everyone at the same time chimed in and said, "Happy birthday, Marcy."

She thanked them, and almost choking up, she stated in her soft, almost childlike voice that she was very thankful to be celebrating her eighteenth birthday with such good friends. There were times when she had wondered if she'd ever survive to reach this birthday or any other day. Clint was somewhat surprised and taken aback a little at her admission of her age because he had thought her to be a little older than eighteen years of age. She certainly looked older than her few young years, and she seemed more mature. This young lady had had a lot of responsibility placed upon her shoulders these past six or seven months—responsibility that an adult would find hard to deal with each day.

Marcy's birthday meal consisted of mule deer steaks, gravy, bread, beans, mashed pumpkin, squash, and fresh coffee with glazed spice cake. After all had eaten and everyone was full and content, the table was cleared of all the leftovers. Hank took a little wooden stool and set it in the middle of the floor. He looked at Marcy and made a low sweeping bow. "My lady, will you have a seat?" He gestured. Marcy crossed the room and sat on the little stool wide-eyed with contentment.

Mrs. Payton stepped forward and said, "Happy birthday, dear. This is from me and the reverend." Mrs. Payton had made a beautiful soft neck scarf for her.

Then Beth said, "And this is from me with a lot of help from Mrs. Payton." It was a beautiful dainty little handmade handkerchief in a pretty blue color.

Hank then presented her with a lovely wood carving of a horse. It was only about five inches high, but it had a great resemblance to Striker. It was smooth and had been carefully carved with detail, and she knew he had spent much time on it.

Clint was anxiously awaiting his turn to bestow his

MARLENE WISE

gift upon Marcy. At last his turn came; he took out a small leather pouch from the inside of his vest pocket and held it out to Marcy. She tenderly reached out and took it very gently in her small hand. It hardly weighed anything at all; it was so light it felt as if nothing was in the bag. Looking curiously at Clint, she slowly and curiously pulled the leather strings and opened the small pouch. Cautiously and with care, as though it might bite her, she poured the contents out into her small-boned, shaking hands. She drew in her breath and sighed as her eyes looked upon a very finely crafted and beautiful necklace. The minute her eyes beheld it, she knew that it had been the work of one of Clint's Indian friends. Perhaps it was Dancing Star who had made it before she was killed. The necklace had been made of tiny dried seeds, little blue stones almost perfectly rounded, and bits of silver and little pieces of leather. She was surprised that Clint would give her such a wonderful present. Marcy profusely thanked and hugged everyone.

While she went to her room to put up the presents, the others cleared the middle of the room. Hank took out his old harmonica and began to play a toe-tapping and hand-clapping song. The reverend and Mrs. Payton started the first dance. Clint asked Beth to dance with him while Marcy was putting her things away. Marcy returned to the celebration wearing the necklace and was about to burst with pride. Clint then asked Marcy to dance with him, and they danced and danced and danced. Clint finally pulled himself away from Marcy and danced with Mrs. Payton and Beth again. The reverend danced with Beth and Marcy also, and then Clint felt it only fair for him to switch places with Hank and play for a while so that he could dance some too. They all whirled and whirled forgetting their problems of the past. At long last, everyone was exhausted and had to sit for a spell to just catch their breath a bit.

Beth was the first one to speak, and her voice seemed to break at points as she declared that this was the first time in a long time that she had liked this land and this place. "This has been a good day for me, but I'm tired and I think I'll go to bed now." She went over and hugged her sister and gave her a kiss on the cheek. She hugged Mrs. Payton and thanked her for the nice supper for Marcy and the cake and everything and then quietly and without further adieu went to her room.

Quietness blanketed the room as they all sat resting and thinking about the events of the day. Then everyone's ears caught the sound of the eerie moaning of the wind. The tree branches began to whip against the cabin, and as time passed, they beat upon it more vehemently. The cold dampness that seemed to follow the wind began to have an effect on the warm skin. It seemed like it pierced the body with its long bony fingers and caused chills to run up and down one's spine. Hank stepped over and put more logs on the fire. Even the fire seemed to welcome the new logs and began to lap at them with consuming fierceness. The fire leaped with fiery bursts of red and orange cinders shooting out on the hearth. Clint walked to the door and opened it slightly. Snowflakes were blowing wildly in every direction like a mass of angry disturbed bees. The forceful wind blew snow all over the floor. What he saw made him quickly slam the door and step back. "I'm glad we filled the lean-to with wood and cut up all those extra logs. Looks like we're in for a really bad storm this time. The temperature is dropping very fast," he declared. "Looks like another blizzard coming."

No one had paid any attention to Marcy. When she saw the snow blowing so hard and knew a vicious storm was well in the making, she went immediately to her room and changed out of her birthday clothes rapidly. She had donned a pair of her father's pants, a warm shirt, his boots and socks, her coat, and the new scarf Mrs. Payton had given her. She was going to the barn to make sure Striker was warm enough and that he was okay. He had been so faithful and protective of her family, and now she only wanted to return the favor to him. But before she reached the door, Clint ran across to her.

"Where do you think you're going in this storm?" he demanded in a harsh tone, which surprised Marcy.

"I have to go see about Striker," she insisted.

"You can't go outside in these conditions!" he argued.

"I'll hold on to the rope, but I have to go, I must," she said adamantly.

Seeing that it was useless to argue with her, Clint said, "Okay, wait and I'll go with you!"

"He's my responsibility! I can handle it all right!" she retorted.

"Hank, keep the fire going," he said as he went to get his hat and coat. She had found the rope and began to follow it up to the barn door. The cold wind whipped fiercely and slashed at her with a cruel, bitter coldness. The trees were heavy laden with a great burden of ice hanging on to every branch, and now the fresh snow topped the already massive branches with an extra load of weight. She could hardly tell where one tree stood from another against the blanket of heavy snow that appeared like a white sheet hanging down from the heavens. It was a struggle, but Marcy finally reached the barn door only to find that the wooden board behind the pin was frozen and wouldn't budge. Marcy beat and pushed until finally the board gave way and freed the door to be opened. But while lifting the board up, she heard a huge crack like the sound of a whip. A gigantic branch from the closest tree to the barn came flying down with great force and hit the barn door. In the twinkling of an eye, Marcy was thrown to the ground and partially pinned down under the cold blackness of this broken branch that looked and felt like a massive icicle. Brave Marcy lay lifeless as though she were dead.

Clint had heard the sound and thought it sounded like a rifle shot, so he hurried through the howling and blowing wind just as fast as he could make his legs go without falling down into the drifting snow. When he reached the barn, he found Marcy lying on the cold snowy ground with part of the heavy branch lying across her. He knelt down beside her, and with all of his might, he tried to push the branch off of her, but the icy weight of the wood, the wind factor, and the snowy ground now getting slippery were too much for him alone. He sensed

MARLENE WISE

that he needed help, and he needed it immediately. He felt for his revolver, but he had been in such haste he hadn't remembered to bring it. Then he remembered the gun he kept hidden in the barn for just such emergencies. He squeezed through the fallen limb and the half-open door as quickly as he possibly could. He went to the spot by feeling in the dark for the place he had hidden the revolver and retrieved the pistol. He went out, fired three shots in rapid succession, and only hoped they could be heard above the noise level of the wind.

Indeed, Hank had heard the shots, and after a short time, which seemed like a whole lifetime, he saw Hank and the reverend along the rope with lanterns swinging in the wind. They bent down and asked in loud screaming voices so as to be heard above the screeching wind, "What happened?"

Fighting for breath and trying to talk loud enough to be heard, Clint told them to take Marcy to the cabin immediately. "Tell Mrs. Payton to take care of her, and I'll be there just as soon as I can. Go on now! Get her out of the cold wind! Be careful with her!" he ordered them. "I don't know how badly she is hurt, but we can't do anything out here in the wind and the snow." So the men carried the unconscious Marcy back to the cabin. They fought for solid footing all the way as they walked against the wind.

Meanwhile, Clint went in and soothingly talked to Striker because he was nervous and antsy. He had heard Marcy's voice and then the loud crash soon afterwards. Striker had stomped and moved around wanting out of

MARCY

his stall to go to Marcy, but he was too confined to do much. Clint patted Striker's head and gave him a little extra corn and some extra grass feed. He saw that there was water in his trough, and he then threw an old blanket over him that Marcy sometimes covered him with on cold days. Clint knew that he'd be okay until morning. He quickly checked over the other animals and fed them and made sure they were bedded for the long cold night ahead of them. Hopefully the storm would have abated by morning.

Clint's adrenaline flowed rapidly as he didn't know how badly Marcy was injured and what would have to be done. His mind was going over all of his medical know-how. He took long steps and held tightly on to the rope. He knew if he just kept going even though it was hard to walk, he would eventually come to the front door of the cabin. Sure enough, he finally reached the front door out of breath and very cold. His chest hurt from all the cold wind he had sucked down in his lungs while walking against the wind. The reverend heard him at the door and ran and opened it wide for him. He reached out to help him inside the warmness of the cabin. Mrs. Payton had a big cup of hot coffee waiting for him. As he drank it and warmed his half-frozen hands, he asked how Marcy was doing.

"She has a cut on her forehead next to her scalp, and I'm not sure about her arm; it may be broken," said Mrs. Payton. Beth had heard all the commotion and had come to see what was happening. She was sitting by Marcy and just staring down at her in disbelief, and all she had said was, "Please, Marcy, don't you die too and leave me all alone." Beth and Mrs. Payton had removed her heavy and bulky clothing and covered her with a warm blanket that had been heated by the fireplace. They had laid her on the table close to the fireplace so they could keep her warm and snug from the cold and keep her from chilling. They were all awaiting anxiously for "Doctor" Clint to give his assistance.

After drinking the coffee to warm him inside and warm up his cold hands, he told Beth, "Please go to my room and bring me my doctor's bag. I'll need clean bandages and some very warm water." The reverend and Hank moved down to the end of the room out of the way until they were called upon for any needed help. Clint listened to her heart, and it sounded fine. Next he attended to the bump on her forehead. There was a small cut on the side of her head, and he sewed it up quickly while she was still unconscious. Her arm was not broken but badly sprained at the wrist and bruised at her elbow. He checked her legs and feet, but they appeared to be all right. Mrs. Payton said that she had a large bruise on her back near her left shoulder. Elmira gently rolled Marcy over on her side, and Clint cleansed the bruise and applied some salve to it. As she turned her back over, they heard a low moan as if she was in pain.

Clint leaned over and said gently, "Marcy, Marcy, can you hear me?" But she did not move again nor did she reply to his question. So Clint sighed and told the others to go on to bed and that he intended to sit by her side all night in case she woke. Clint sat silently on a little wooden stool next to the table by Marcy and watched the glow of the fire. His memory flitted from one thing to another. He thought of the wagon train going to California, about his parents, about medical school and more training, his father's practice, his life here for the last two years. Then his mind wandered back to Marcy. How beautiful she was, how strong and courageous, her stubborn determination to make things better for her and her young sister.

Marcy stirred and gave a small moan but didn't wake up. It was when Clint stood thinking she was waking up that he looked down at her and realized how much he really loved her. He had loved her that first day they met when she held the rifle on him and said, "That's far enough!" She was only eighteen, and he was twenty-six, and yet he knew beyond all doubt that he truly loved her. He had felt this even stronger when she had helped carry the food to the table today and they had started to celebrate her birthday. He had wanted to tell her then, but he wasn't sure how to go about it. He knew that Mrs. Payton had sensed something too about the way he had looked at Marcy when she had entered the room in the early evening. Clint laid down his head and all of his swirling thoughts and memories on the side of the table by Marcy and fell fast asleep. He had not realized just how very tired he really was.

The damp grayness of the morning seemed to shake Marcy awake. She opened her eyes and suddenly felt very strange, even confused. *Where am I?* she thought silently. Then she raised her head slightly and saw Clint's head leaned over on the side of the table beside her.

MARLENE WISE

She tried to stir a little and asked out loud, "What am I doing on this table?" As she began to stir about more, Clint suddenly awoke.

"Well, how are you feeling?" he asked gently.

"What happened to me?" she asked in a hushed whisper. "My head hurts and my arm is terribly sore."

"You don't even remember the raging storm last night and the accident?" he inquired of her.

"Well, yes, yes, vaguely, I do," she slowly replied as though she was trying to pull it all together. "Striker. I was going to check on Striker. How is he?" she asked with great concern.

"He's fine. I gave him some extra food and covered him with the old blanket."

"Oh, thank you, thank you," she said drowsily. Clint spoke with great concern and warned her that her head would probably be sore for a few days.

"You've had a nasty bump on your head and also a little cut. I had to put a few stitches in a cut on the side of your head."

"Now I remember. The branch fell on me at the barn door and hurt me. Yes, yes, I'll be okay. I know that I will be."

"But," Clint reminded her, "you must rest for a few days and not be up and around much. Maybe by Thanksgiving time, you will be up and around and doing a lot better."

"That's only a few more days away," she gently reminded him. Clint carried Marcy all rolled up in the warm blankets to her own bed so she could rest better and get well.

THE DOCTOR'S PROPOSAL

Thanksgiving time came and went with a wonderful celebration of thanks and a table of great abundance. Everyone had a lot to be thankful for this past year. The last days of November was ushered in with surprisingly warm days of sunshine. The sun came out, causing the remaining snow and cold weather to vanish for a short while. At times, it was still cold enough for a coat, but there were no blizzard-like conditions.

The first few days after Thanksgiving were nice enough to get out of the cabin, and Beth wanted to go out after being closed in for so long a time, but they told her not to go too far, as the weather was unpredictable and had been known to change in the twinkling of an eye. The first place she went was to her parents' graves, and since no one was around to hear her, Beth began to talk to them as though they were right in her presence. To her this was like cleansing her wounded heart and soul. She always seemed to feel better after one of these long talks at the graveside. Casually, she walked toward

MARLENE WISE

the big juniper tree that sat among the firs where she used to pick flowers all the time in the summer. She heard a big commotion up in the branches of the tree and looked to see a gray squirrel that had also ventured out of his hiding for a little breath of fresh air. Perhaps the birds had disturbed him from his sleep by trying to steal a few nuts from his cache of food. He angrily ran from one branch to the next chattering as he ran back and forth. Beth found an old large fallen log nearby and sat down for a spell to watch this entertaining little character as he put on quite a show for her.

Marcy soon joined Beth, as she was completely mended and well now, and it was good that she too could come out and breathe the fresh clean air. Then she too seemed to feel the strange sensation of being pulled in the direction of the burial plots. Standing and looking down at the graves of her parents for quite some time, she couldn't help but wonder what it would have been like to have been in Oregon right now. Perhaps she should have suggested more strongly that they stay with the original wagon train. Would her parents be alive today if they had remained, or would death have snatched them in another way? She was saddened a little to know that she would never celebrate another birthday with either one of them, nor would Beth. With this thought in her mind, she leaned against the fence that surrounded the graves and let the hot tears slowly trickle down her rosy cheeks.

"Oh, Father, I wish you were here. I don't know what to do. I don't know what Beth and I will do, and I know that I promised you I would take care of her and see that she was provided for. We can't take another train until late August of next year. I have the money you so wisely had hidden away, but it won't be enough to travel on to Oregon and then live on when and if we ever reach our destination. Perhaps we won't even survive this horrible winter and we'll be with you and mother soon." She sobbed.

Marcy was so carried away with thought that she didn't hear Clint walk up behind her. "Hello, Marcy," he spoke softly.

Marcy quickly dried her face and only half turned toward him. "Hi, Clint," she said hesitantly as though she feared and was ashamed that her voice might crack and give away her inner thoughts. She didn't want him to know that she had been crying because he would probably ask her why and want answers to a hundred other questions. Right now she didn't have any answers, not even for herself and Beth. How would she ever explain her feelings to him?

"I hope I'm not interfering with your private moments," he said.

"Oh no, you're not. I was about to leave and go for a little walk," Marcy said, trying to keep the quiver out of her voice.

"Would you like to go for a ride with me? Mrs. Payton made us some food to take along. I have the horses all saddled."

With great surprise she asked him, "You mean that you saddled Striker?"

MARLENE WISE

"Yes, I did. Is there a problem with that, Marcy? Should I not have?"

"No, oh no, it is okay. It's just that he must really like you, as he is very picky about who puts a saddle on him." She chuckled and shook her head.

"Mrs. Payton said she would take care of Beth and keep an eye on her for you." Everything seemed to be taken care of and plans arranged quite carefully, so they mounted the horses and began to ride off to the north.

"Where are we riding to?" asked Marcy.

"Hank has gone off for a few days to hunt for fresh game for us. I thought that we'd check his cabin for him while he's gone. Also I want to show you a place called the Outer Rim. There is a sight near there that I want you to see."

"Give me a hint, Clint. What is it?"

"No, you will just have to be patient and wait and see for yourself," he said with a broad grin across his face.

They talked all along the way, and the cabin soon popped up among the fir and spruce. It was a neat, small cabin just the right size for one man. Clint dismounted and then reached up to help Marcy down from Striker. As they entered the cabin, Clint realized that someone had made use of it and had left it dirty and cluttered. It had to be Raney when he was hiding out because he left dirty dishes and food scraps on the table. Mud had been tracked in, and scattered bits of grass and twigs were found here and there on the floor and next to the fireplace. The fireplace had not been cleaned after being used for several times. Clint knew Hank all too well and

180

knew that he was a very tidy man and hadn't left such a mess when he came down to stay with him. So Clint and Marcy cleaned up the mess. Marcy washed the dishes, cleaned the table, and then put the dishes and pans away. Clint cleaned out the fireplace thoroughly and put fresh wood in ready for a new fire. He had Marcy make some fresh hot coffee to go with their lunch that Mrs. Payton had packed for them.

For the first time, Marcy asked Clint about his family and the ambush that he had survived. Clint told her the whole story about the massacre of his family and also Hank's family two years ago. Hank was only about twenty-eight years old and had a wife and two children. He buried his family over on the little peaceful knoll just a short distance away from the cabin. They sat on a nearby log and talked for over an hour. Clint revealed all the details of the ambush and massacre of both families. After Clint finished his story about Hank and himself, Marcy had tears in her eyes again. His story was almost identical to hers, and she suddenly realized that they really did have a lot in common. But Marcy did not want to cry in front of Clint, so she fought back the tears with all that she had within her. She had to think of Beth. She kept hearing her father's dying words to her, and this always gave her strength and courage to move on.

As she thought about her sweet and beautiful mother, the burning tears came rushing to her eyes furiously wanting to overflow the brims that contained them and release themselves down her rosy cheeks. She was remembering how that morning of the attack she had braided her mother's hair and then left to go take care of the horses as she had promised her father she would do. She had been in a big rush and had not told her mother that she loved her as she had done on other days. This thought seemed to eat at her and make her very unhappy, but then it was as if someone from behind her said, "She already knew that you dearly loved her by taking time to braid her hair and do something special for her that very morning." She turned quickly thinking that someone was there, but no one was near her at the time. The gooseflesh raised on her arms and the back of her neck, and then her eyes were again like full lakes after a rain, and she could not contain the tears no matter how hard she tried. The hot tears now overflowed the rim of their red, swollen boundary and cascaded copiously down her soft lovely cheeks. Marcy jumped up and raced from the cabin not knowing where she was racing to. She didn't care where flight was taking her; she just wanted to get far away. Her flight was like a swift deer when a hunter was closing in upon it, and there was no place of safety to hide. It used its speed to flee.

But she was not fast enough to find a place of solitude to hide. She heard Clint's voice coming fast behind her. "Marcy! Marcy! Wait, please wait for me. It's okay. I understand why you are feeling the way you do. It's all right to cry; let it all out," he advised her tenderly. He stopped abruptly right behind her and placed his hands on the back of her shoulders and just stood there as Marcy cried. Then gently he turned Marcy around in order to face her and gently removed a wisp of hair that had fallen across her tear-stained face and smoothed it back across her forehead. "Marcy, of all people, I do understand perfectly your feelings," he declared with a smooth and soft lilt in his voice. "I understand your anger, pain, fear, hurt, and all the emotions you are feeling this moment."

She turned without looking at him and fell upon his chest feeling the strength of his arms gathering her to him. He held her close and let her cry out all the mixed-up feelings that she had buried within her. "Marcy, I must confess there is another reason I wanted to bring you up here. There is something I have wanted to tell you for a very long time, and I have not been able to find the right time nor the proper place with everybody around," he confessed.

"As I hold you close to my heart now, it is even more important for me to share my deep inner feelings with you and say what I have wanted to say for a long time." Marcy became very quiet now but was in no hurry to lift her head from Clint's shoulder or remove herself from his strong arms. "Marcy, Marcy, I love you! I believe that I've loved you since that first day we met right after the attack when I found you wandering aimlessly around in your wagon. I want to marry you and take care of you and Beth too. If you want, come this next year, we can catch the train at Fort Hall as it goes on to Oregon. I could establish my medical practice there or whatever it would take to make you happy. I truly love you with all of my heart," he whispered in her ear.

"Yes, and I love you too, Clint. I have known for a long time that I did. However, I have had a lot on my

MARLENE WISE

mind and worries about what we would do, Beth and I. I have to think more of Beth than for myself because I promised my father I would take care of her, and this is one promise I must keep. Beth seems so fragile, and she's had to bear so much sadness and burden for such a young girl. It is so difficult for me to know what to do, and I must not make another mistake that will compound the mistakes that have already been made. But if I had someone like you to share with and love, it would be a lot easier to cope in this life," she said softly.

"Well, will you marry me?" he asked her as he pulled her to arms' length so he could see her face. Marcy felt like she was going to faint as she looked up into his kind and smiling eyes.

"I think my answer will be yes, but give me a little while. I need to talk with Beth," she reminded him. "I'll let you know very soon," she promised.

"Marcy, the reverend could marry us anytime, I'm sure. Let's think it over. We have all the time we need to decide and let everyone know. It's just that I truly do love you and I want you to be all mine simply because I want to be with you every minute of every day, and I want to share my life with you. I want to make life a little more bearable and a little easier for you, and also for Beth." Marcy stepped back feeling like she was floating on a lovely fluffy cloud and finally said that they must be going. Clint lovingly pulled Marcy to him and kissed her, saying, "I hope it won't take too long, as Christmas is only a month away and that would be a perfect gift for me."

Marcy smiled a contagious smile at Clint and began to reach for Striker's reins. "Let's go now, Clint."

184

Before they left the mountains, they rode over to Outer Rim, and Clint showed her where their Indian friends lived. The teepees were sitting in a close-knit circle. The view looked like a home scene with children outside playing, the daily chores being attended to, and fires burning with the smell of fresh meat being cooked and the scent rising heavily into the air. Marcy asked, "How do they stay warm in the snows and blizzards?" As Clint gazed off in the distance, he simply replied that he had been in their teepees before on snowy days, and they were pretty snug and warm. A fire burned inside, and the snow made for good warm insulation, and they buried down under their fur blankets made from the hides of their hunts. Most of the Indians moved on to new hunting grounds and warmer climates for the winter, but some chose to stay and brave the storms.

Clint and Marcy rode back toward the cabin with only a few words spoken but with many thoughts running through their minds. As these thoughts ran through Marcy's mind, she tried to figure out exactly how Beth would feel about all of this sudden news of marriage. When they reached the cabin, Clint helped Marcy down and then took the horses to the barn to care for them.

Marcy noticed the gate to the burial plots was open, so with curiosity she softly walked toward the open gate and found Beth laying fresh cut spruce and fir across the graves. It was still some time off until spring would peek through the cold and snow. Consequently, the only thing that had any green and life to it was the fir and spruce trees, but this seemed to please Beth, so it made Marcy happy for her.

"Hi, Beth," said Marcy. Beth jumped nervously, as she had not heard her sister's footsteps. She had been far away in deep thought about her parents and life back home in Minnesota, as she would often do since they had come here to Clint's cabin.

Beth looked up at Marcy with childlike innocence and stated that she was adding some branches of spruce to make the barren ground look better. "It looks so dull and lifeless with no color on the graves," she stated sorrowfully. But after a while, Beth had completed her task to suit her, and she asked Marcy if she would go for a walk with her. This seemed very fitting to Marcy as she really was anxious to speak with Beth about her ride to Outer Rim and the conversation she had had with Clint. As they walked about, Marcy thought this might be as good a time as any to discuss Clint's marriage proposal.

Beth asked her sister if they would leave this next year and go on the wagon train to Oregon from Fort Hall. "I don't know, Beth. Is that what you would like to do?" she asked quickly. Beth thought silently as she slowly twisted a little twig in her hands.

"I don't know, Marcy. Sometimes I really miss our home in the big woods of Minnesota," she cried. "But we don't have a home there anymore, and we don't have a mother and father anymore. All we have is each other to depend upon," she said as she wiped her eyes and sniffed.

"Beth, I want to talk to you about that very thing. Do you like it here?" she asked her softly.

"Yes, I guess so," she said sadly. "Our family is here

even if we are the only survivors, and it reminds me some of back home," Beth finally said. Marcy reached out and clasped Beth's hands.

"Beth, Clint has asked me to marry him. He loves me, and I love him too. He wants to take care of both of us. How would you feel about this?"

At first Beth's face took on a look of unbelief, and she sighed heavily and said as if in pain, "Oh, Marcy, I'm going to lose you too!"

"No, Beth! You will not lose me too because we will always be together until you decide differently," she told her. "Someday you will want to marry and have children and your own home," she said with great pride. Marcy then related Clint's story to her.

Beth hugged Marcy tightly. "Sister, if this is what you want, then I am happy for you and I want it to be so. We shall always be close to each other like we are now not only because you are my sister but also like a mother to me. I do love you so, Marcy," she said to her with outstretched arms. By now, the wind had picked up a little, and it was getting late in the evening, so both girls walked hand-in-hand back to the cabin with big smiles on their faces and a spring in their walk.

A few days later, while Clint did chores down at the barn, Marcy informed him that her answer was a very definite yes. She would accept his proposal now and marry him, and they would discuss the date at a later time. Clint declared with great joy and exuberance that they would announce it as soon as everyone was together again. Marcy was happy, but at the same time, she had a

MARLENE WISE

nervous knot in the pit of her stomach. She had been a daughter, a sister, a friend, and even like a mother to Beth, but she had never been a wife. Consequently, this made her feel nervous, as she had no mother to ask questions or to get advice from about anything that bothered her. Mrs. Payton was the closest one she had now, and she had been so sweet and so comforting to her that she almost seemed like a true mother. Marcy knew she would have to lean upon Mrs. Payton and ask her about anything she had questions about.

Two days later when everyone gathered around the supper table to enjoy the delicious fresh meat from Hank's recent hunt, Clint said he would like to say something. He then proceeded to tell them he had asked Marcy to marry him and that she had said yes. Hank and the Paytons did not look at all surprised. They seemed to have already figured it all out but didn't realize it was official until Clint had said so. Reverend Payton agreed to perform the ceremony, Hank and Mrs. Payton would stand as the witnesses, and Beth would be a bridesmaid and stand with her sister. Mrs. Payton said that if they would set the date and let her know, she would be happy to bake a special cake and have a wedding celebration. In light of this news, Mrs. Payton had many things to do, one of which was that she offered to help Marcy make a new dress for her wedding. They had enough material and sewing items from the wagons that she could make both girls a new dress. This she did indeed! She worked hard by day and several nights in a row by lantern light in order to complete the promised girls' dresses.

188

Clint invited Silver Moon and some others to the ceremony. If the weather stayed nice, they would have the ceremony outside under the trees. Silver Moon said that after the white man's ceremony they should come to their village for another ceremony with their Indian friends. He wanted them to stay for two moons at their new marriage lodge. Clint looked over at Marcy to see if she approved, and he knew so by the nod of her head. Clint turned and spoke to Silver Moon in his native tongue and said that he would be very honored for this ceremony to take place. The Indians left and returned to their village close to Outer Rim with many things to do and much preparation for the ceremony.

Several days passed with great anticipation. On the morning of the wedding, everyone rushed about with much excitement. Mrs. Payton baked a cake and cleaned the cabin with special care this time. The weather didn't look at all favorable for an outside wedding because the clouds were moving fast and beginning to take on a dreary gray sadness that wasn't appropriate for a beautiful wedding day. Marcy had so hoped the weather would cooperate and stay nice for a few days more. She had truly looked forward to Mother Nature providing the stage for her special day. But with all her wishing and hoping, the wind began to moan and howl like a lonely coyote way off in the hills. They could see rain coming over the higher mountains and down into the lower hills to the north like someone gradually covering the earth with a sheet of darkness.

Marcy, knowing the inevitable course of the storm,

left for the barn immediately to check on Striker and the other livestock. She had planned to leave Striker outside for a while longer to enjoy the fresh air and to nibble the small amounts of grass that could be found in the corral. While she was gone, Clint asked Beth if he might come in and speak to her privately in her room. Beth was quite surprised to hear Clint request this. He said that he had a surprise for Marcy but that he needed Beth's help to keep it a secret. Beth's eyes lit up, and she asked, "How can I help with a secret, Clint?"

"I have a gold band that I want to give Marcy when we are married, but I don't know if it will fit her or not. Your hands are a little smaller than Marcy's. Will you try this on and see if you think it will fit her hand?" he asked her.

Beth took the little gold band and slowly slid it on her finger. "Yes, I believe it will fit her okay," stated Beth excitedly.

"Good, now I want you to keep it wrapped up in this piece of cloth until I ask for it at the ceremony," said Clint with a big smile on his face. "Can you do this for me and keep it a secret too?"

"All right, Clint, I will do it for you and keep it a secret too," she promised him.

"Now, be sure you don't tell Marcy about this. I want her to be completely surprised about the ring."

"Clint, may I ask you, where did you get a ring way out here? There are no stores around here to buy anything," Beth said in puzzlement.

Clint lowered his head and blinked several times to

keep back the hot tears that wanted to rush down his face. In almost a reverent whisper he said softly, "It was my mother's wedding ring. I thought Marcy would like to have it."

Beth stood silently for a long minute. "That's very nice, Clint. Marcy will be very happy to wear the ring, I'm sure. I'm glad she is marrying you."

Clint stepped a little closer to Beth and placed his hands on Beth's shoulders. "Beth, I love your sister very much, and I love you very much also. I want us all to be a family, and I want you to know that you will never have to worry as long as I am around. I intend to care for you and your sister always. It's strange how such horrible happenings can bring two people together." He gently pulled Beth to him and gave her a kiss on the top of her head. Beth felt a strange sense of warmness that she had not felt in a very long time. It was almost like when her father had hugged her and said that everything was going to be okay. She felt safe and secure with Clint just as she had her father.

She was so happy for Marcy that she felt like she was going to burst. If anyone deserved any happiness and kindness, it was Marcy, her beloved and courageous sister. Beth knew that her mother and father would be very proud of Marcy and all that she had done. Beth looked up to her older sister and was so thankful that Marcy's life hadn't been taken with her parents. What would she have done without Marcy to lean upon and look to for help in their troubled and hard times? Beth knew in her heart that if it had not been for pure raw courage and

MARLENE WISE

faith they would probably not have survived. Marcy was strong, brave, and very determined. She was a survivor and an inspiration to all around her.

QUAINT CABIN WEDDING

The ceremony had to be held inside the secluded and sunless cabin, but even so, it would be very nice inside, as Mrs. Payton had done her very best to make sure it was wonderful and memorable for Marcy and Clint. Marcy had hoped to have the outdoors as the stage for her very special day, but it would not come to pass.

Her dress was made from a pink material with tiny red and pink roses. It was fitted in at the waist and had a large bow at the back of the waist. Mrs. Payton had been saving the material to make herself a dress when they reached the new mission that they were to take over. She also loaned Marcy a beautiful old brooch to wear at the neck of her dress. Marcy's long hair was pulled back with two beautiful gold-colored combs that had belonged to her mother. The groom looked exceptionally handsome this day with dark pants, a pale shirt, and a dark-colored vest. His dark hair was combed and neatly in place, and his bronze skin seemed to shine and glow even as the smile on his face seemed to light up his complete countenance

MARLENE WISE

with genuine happiness. Beth looked equally lovely in a soft blue cotton dress with a blue ribbon in her fresh-washed soft hair. Mrs. Payton had helped put some curls in her hair and pinned some on the top with a pretty comb and made little tendrils of curls that hung down around her face. Marcy had found new ribbons and hair combs hidden down in her mother's things in the secret bottom of the wagon. These perhaps had been purchased for a birthday gift or for Christmas gifts for the girls. Everyone looked very nice for the wedding; even the eleven Indians were all brightly dressed in their best beads, moccasins, and deerskin clothing. They appeared to be in a gay and festive mood.

Reverend Payton married Clint and Marcy on this cool gray day at mid-morning. Reverend Payton knew about the surprise Clint had for Marcy, his mother's ring. When he spoke the part, "Clint, will you say, 'With this ring'..." there was a pause as Beth took it carefully from the cloth almost bursting with pride that she had kept the secret so well. Marcy's eyes were wide with astonishment.

Clint took the little gold band and slid it on Marcy's finger and repeated, "With this ring, I thee do wed. I pledge all my love to you." Marcy was completely overwhelmed. She looked first at Beth and then back at Clint with a look of "Where did this come from?"

After the ceremony, Clint told her about the ring, and Marcy said that she felt honored to wear it. "It even means more to me now that I know the whole story about the ring. Oh, Clint, I will cherish it forever and forever."

There was cake and celebration, harmonica music, dancing, giving of gifts, and a happy and festive mood throughout the cabin. One of the Indians left and then returned quickly, bending down to Silver Moon and whispering something in his ear, and then immediately the room of celebration became very still and quiet. Silver Moon said with urgency in his voice that they must all leave now because another storm was approaching and would be there in a day or two. He wanted to have a celebration for the happy couple in his village too. Silver Moon would be offended if he could not have his own celebration to start Clint off in his marriage. Clint meant a lot to him and had seemed like a son to him on so many occasions. Clint had heroically saved his son, helped others in the village and aided them medically when he could, and freely given to them knowledge to help them live and survive better and longer lives. However, Marcy had serious doubts about going to the village at this time because of the upcoming storm. Clint told her it would not be too far to travel and that they would be fine. He didn't want to take a chance of offending his Indian friends after they had gone out of their way to make a nice celebration for them. So, they bundled up in their coats and took a blanket to throw across their legs for warmth and headed off for Outer Rim with the Indians.

Marcy kissed Beth and Mrs. Payton good-bye and said that she would return in a couple of days. Upon arriving at the Rim, the Indian maidens had a large fire going in the center of the circle. There were many decorations of things from the earth and from animals.

MARLENE WISE

There was dancing, drumming, singing, pipe smoking, and talking, lots of talking. The medicine man sprinkled some scented water on them and chanted a good-luck chant. They both were given a special good-luck and good-fortune necklace to wear. Several maidens came and presented gifts to them on a stretched-out buffalo blanket and then placed an eagle's feather in the hair of both Marcy and Clint. Then as the fire roared high and bright, everyone was served a plate of food. While eating, the wind began to howl a little harsher and the fire began to flicker, so immediately Silver Moon arose and asked Clint and Marcy to follow him. He took them to a brand new teepee off to one side of the village. He motioned to the flap of the teepee, which one of the maidens held open for them.

He said in his native tongue, "Here is your marriage bed. We will bring you food and drink, and you will not have to leave the lodge." There was nothing else to be said, so they entered the warm and snug lodge. Marcy was amazed at the warmness and coziness inside the Indian home. A small fire burned off to one side making a yellow and orange glow upon the inside of the teepee. They listened as everyone left to go back to their dancing and drums, which would last well into the night. Come morning the tent flap was barely opened and a plate of food and drink was set down at the opening of the teepee. Both Clint and Marcy ate and drank the warm liquid that was served to them. Clint said the drink was probably made from the root of a plant the Indians gathered at the foot of the mountains.

MARCY

Clint and Marcy stayed inside getting to know one another and just talking. Late into the morning of the second day, Marcy fell asleep snuggled up close to Clint underneath the warm buffalo robe and blankets. It seemed like she had been asleep for a long, long time. When she awoke, Clint was propped up on one elbow and watching her as she ever so softly breathed and slept. She opened her eyes only to meet with the soft dark eyes of her husband. He was smiling ever so contentedly. He told her how beautiful she was and what a lucky man he was to have found her that day. They talked about both of their tragic misfortunes and how good had come from something so terrible. He suddenly felt very blessed and quite happy and knew that he was indeed a lucky man to have found someone like Marcy, his sweet, young, beautiful Marcy, so full of courage and determination.

A fierce wind began to blow, and chills ran up and down Marcy's spine, making her shiver. They could hear loud voices outside and the scurrying of people and children all about. Clint wondered what was happening, as it had previously been so calm and quiet. Soon he heard the voice of Silver Moon as if he was giving instructions in an urgent manner. Clint dressed quickly and moved to the flap of the teepee in order to try to see what was taking place. Silver Moon came to the outside of the teepee and spoke briefly, and then Clint hurriedly came back in. "Marcy, we must hurry! A bad storm is blowing in from the north again. It looks like a really vicious one this time, and the black angry clouds look like they could bring a blizzard. Silver Moon says it will be one of the worst storms yet," he relayed to her.

197

MARLENE WISE

The Indians were rounding up their livestock and getting them over to protection in the corrals. Clint and Hank had convinced the Indians to build a corral with shelter for their horses and to stock in some grass, food, and water for them if they were going to remain here and not with the rest of the tribe farther to the south. Hank and Clint had gone over when the weather was nice and had helped to build the shelter so they wouldn't lose all of their horses from the freezing cold. Hank and Clint worried about the Indians in their camp and were concerned that the blizzard conditions would take their toll on them. Clint had made an offer for them to lodge in the barn and use the corral to set up their teepees if they needed to. But they had kindly rejected his offer and said that they would be okay as they had been for every winter. They were more concerned for the animals than for themselves, as some years ago they had lost a lot of their horses due to the severe winter conditions. They would bury into the teepees and stay until the storm passed over, only coming out to check on the horses and get necessary items. Most of the Indians that had remained behind were the younger ones who were well able to fend for their families and themselves and withstand much more of the harsh weather. Only about a dozen had stayed behind to challenge the winter and the severe cold.

In the meantime, Clint and Marcy hurriedly dressed and put on their coats, hats, gloves, and readied their blankets to cover their legs. One of the maidens came and rolled up the bed and all the gifts in a large piece of skin. They were loaded on the horse for the cold and windy trip back home. Two young braves were sent with Clint and Marcy as they traveled back to their cabin. They hurriedly started their trek to the cabin in a great swirling and darting snow that had started to fall. The blinding snow came harder and harder. It stung their faces, and they could barely see where they were going. The wind whipped viciously and slapped their cold bodies and their horses like a trained fighter. When they reached a distance from Outer Rim, Clint told the Indians to go on back to their village. Clint said they could get home all right from here; the horses would lead them the right way.

They halted and hated to go because Silver Moon had given them an order and they did not wish to disobey for they knew the relationship was very close between Silver Moon and Clint. "Tell Silver Moon that I said it was okay and I'll talk to him later. May the great spirit keep you and watch over you," he yelled above the screeching wind. Marcy and Clint put their heads down and headed on in the direction of home. They rode in silence most of the way, as it was impossible to talk without screaming at each other. After a while, Clint pulled on the reins of Striker so he could get as close as possible to Marcy. "Marcy," he yelled. "Are you all right?"

She hollered back as loud as she could, "Yes, I'm fine, just a little cold."

"Well, we are almost there now, just a little distance to go. Hang on!"

They turned the horses and could finally see the

outline of the cabin a short distance away. The smell and sight of smoke billowed up toward the enraged white sky. A whiff of hot food could be smelled as it wafted through the cold air. Hopefully Mrs. Payton was fixing some of those delicious mule deer steaks again. Suddenly, they were both very ravenous. The hard ride in the forceful blowing wind had exhausted them. They were anxious to get inside their cabin again and feel the relief from this horrible storm. But just as they neared the cabin, the horses began to shy and snort.

Striker became very nervous and jumpy and tried to rear up. He acted as though he wanted to strike something or somebody with his front feet. As they slid down off the horses, Striker began to rear up even more and kick with his front hooves. Marcy had never seen Striker do this unless he was mistreated or in some danger. Clint looked in the direction of the cabin off to the left, and there was the problem right there in front of them. A large, lone silver wolf was very close to the lean-to sniffing and searching for something, probably the food he could smell from the inside of the cabin. While Marcy tried to calm Striker and Clint's horse, Clint drew his rifle and tried to steady it in the wind. He didn't really want to kill the wolf, only to scare him away and settle down the horses. He aimed and fired right above the head of the wolf, which did indeed frighten him away.

The door opened, and Hank came out followed by the reverend. "Well, welcome back. Are you still celebrating?" they all asked.

"No, a large wolf spooked the horses," he replied

while looking all about the cabin area. "He must have been caught out in the storm like we were. He must be quite desperate for a meal, and perhaps the smell of the food was tantalizing to him. He is either very brave or very hungry to come this close looking for food or shelter. I'd say that he better go find shelter right quick as this is going to be a really bad storm. In fact, it may last for several days," he stated. "Silver Moon says that it will be the worst one yet."

Hank took the horses and said he'd go bed them down in the barn for them. "You all go on in and get warm and get something to eat and some hot coffee in your bellies. I'll be back shortly after I've rubbed down the horses and fed them," he replied with a bit of shakiness in his voice from the cold wind. Marcy just wanted to get in where it was nice and warm, so as they walked to the door, Reverend Payton held it open for them.

Marcy quickly started to go in, but Clint said, "Hey, hold on a minute." He then swept her off her feet and continued to carry her across the doorway.

"Welcome home, Mrs. Brody," he said as he passionately kissed her. This sounded really strange to Marcy, as she had never called Clint by his last name. But she would get used to it.

"Marcy Brody." She liked the sound of it, but she'd have to get accustomed to being called Marcy Brody instead of Brewster. Beth ran and gave both of them a big hug. She was happy to have Marcy back and Clint too. It had only been two days since they had left, but she had missed them the moment they had started to ride away to the Outer Rim with the Indians.

MARLENE WISE

Clint started for his room to put his things away but was gently informed that it was no longer his room. Mrs. Payton, the reverend, and Hank had all worked hard to fix Beth and Marcy's room for the newlyweds. Hank had moved all of Clint's things into Beth's room, and Beth now occupied the small room all by herself. The reverend and Hank had made a couple of chairs and a small table for the room. Clint's things were neatly stored in one corner and Marcy's in the other corner. Beth had made a new cloth to go over the rough-hewn little table. She was happy with her own room, but she felt bad that Hank had to stay in the small front part of the cabin. He took one corner of the room and placed his meager belongings and his handy old rifle there. He would soon be leaving at the first hint of spring, so he didn't intend to be there very long.

The day slowly wore on as though there was no relief in sight. The snow continued coming down in a shower of white fury along with its friend the shrieking wind, which beat against anything in its path. Hank brought in more wood and stacked it against the side of the fireplace. The temperature was dropping fast, so the fire would have to be kept going all night long. Since Hank was already close to the fireplace in his little corner, he took on the duty of adding the extra wood through the cold night. They hoped to have hot coals by morning so the room wouldn't be so frigid and uninviting. Hank also knew how hard it was to restart fires with damp wood when it was so cold. He would do his job well!

Marcy was worried about Striker and the other horses, so naturally, Clint said he planned on going down to the barn early in the evening to care for all of them. About four o'clock he and Hank wrapped themselves as warmly as possible and went out in the direction of the barn. They held on to the rope attached to the door so as not to lose their way and the direction to the barn. The wind was still so strong and vicious that they could hardly hold on to the rope and walk too. Gratefully, they soon reached the welcome shelter of the barn. Hank opened the barn door, and the wind was so violent that it took both men to handle the door. Once in, the door banged shut heavily and spooked the horses. The men were dressed in heavy buffalo coats, gifts from Silver Moon the first year, and with hats and scarves, so Striker wasn't for sure who was approaching until Clint spoke his name in an easy gentle voice. But even then, it took Striker a few minutes to make up his mind that it was indeed Clint.

The men made sure there was water in the trough, and they put out extra corn and grass for them just in case they might not be able to get back in the morning at a decent time. The horses were checked over thoroughly, and they made sure that each one was in good shape. Before they left, they took shovels and cleaned the horse stalls and then spread new dried grass on the barn floor. They threw some old blankets across the backs of the horses to help keep them a little warm.

The walk back to the cabin was treacherous as they faced the wind's full-blown terror. Hank was glad that Clint had had the sense and forethought to attach the rope to the front door of the cabin. Otherwise, they might be aimlessly wandering around in a circle in this wicked

MARLENE WISE

snowstorm. Nothing could possibly live out in this kind of storm for very long. When they finally reached the cabin door and opened it wide to enter, the smell of food and hot fresh coffee permeated the air and saturated their nostrils with great temptations. They were suddenly famished from the cold and the hard work. The snow had drifted and was over five feet in some places. The snow had to be cleared from the barn door every day in order to open it. This consumed a lot of energy, so the hearty deer stew and hot biscuits that awaited them were most enticing.

Stomachs all full, everyone was content to sit close to the hearth and talk or read until bedtime. Marcy found her new husband's medical books and papers quite interesting. The more she read, the more she liked and entertained the thoughts of Clint having his own medical practice someday. She could even assist him as a nurse just as Clint's mother had done for his father. The sight of blood and sickness had never bothered her, so in reality, Marcy considered herself to be strong in more ways than one.

The reverend was slow to get up and move around one morning. Mrs. Payton was up preparing breakfast and had made a big pot of boiling coffee, and the flapjacks were just about ready. She went in to tell the reverend that breakfast was just about ready and that he needed to brave the cold and get up, but she found him sitting on the side of the bed shaking with his hands pressed to the side of his temples. He was not shaking from the cold alone because he also had a fever and a pain in his chest. Mrs. Payton went over and laid her hand on his forehead.

"Well, dear, you are burning up with fever; no wonder you are shaking so. You should get back in bed and rest. I'll call Clint to come check on you. You have taken the grippe," she told him as she helped him back into bed.

Clint had reluctantly climbed out of bed this morning, but the cold brisk day had caused him to dress a little faster than usual. Just before he left to go do his chores, Mrs. Payton stopped him and told him the reverend was ill. "Could you come check him after your chores?" she nervously asked.

"What seems to be the matter with him?" he asked Mrs. Payton with concern.

"He has a fever and pain in his chest," she said anxiously.

Hank told Clint, "Go ahead and tend to the reverend, and when you finish, you can come down and help with the remainder of the chores." Clint called for Marcy and asked her to bring his medical bag to him. She hurriedly brought the bag and was surprised and somewhat concerned to see the reverend so ill. He shook hard with chills and complained about a severe pain in his head and chest. Mrs. Payton said it was not like the reverend to complain, as he was hardly ever sick. Clint saw the look of worry on both of the women's faces, so he tried to be reassuring.

He said he would do what he could for him and try to make him more comfortable but that he would need to rest. He gave Marcy instructions to take a container of yellow powder out of his bag and use about one or two tablespoons of the dry fine powder mixed with other ingredients to make a poultice for the reverend's chest. Next, he dug down into a small tin box and took out what looked like some dried leaves and a little vial of some dark brown powder, which had the texture and look of fine sand. He requested that Mrs. Payton bring a small pan to him, and she did so. He placed two leaves and about one half teaspoon of the strange powder into it. He gave her instructions to place about four cups of water in it and let it simmer for about ten minutes. "Pour about one half cup of the liquid and add about one half teaspoon of sugar so it's more palatable. If he can drink it all at one time, it will be better for him. If he can't, then feed him with a spoon every ten or fifteen minutes as much as he will take. But he really needs to have the large dose at one time, if possible. Since the taste won't be so pleasing, try to get him to understand that it is for his benefit if he takes it all now. He needs to start on this just as soon as you can get it brewed."

In the meantime, Clint applied the poultice on the reverend's chest. As soon as the liquid was ready, he drank about one half of the concoction making faces as it went down. The very ill reverend placed his hand up to his mouth and shook his head back and forth and then gulped for a big breath of air. "I'm not one to complain much, but I have tasted much better brew than this stuff," he said through his coughing and sputtering.

"Now, now, my dear, he is only trying to help you get well. He has helped a lot of people, and they have all been grateful to him for his help, and you will be too in a few days. I'm sure even if you don't like the medicine you must know that it is the best thing for you, if you want to get well."

The reverend was sick for about five days. His fever came and went, especially at night. Clint continued the medication and the "horrible brew," as the reverend called it. On the sixth day the reverend woke feeling much better. He had no fever and felt like he wanted to get up and have breakfast with everyone. Mrs. Payton told everyone, "Well, if he's wanting to get up and eat, then I think he must be all well again." Clint checked him and agreed that he could probably get up. But he cautioned him that it would not be wise to go outdoors and he must keep himself warm and not tire himself. He would have to be satisfied staying indoors and helping with light work or assistance around the cabin. The reverend agreed to Clint's suggestions.

There was a break in the weather, and this made the good reverend feel even better. It was cold, but the snow had finally vanished for a little while. Even the sun came out for short periods of time which put a big smile on the face of everyone.

It would be Christmas in less than two weeks. It was hard to work on any Christmas surprises in such confined quarters. One only had a few stolen moments here and there. Sometimes Mrs. Payton went to Beth's room to work, or Marcy went to Mrs. Payton's room and so forth. The women could work on things when the men were at the barn for longer periods of time. When they heard

MARLENE WISE

voices and stamping of feet, all surprises and work were then immediately put away until the next few stolen moments of time.

CHRISTMAS WOLF

At breakfast Clint asked Beth if she would like to go with him and bring back a surprise. Beth raised her head and looked at Clint quizzically. "You have a surprise? What is it?"

"You have to trust me because if I say what it is now it won't be a surprise for anyone," he said with a wink of his eye. "Are you game? Do you want to go with me?"

"Okay, right after breakfast I'll get ready to go."

"Oh, dress warmly, and you'll need a pair of gloves too," he said mysteriously.

The reverend called to Beth, "Use my gloves since I won't be up and around for another day or two, or this is what the good doctor tells me."

The table was cleared, and Beth rushed around and readied herself to go outside. She did dress warmly by putting on a heavy coat, boots, a scarf, and the gloves, which seemed to swallow up her small hands. But they would serve the purpose for wearing them. She opened the door and found Clint all ready and standing beside

MARLENE WISE

the two mules. "Are we ready to go now?" he asked with anticipation.

"Yes, I guess we are," she answered. He explained to Beth that they weren't going to go far so they would just lead the mules. "Then why bring them at all?" quizzed Beth.

Clint's eyes beamed brightly as he smiled at her and said, "Well, how else can we cut a Christmas tree and green boughs and get them home?" He chuckled. Beth stopped in her tracks and drew in a sharp breath.

"A Christmas tree! Oh, a Christmas tree! I had forgotten all about a tree! What a wonderful surprise! Marcy will be happy too and just as surprised. Does she know what we are doing?"

"No," said Clint. "Your job is to search until you find the prettiest one. We better get started on our mission as this could take some time. It's still pretty cold out, so I don't want to keep you out here too long. I don't want you to get sick too right before Christmas."

With excitement, they started down the northwest trail and followed a small path for a short distance. Then they wandered off that little path and down to where there were lots of fir and spruce trees, big ones and little ones of various shapes, sizes, and widths. Beth searched high and low looking at each one she came upon for the perfect tree. Most usually she considered them either too big, too little, too scraggly, or if there were any signs of a bird nest, new or old, she would pass right on by, even if it was the perfect tree. Finally, after searching back and forth, she said, "There, Clint, that one over there. See it?

210

It's not too big and not too little; it's just right for us." She squealed with delight.

"Are you sure this time this is the one you want?"

"Oh yes. Yes, it is, Clint." Clint went to the mules and took down the newly sharpened axe that he had sharpened just for this purpose yesterday after he had done the chores. Beth had chosen a pretty spruce tree that was well formed and had very even branches on it. Clint laid the axe to it a few times, and the little tree finally gave up and toppled over. They spread out an old gray blanket and laid the tree on top of it and rolled it up. The mule could carry it a little better without the branches rubbing and pricking against his hide. They then gathered some big cones and green boughs and wrapped them in another blanket and placed them on the other mule.

Clint carefully put the axe away and said, "Well, Beth, I guess we are ready to go back and share our surprise with the others. We've got what we came to get, and I must say that you did a fine job of choosing the most perfect one for us."

"Everyone will be surprised, won't they?" said Beth.

"I hope they like your choice because you must have looked at thirty of them, and I began to wonder if you would ever find one."

They turned to go and Beth seemed to hesitate a bit. "What's wrong, Beth? Aren't you ready to go yet?"

"I, I was just wondering if, oh, nothing, we better go now."

MARLENE WISE

"Beth, what is it? You were going to say something. You can talk to me and tell me."

Finally she looked away from Clint and said in a hushed voice, "I was just thinking that maybe we could cut a little tree to put on the burial plot for our parents, just so it wouldn't look so barren and drab."

"Sure, we could do that; I was just thinking about doing that myself," he confessed. So they returned to the field of trees and cut a small fir tree and took it with them.

By the time all was loaded and they walked back, it was almost noon before they came in sight of the cabin. They stopped first at the small cemetery and placed the little tree between the graves. The green tree did seem to break the drab and icy silence of the cold snow-spotted ground. Beth stated that her father was always fond of the green fir, pine, and spruce trees. He had so liked their home in the big woods of Minnesota, and this had been one of the reasons, the big beautiful trees and the forest.

Clint took the mules right up to the door, and Beth immediately began to help unload the tree and boughs. She ran excitedly to open the door of the cabin so that Clint could carry in their surprise. Her face glowed and showed its happiness. Everyone's attention was on the door as it was held open widely for the tree and boughs to be brought in. Clint carried the tree to the far corner and sat it down.

"Well, it's almost Christmas time, and we needed a tree to trim for the occasion. Beth has picked us out a real pretty one, don't you all agree?" he asked like an excited

MARCY

child. "We're going to leave all the fixing up to the ladies since they are better at this kind of thing. The men need to go do chores and cut some more wood while it is still half decent weather and not snowing," he said. The men all agreed and began to make ready to go outdoors and get started. Marcy and Clint both reminded the reverend that he could only help with the light work and could not be out in the cold weather.

As Clint turned to go, he looked back at Beth and said with a twinkle in his eyes, "Beth, we'll put you in charge of the tree and some decorations for it."

"Okay, I'd like that very much. I'll see what I can find to decorate it with."

Since that was all settled, Clint and Hank had already started out the door when Hank paused and called to Beth. "Here, maybe this will do for the top of the tree," he said with pride. Beth reached out almost with reverence and took a beautifully carved wooden star that Hank had made from a light piece of wood for the treetop. Hank was quite the wood carver and was always whittling something. Her eyes were filled with amazement and delight at the star she held in her soft little hands, but this told her that Hank had been thinking about Christmas too. There was a tiny little hole in one of the points of the star with a piece of rawhide string in it to tie to the tree.

This inspired Beth to begin a search to collect things to put on the tree for decorations. Clint had given her a little tin box with some colored beads in it to use however she wished. She collected pieces of ribbon, buttons, small cones, and other little items that Hank whittled for her in his spare time in the evenings. Mrs. Payton found time to make two little angels out of bits and pieces of cloth left over from the wedding dresses. With the use of a scraped corn cob, she had something to use for the face and arms of the angels. Mrs. Payton also said they could pop some corn in the evening and that she would show Beth how to take a needle and thread and string the popcorn for the tree.

"Oh yes, Mrs. Payton, I want to do this so the tree will look like it has snow on it," said Beth with delight. Beth stood back with admiration and smiled with glee as their tree was beginning to look pretty and look more like Christmas. The boughs of green were hung around the room on the walls and over the doors with anticipation of Christmas arriving in a few days. Beth and Marcy felt the Christmas spirit, and they were happier now than they had been in a long time since they had left home. Things were beginning to look up, and it was about time.

After that tragic day in August, Marcy could not believe in her heart that their situation would ever turn into anything but misery. But how wrong she had been; life was good to them again. She realized that this was all due to them meeting Clint when they did. She had been really scared the first time she saw him riding up on his horse because she had supposed he was one of the thugs who had killed, robbed, and burned some of the wagons, but how wrong her thoughts had been. Clint and Hank had been literal life savers for all of them. She could not imagine where they would be this day if Clint had not appeared and rescued them when he did. They all had again found life, shelter, food, and clothes for the upcoming winter and had indeed found good friends. Marcy had found a husband, someone to help share her heavy load and love and support her. The thought of finding or even looking for a husband had never even entered her mind. The only thoughts Marcy had allowed her mind to entertain were thoughts of survival and getting on to California to begin some sort of life, to protect and raise Beth, and see that she had what she needed.

Because of Clint, Beth was slowly coming out of the shell she had built around her these last few months. Clint was strength and a father figure for her, something she had so dearly missed after the death of their beloved father. Marcy was so happy that Clint had come into the picture. Marcy had tried to be mother, father, and sister all at the same time these last few months, and it had been overwhelming. At times it had seemed almost more than she could bear at the tender age of seventeen. She had to lean upon the reverend and his wife so many times just for strength and to ask of their wisdom in hard situations.

The cabin was generously engulfed with the clean fragrance of newly cut spruce. A new freshness mingled in with the smells of cooking, and baking aromas were most pleasant to the sense of smell for all. It brought back old memories for Marcy of the good days gone by with family and friends. Christmas was all about peace, and Marcy was beginning to find a sense of peace in her newfound life. Her inner peace of heart and mind

MARLENE WISE

gave her a sense of strength and great joy. God's peace, provision, and protection filled her heart and mind with his promise from his Word when he said, "I will never leave thee nor forsake thee, even until the end of the world." In the quiet evenings, Hank and Clint serenaded them with Christmas music from the harmonica.

Ready or not, Christmas day would emerge across the land like a swift moving shadow. This pioneer Christmas would be much different from any they had ever celebrated in the past with family. Nearly everyone living here had lost close family members except the Paytons, and they had lost close friends on the wagon train. The work they were traveling to in California had probably found others to take their place, thinking they had died along the trail somewhere. Even Silver Moon and his people would share a different Christmas season, for they had lost loved ones this year too, those who were immediate family and very close to them.

Christmas morning crept across the land on the wings of a gentle wind with a breath of winter behind it. There were still places with patches of white frozen snow; however, the skies looked like a mixture of gray rain clouds and snow clouds. It was never surprising when the heavens flooded them with an abundance of snow or just a shower of sparkling and shimmering snowflakes that looked like dancing white leaves falling to the earth, but soon they would melt away into oblivion without many knowing they had even touched the ground in their softness.

Clint was up early before anyone else, and he quietly

opened the door and headed for the barn. He had been excited about his own surprise and in the rush had not taken his gun with him. He tended to the horses pitching them a load of fresh grass and watering them and then gave each horse an extra special Christmas helping of grain. Clint stroked and patted each of them as he was on his way out then talked to each of them in a soft and reassuring voice.

He and Hank had secretly made two rocking chairs, one for Marcy and one for Mrs. Payton. His intentions were to move the chairs out of their hiding place and into the lean-to for Christmas giving. But just as he started out the barn door, he heard a low deep growl like the sound of a dog. He quickly turned toward the direction of the growl and was suddenly faced with one of the largest wolves he had ever seen in these parts of the country. His mind raced back to the wolf he had shot at when he and Marcy had returned that day from the Indian camp. He had shot above his head not meaning to kill him, as it had been a very cold day with snow blowing. Clint figured the lone wolf had been caught out in the weather and was looking for food and shelter. He now wondered if this was the same large wolf that was returning to get his missed meal.

The wolf was in a crouched position ready to pounce at any time. His lips were curled back, and all of his teeth were showing as he continued to growl at Clint and size him up. Clint was close enough to view the face of the wolf and observe his desperation and the hunger that gnawed at his being. The wolf was determined to get

MARLENE WISE

inside the barn where he knew that a fresh meal could be found without too much of a chase and struggle in the cold. However, he had not counted on Clint being in his way when he spotted the door standing wide open. The wolf paced anxiously back and forth growling nervously all the time trying to find a quick opening to get through. Clint tried to move cautiously and slowly backward, but this seemed to irritate the wolf even more. Clint had remembered the revolver that he kept in the barn for special emergencies, emergencies just like this, but there was no way to reach the revolver without moving. Clint knew one sudden move or a quick jerk could make the wolf lunge at him.

For the moment, it was a standoff. Clint could hear Striker getting nervous and stomping around in his stall because he could smell the scent of the wolf and hear the low throaty growl coming from the doorway. Striker could sense that this was danger for Clint, so he began to kick the stall, butt the logs with his head, and stomp the ground viciously. Striker wanted out of his stall, and Clint could only hope that he would settle down and not injure himself with this wanting to be a protector for him. So very slowly, Clint set the rocker down and inch by inch began to move backwards, but keeping a sharp eye on the wolf. He had moved only about four steps back when the daring wolf lunged high into the air and started coming through the door. All in the twinkling of an eye, Clint jumped to the side and backward, falling to the ground. A rifle fired, and the big silver wolf came crashing to the ground and lay lifeless just in front of the rocking chair. Clint trembled and slowly rose on his shaking feet.

Then he saw two Indian braves, Swift Bear and Gold Eagle, come around the side of the barn smiling. Clint gave a deep sigh of relief and bent down on one knee feeling a bit weak and nauseous. Hank had heard the boom of the rifle and came running with his own rifle in hand ready for whatever might face him. Hank too was astounded at the size of the huge wolf and his beautiful silver coat. Hank had hunted all over the mountains surrounding the cabin and the Indian camp and had never seen anything like this. The wolf had probably not had a decent meal in days and now needed something of size to sustain him for the next few days because another storm was slowly brewing in the far northern skies. Perhaps the wolf could read the weather signs as well as humans and knew that he must find food even if he had to take desperate steps to obtain it.

The Indians went over to their horses and returned with a skin sack. They offered the sack to Clint and Hank and stated, "Silver Moon said this was a present to be given to you on this special day. The Great Spirit speaks well of you and your friends." Clint asked them to wait for a moment, and he went back into the barn and then returned with a blanket rolled up in a rather odd shape. He never spoke about what the blanket contained, only that it was a gift for Silver Moon. He asked that the blanket be given to Silver Moon today as soon as possible. The two Indians bid the men good-bye, picked up their silver wolf trophy, and threw him across the back of their horse, but the horses were skittish and reared and did not want to be around the dead wolf with the smell of fresh blood. The Indians were forced to make a travois to haul their prize catch home so as not to excite the horses to run away or rear up and throw them to the ground and hurt one of them. The Indians soon disappeared around the barn just as they had quietly appeared at the crucial time.

The two rockers were taken and stored in the lean-to for the time being. The men finished their chores and finally were ready to go share their well-kept secret with those inside. As the men ravenously consumed stacks of hot flapjacks, little strips of crisp fried meat, two cans of peaches, and hot fresh coffee, they told everyone about the big silver wolf. Everyone ate heartily this Christmas morning, even the reverend. He was well now after his week of sickness, but still seemed a little weak at times. Mrs. Payton made him rest often and did not allow him outdoors very often because she didn't want him to have a relapse.

After breakfast was cleared away, Clint told Marcy and Mrs. Payton to stand by the hearth and he and Hank would return in just a few minutes. They went into the lean-to and brought back the two rocking chairs. Hank set one at one end of the hearth, and Clint sat the other one at the other end. In unison they both said, "Merry Christmas!" Marcy was elated and very surprised at their well-kept secret, especially the fact they had been hidden in the barn. She made daily trips down to the barn to be with Striker and care for him; however, she had not noticed the rocking chairs there.

Mrs. Payton sat down in her chair and said with a

look of contentment on her face, "Oh, this is so nice. I don't think I'll ever want to get back up."

Marcy sat down in hers and then slowly began to rock back and forth. She suddenly realized just how happy she really was. She walked over to Clint, wrapped her lovely arms around his neck, and gently kissed him. "Thank you, Clint. It is such a fine gift and made with your own hands," she said as she walked back and stroked the smooth arm of the chair and then sat down in it again.

As the others sat around the table, they could feel such an atmosphere of great love. Mrs. Payton finally said, "If I don't get out of this rocker right now and get busy, we won't have any Christmas dinner."

Hank spoke up and said, "I have a little something for you all, but I'll wait until after our Christmas dinner."

"So will I," added Clint.

"Then we will wait also," said Marcy and the Paytons, and they immediately went to get started on their special dinner. There was much to be done and a lot of food with extra special trimmings to be prepared for their special day of celebration. Hank took out his harmonica and played some Christmas music for everyone. While the music wafted throughout the cabin, Clint walked over to the tree and stood as though he was in deep thought.

"Beth, this is a very beautiful tree. You did a good job with the decorations, and I love the smell of the spruce boughs." He glowed with happiness. The men sat by the fire and reminisced about the time they had been there. They discussed the idea of leaving in the late summer and what they would have to do if they did. The wagons would

MARLENE WISE

have to be repaired and made ready for travel, as well as the canvas tops for each wagon. The reins and harnesses would need attention and to be thoroughly checked and softened a bit as they had all been stored in the barn these long months. Clint realized that now he would have to discuss this all with his newly acquired family and friends and get their ideas and thoughts. They were not too far from Fort Hall, and they still had plenty of time to talk and make up their minds. Another wagon train wouldn't reach the fort for another six to eight months. He only wanted to do what was best for his family now and see that they were happy and content in this life. He wanted Marcy and Beth to have life a little easier than the harsh things that had been dished out to them these last few months. He intended to protect and provide for them as best he could in whatever situation or home they chose to live. He loved Marcy deeply, and he would fight for her and Beth and try his best to see no more harm came to either one, physically or mentally.

Every time Mrs. Payton or Marcy uncovered a kettle or a pot and stirred the food, the smell was very much overwhelming. Several hours had passed, and it was getting close to time to eat. This would be a very special day that would always be remembered in all their thoughts through many years and Christmases to come.

Clint had requested that Mrs. Payton again use his mother's dishes. The bright-colored cloth that was used at Marcy's birthday party was again used on the dinner table. The beautiful white dishes with gold and blue flowers graced the table and gleamed in the light from the fireplace. Marcy had laid a piece of spruce in the center of the table along with a few cones on either side. As the food was brought to the table, Marcy stood gazing at the setting with a look of wonderment on her face. She slowly stretched her hand forth and picked up a plate. She ran her fingers over the edge of the gold and blue flowers, and as she did so, Clint had stopped talking and was intently watching her. Marcy's gaze raised and caught Clint watching her. "Did these belong to your mother or grandmother, Clint?"

He rose from the little wooden stool he was sitting on and whispered to her softly. "Yes, they belonged to my mother. They first belonged to my grandmother, Corinna Wilton. When we were getting ready to leave Missouri, Mother would not leave them behind. She said that she would leave other things but not her mother's dishes. Father was never one to argue much with Mother or even tell her no, so he built the wooden box they were in and wrapped the dishes in old newspaper and straw. He never really thought they would make it in one piece, and if the truth be known, neither did I. But we didn't have the heart to tell her that we thought that. But surprisingly, they did make it, or most of them did, and I was always glad they did because they meant a lot to her. She is gone now, so they belong to the new Mrs. Brody," he said tenderly.

Marcy set the plate down very gently. "I shall cherish them for as long as they are in our family."

Mrs. Payton asked that everyone gather around the table. Reverend Payton asked the blessing on the food and thanked God that he had kept them thus far and

MARLENE WISE

allowed them to be together on this day. It did not take long after the reverend said "amen" for the plates to be piled high with big pieces of roasted meat, gravy, cooked squash, spiced pumpkin, beans, hot bread, and roasted corn. Mrs. Payton had even made some pies, a cake, and some mint candy. She had found the wild mint leaves growing along the way at one of their stops. She had picked a lot of it and dried it to be used later on down the trail for some hot mint tea and to use as a spice for cooking, and of course, it had its medicinal uses too.

On this Christmas day, voices chatted and laughed and sang and remembered out loud stories about their travels and life. The food was then put away until suppertime, that is, if anyone would still be hungry by that time. No one really felt much like doing anything except being lazy after such a big meal. Beth spread an old gray blanket and a buffalo blanket close to the hearth and settled down to watch the logs burn and glow with their many colors. Hank had showed Beth a trick about putting a large pine cone in with the wood and watching it make pretty colors as it burst forth from the heat. Marcy and Mrs. Payton sat in the two new rockers and very contentedly rested from their day's work of preparing the big meal. The three men sat on the wooden stools. Everyone drank in the quiet and peacefulness for the moment. The only occasional sound was a pop and crackle of the burning logs and the pine cone or a little creak from the new rocking chairs.

However, after some time, the silence was broken by Hank pushing his wooden stool from the table. He walked to the far corner of the room and picked up an old sack that he had laid near the Christmas tree. He laid it upon the table and began to take gifts out of it one at a time. Smiling at Beth, he stretched out his hand and said, "This is for you. Merry Christmas." He had handed her a small leather pouch that Beth took and carefully opened up. She poured the contents out in her small shaking hand.

She sighed. "It's so very beautiful. It's so beautiful." She held the long strip of black velvet with a cameo fastened to the middle of it. She stared at it for a long time with great astonishment and surprise. The cameo would lay just above the throat and look very nice on her long slender neck.

He turned to Marcy and said, "And this is for you, Marcy." Just as carefully as Beth, she emptied the little pouch out into her hands and beheld something so wonderful she could hardly talk. She looked at the gorgeous brooch that lay in her hand and observed the brilliant small colored stones of different shapes and sizes. Marcy surmised that this must have belonged to the wife that was buried along with his two children on the knoll next to his cabin.

"Thank you, Hank. It is very beautiful!" But thank you seemed such a small thing to say, especially when someone had just given her a little piece of their most precious memories.

"For you, Mrs. Payton. I hope you like it." Mrs. Payton's long-fingered hands stretched out to accept her gift that was wrapped in a piece of cloth. She opened it gently and found that it was a little dark blue tin box with hand-painted flowers on the top and sides of it and that it contained some needles, thread, buttons, scissors, ribbon, and some yarn.

Mrs. Payton was so surprised that her eyes became teary, and she said, "Thank you, Hank. I shall always remember with fondness this Christmas gift." He simultaneously handed the Reverend and Clint their gifts. Clint received a handsome wooden shingle that read, "Clinton R. Brody, M.D." He was surprised but very well pleased. The reverend also received one which simply said, "Reverend Caleb Payton." He also was amazed but very well pleased. The ladies had made hand-sewn gifts for the men—shirts, socks, and scarves.

Time had passed on while everyone was exchanging gifts. The ladies took a break to go prepare some hot mint tea to serve with the cake and pie. While the ladies buzzed like bees getting the treats ready, Clint disappeared into the bedroom. After a short while, Mrs. Payton carried the big metal pot to the table, and Marcy brought the pie and cake. Clint appeared in the doorway and then leisurely walked over to the fireplace. He glanced at Marcy with a mysterious smile spread across his face. She poured him a cup of mint tea and graciously held it out to him. He slowly walked over to her and took the cup. He sipped and savored the flavor of the mint tea, and he remarked how good it tasted on a cold day like this.

As he continued to sip his tea, he held a book out to the reverend and said, "This is for you, Reverend. It was my father's favorite book, and I thought you might enjoy reading it." The reverend accepted the book and stepped closer to the hearth where the light was brighter so he could see it better. For Mrs. Payton, he reached in his vest pocket and pulled out a thimble, a thimble he had seen his mother use so many times. He then drew Marcy and Beth close to him. He leaned down and kissed Marcy on the cheek and Beth on the forehead and told them both how much he loved them. From his right pocket, he took something out and placed it in Beth's hand. Beth felt something like new cloth, and she stood gazing upon a beautiful lace-edged handkerchief. Inside was a very small figurine of a child no taller than three or four inches high. From his other pocket, he took out two beautiful hair combs and placed them in Marcy's small hands. They were dark in color and had raised flowers of pink with little green buds around the flowers. Marcy had never seen anything so beautiful, and in truthfulness, she had never owned anything quite so delicate and pretty as these combs.

Clint explained that these things had belonged to his beloved mother. "It's all that I have left of her things, and it is indeed fortunate that I was even able to salvage them from the burning wagons. My mother and father had hidden some things so well that the thieves had not found them. If the thieves had found them in the secret hiding place, I am sure they would have taken them too and probably sold or exchanged them for items they wanted to survive the winter. I want someone I really love to have her things, and this means you and Beth and Mrs. Payton. You are all my family now. We've had hard times, but we are now together. We've got each other," he

MARLENE WISE

declared in a choked-up voice. Knowing he was almost on the verge of tears, he suddenly cleared his throat and said loudly, "Merry Christmas to all. I love you dearly."

ARMY DOCTOR

It was now into the first week of April, and spring had made its entrance in a calm and serene manner. The past months had been cold, snowy, and full of winter storms, and it had been a hard winter to come through. However, life was budding all around, the flowers were coming back, grass was turning green, and the trees were vibrant. The animals had left their drab and dark shelters and were out for strolls in the sunshine, and even the horses kicked up their heels and ran freely in the corral. Birds were building nests and singing happy songs to their young. The whole earth was alive again, and even Marcy carried life. She had found herself with child in February, which frightened her, but then she remembered she had a husband who was a doctor. Mrs. Payton was with Marcy and had seemed like a mother to her since her own mother had been killed. It had been a long time since she had been around little children and cared for them. The baby was not due until late fall, so she had plenty of time to prepare herself. Beth was excited that she was

MARLENE WISE

going to be an aunt, so this was all she could talk or think about. She would ask questions about it when they were together by themselves.

The ladies gave the cabin a thorough cleaning and scrubbed everything in sight. They shook all of the fur rugs, robes, and blankets and aired them outside. The windows and doors were opened, and fresh air blew into the cabin and brought the refreshing smell of sweet flowers and spruce-scented air. The cabin had been closed up for so long it had taken on a damp dank smell. Spring, Marcy's favorite season, seemed to be such a mellow, beautiful time of the year because to her it always meant new life and new beginnings both for animal life and people. She even felt somewhat like the new flowers pushing up through the newly uncovered earth. Mother Nature had removed her white carpet and replaced it with a lush green one sprinkled with color here and there. What freshness, newness, and beauty for the viewer to behold.

In late April, Hank rode in from hunting one day with an abundance of fresh meat and game he'd caught for them. He said he noticed not far away a lot of hoof prints that looked like army horses because they were shod and made imprints in a double row of tracks that looked like the familiar old army formation. "There must have been fifteen or twenty riders or even more, the best I could see." Hank wondered why they had crossed the Snake River and come in this direction, as there were no Indian problems that he knew about.

Clint said, "We should all be aware of what's going

on around us and keep our eyes and ears open. Always know what's going on around you and in our area. Hank, you should always let us know where you are and in which direction you go hunting." Faithful Hank went hunting again a week later as he usually did to provide them with more fresh meat. Just as he had a large mule deer in his sights and was ready to fire, he heard the sound of nearby riders. He stood up and looked below the ridge and viewed a patrol of soldiers coming his way. They halted abruptly and looked in Hank's direction squinting against the sun and trying to make out who Hank was. Three men rode toward him a ways and suddenly stopped as if they had lost view of him.

The soldier cupped his hand to his mouth and shouted, "Are you Joseph Brody's son?" Before Hank could answer, the soldiers were riding up the hill toward him. Hank picked up the horse's reigns and began to walk toward them, finally meeting them face to face about halfway down the hill. The sergeant asked again, "Might you be Joseph Brody's son?"

"No. I'm a friend of his though. Why are you looking for him?"

"We understand he's a doctor," said the soldier.

"Yes, he is. But he has not had a practice in over two years now except that he's doctored the Indians at times and the family and friends that live with him."

"Can you show us where he lives?" they inquired of him diligently.

"Yes, sir, I can."

"I need to talk with him myself, as Colonel McCord

MARLENE WISE

has sent me with an important message for him to be delivered by me personally," he told Hank. "We've been searching for him all over these lower mountains for the last three days. The troops thought they saw smoke, but then it disappeared before they could make out where it came from. Gun shots were heard several times too and thought it might be Mr. Brody, but there were not enough shots to follow the sound."

Hank beckoned for the soldiers to follow him, and as they rode along, they talked and Hank relayed the story of what had happened to them. The sergeant rode along in quietness and could not believe what he was hearing from Hank because the stories seemed a bit unreal. The soldiers confessed that they had recently found some burned-out and looted wagons but had always blamed the Indians for the wickedness and wrong done. They had supposed that there were no survivors or they had been taken captive by the Indians as they never found anyone from these wagons alive. The sergeant said that one day not long ago one of the soldiers had remembered a Brody coming to the fort for some supplies that had been left there for him by the wagon train. He said that he then headed off in this direction by himself. He always picked up supplies like what a doctor would use. He had mentioned to one of the soldiers that he lived in the hills and the small mountains south of the fort. So consequently, we decided to start our search here first."

Upon entering the front yard of the cabin, the door opened, and Clint and the reverend came outside followed by Marcy and Beth.

"Sergeant, this is Clint Brody, the man who you're searching for."

The sergeant dismounted and firmly shook Clint's hand. "Good to meet you, Mr. Brody. We've been searching for you for days." Clint introduced everyone and asked the sergeant to come in.

"Hank, please show the men where to water their horses and rest them, if you don't mind."

In the meantime, realizing it was nearing lunch time, Clint asked the sergeant if he and his men would like some food prepared. The sergeant replied, "That sounds good, but there are fifteen of us, and we don't want to put anyone out or cause an extra burden on you as you've already been through so much." But the women, not waiting for further instruction, hurried to cook some food while the men waited and visited with Clint, Hank, and the reverend.

"Mr. Brody, my mission was to find you and see if you would come to the fort and fill in as doctor until we are able to have another army doctor sent in. A month ago there were some Indian issues north and northwest of the fort over around Silent Springs. Our army doctor was severely wounded and died before we could return to the fort. The soldiers have no doctor at this time, and we are in great need of medical assistance. Some of our wounded men are not responding to our doctoring and care since we are not doctors and have no medical knowledge of what to do. It will take a long time to notify the army of our loss and have a replacement sent to us. Would you consider moving to the fort and doctoring our troops until a replacement can come?" he asked him. "If you can come, housing and a small salary will be afforded you."

"Sergeant, we would all have to come, as we're in this together. I would not leave my wife and friends here alone. There are six of us altogether."

"We would not ask you to do such a thing, and of course, all of you would come and be welcome," said the sergeant with urgency and gratitude in his voice.

"We have our wagons and canvasses stored near the barn, so we could move to the fort with few problems. Let me talk with my family and friends, and we'll give you some kind of decision after lunch."

Mrs. Payton and Marcy had prepared the fresh meat from Hank's hunt along with cooked pumpkin, squash, heated beans, biscuits and gravy, and a pot of hot coffee. The men filled their plates with hearty helpings of food and went outside to sit under the trees to eat. The sergeant went with his men to partake of the hearty helpings of fresh home-cooked food, which they rarely got any of in their line of work, and they left the family to talk the situation over. By now, everyone was well aware of what the visit was all about. Clint wanted to hear what everyone had to say, as each one's thoughts were important to him.

"We had planned to go in late summer to catch the wagon train on to Oregon," said the reverend. "So we could go now while we have an escort, for who is to say the bandits aren't lurking around again?"

Marcy said, "I feel that we should go. Clint, you're a doctor, and they need your help."

"What about you, Hank?"

"Well, I was figuring to move on later, but I guess I could go now too," he admitted with reservations.

"Beth, you've not said anything at all. How do you feel about all of this?"

"I want to go too, but I also want to stay because Mother and Father are buried here and I hate to leave them."

"Beth, if Father was here, he would say to go; I know that he would. We must also think of the baby; we'll be in a better place for medicine and medical care."

"Yes, I feel it is the right thing to do," muttered Beth slowly as though she was not really sure about her own feelings.

"Okay," said Marcy.

"We'll let the soldiers know we'll be going along with them. Let's see when they wish to leave," Clint told them, and he quickly went to find the sergeant.

"Okay, it's all settled; we'll all go with you. Everyone is in total agreement, so that makes it much easier. When do you want to leave here?"

"Just as soon as it is possible. The men will help prepare the wagons for travel, and I will have some of the men help Mrs. Brody and Mrs. Payton with the packing and lifting," he offered. The sergeant divided the men into groups for various duties, and as soon as the sergeant gave the orders, the work began quite quickly. Several worked on restoring the four wagons for travel to the fort, which included the repairing of the canvas tops, greasing the wheels, minor repairs that were needed to

MARLENE WISE

make the wagons able to travel, and the repair of some of the burned or splintered boards.

Hank took two men to his cabin to make ready his wagon and his belongings. His helpers were really of great assistance, and by dusk they drove his wagon down into the front yard of Marcy and Clint's cabin along with the others. "It shouldn't take very long to load all the wagons with all the help we have," said Hank.

At daylight, Hank and Clint informed the sergeant that they had one last thing of importance to do. Clint said, "We must go tell Silver Moon that we're moving on so they won't wonder where we've gone. It should take us no more than an hour at the most." They found the Indian camp bustling and busy with their usual everyday affairs. Their fires were going, and the ladies were cooking food by each teepee for the day's eats.

They were already aware of the blue coats; however, they didn't know why they had come to this area. Clint revealed that they had known that day would eventually come and that they would move on farther west. He shook Silver Moon's hand with the traditional Indian handshake by grabbing the hand and arm and making the sign for friendship. Clint relayed to Silver Moon that he and Hank would always be their "brothers." Before leaving, Clint presented Silver Moon with a sack filled with pumpkins, beans, squash, and some flour and sugar and some seeds. He accepted their gift, and then in return he gave Clint a necklace from his own neck, and to Hank he offered a beaded pouch to wear around his neck. With great reluctance, Silver Moon gave the friendship sign and said, "Go in peace and may the Great Spirit watch over you and your family always. You are both very brave men."

With reluctance and a deep sadness, both Clint and Hank climbed up on their horses and began the trek back to the cabin. They sensed a hollow feeling inside, and neither one had much to talk about. The Indians had not been savage killers as many liked to say they were, but they were good friends and teachers. They had taught the two men many survival tactics, and the Indians had learned many valuable lessons from their white friends too. Silver Moon had learned much about the white man's medicine and caring for their children and easier ways to care for their sick. In return, Clint had learned about medicines that grew in the area that he never knew anything about like medicinal roots, leaves, bark, and other things that could help cure different ailments, even those of their livestock. Roots, leaves, and bark in this area were much different than the roots, leaves, and bark in Minnesota or Missouri. So it had been good to have a good teacher who knew about these medicinal helps and could assist in teaching others of their proper use. Their lives had literally been in the hands of the Indians for those first few months that they lived in the mountains. It had been a rich learning experience for both the Indian and the whites.

The two men returned in a little less than an hour as they had stated, and found that the wagons had been repaired and were all ready to go. They would leave early the next morning when the last items were loaded. They ate cold biscuits, meat, and hot coffee for supper, and then everyone went to bed early awaiting the early morning to peek through the skies. But it was hard for everyone to close their minds and eyes and go to sleep. So many pieces of life were being left behind along with the many memories that had been forever etched in their minds. But each one realized that if those memories and pieces of life were not taken captive and pushed far back in the mind for this night, no one would get a good night's sleep for the long, hard journey.

A beautiful morning of silence dawned upon them along with a gorgeous and glorious sunrise. Mrs. Payton made coffee and flapjacks and cold little pieces of fried leftover meat from the mule deer steaks. Everyone ate their fill and then loaded the remaining items that had been left until last. As the loaded wagons proceeded forward, Marcy and Beth felt the same old familiar roll in the pit of their stomachs. They had felt this strange sensation long ago when they had left the big woods in Minnesota to visit family in Missouri and then again when all the wagons departed on the first miles of their westward journey. They were sure the others must feel the same as they did.

Beth's eyes were fixed on the fence around the cemetery, and she watched with tears rolling down her cheeks until she could no longer see the fence and until they were completely out of view of the cabin that she had called home for these past few months. But even then, she strained to get even just a last glimpse of what she was leaving behind. Marcy laid her hand over on her sister's small hand and whispered to her that all would be all right. She told her that Clint had made arrangements with Little Dove to come once in a while to place flowers on the grave and check on it for them. "They will be in good hands with Little Dove because she understands our feeling for our loved ones who have passed on, so there is no need to worry, Beth." She consoled her sister with a big hug and a kiss on the cheek. Beth snuggled closer to Marcy and said she was so glad Little Dove would do such a thing for them. She suddenly felt better and even lost her worried look and the sad face she had started out with.

Beth had found some flowers and had placed them on the graves before they had to depart. She knew this would be the last time she could do this for her parents. But she was content, as she had found some flowers shooting up on the graves of their own accord. The seeds must have come from all the flowers that she had placed there before. Little Dove might not have so much to look after when the flowers came into full bloom. This soothed her to know that the graves would not be bare but that something would grow to make it look prettier. They would have Mother Nature to care for them too with her radiant flowers of all colors and shapes. Some of the same kinds of flowers that her mother had cherished and picked along the way and that had brought a little happiness to the long dreary days of travel would soon bloom on her mother's grave.

RETURN OF THE EVIL MEN

The trip to the fort with the four wagons took almost two weeks of travel time. The soldiers had made it in about one week, but it was a mission of urgency. The travels were uneventful and peaceful, and the early spring with its warmness and sunny days made the best time to travel, as it was a whole lot easier on all.

Striker was tied to the back of Marcy's wagon but seemed a little discontent because he wanted to be free to run and kick up his heels. Striker had been confined for so long to small quarters that he longed now to have freedom out in the warm spring air. Clint felt sorry for this faithful horse and finally saddled and rode him giving him a chance to stretch and exercise. Clint and Marcy could both tell Striker was not happy at a slow gait but wanted to break free and run wildly through the fields and grass. Finally Clint let him run for a distance and then went back to the same gait as the other horses. The sergeant had been eyeing Striker and watching him with great interest for quite some time. Finally the sergeant

MARCY

rode back to the Brody wagon and offered to buy Striker, but Marcy said, "This horse is not for sale at any price and never would be. There is no amount of money or goods that could ever replace him. He'll be with our family until we are all dead or until he dies. Striker's a very special horse and a precious part of our family and our life."

In the distance, they could see brown log buildings and a tall building rising up above the others. It was the watch tower for the guards at the fort that kept watch in all directions for Indians, trouble of any kind, or returning patrols. The soldiers were anxious to get back to their "home," their quarters; therefore, when the buildings came into view, the speed of the soldiers and the wagons picked up.

They could see dust swirling in the westward direction and make out horses and riders, which was another patrol returning to the fort with the flag waving in front of them. There were at least forty soldiers riding in the patrol. Hopefully, there hadn't been more Indian problems in the area again. The army patrol reached the big gates first, and the man in the tower hollered, "Open up the gates; west patrol coming in and soldiers and wagons coming in from the south too." Upon finally reaching the fort, Marcy and Beth were delighted to have reached their destination without any problems or situations that delayed them.

The fort and the soldiers gave them a sense of security, comfort, and well-being. Marcy felt extremely tired and only wished to lie down. The travel these last days had caused her to be very exhausted from riding

MARLENE WISE

in the wagon. The wagon, even though loaded heavily, seemed to jostle and hit all the holes, bumps, and rocks, not to mention the unending uncomfortableness of the hard wagon seat. She hoped that soon she would be able to take a good uninterrupted nap and rest her pregnant body some with a little more comfort.

The sergeant had sent three soldiers ahead to tell the colonel they were coming and what accommodations they would be in need of. The remaining soldiers at the fort had added on rooms to house the new visitors. In no time, the soldiers had unloaded the wagons and set things up in their quarters for them.

Clint told Marcy the trip had been long and he wanted her to go rest and take a nap. "Beth, please see that she lies down before suppertime. I'm going to wash up, change clothes, and go check on the sick," Clint stated.

Without further adieu, Clint took his doctor's bag and went to the infirmary to locate the wounded men that needed his services. First, he began his work with a man with a nasty red infected leg wound who seemed to be the worst among the sick. The leg was inflamed, swollen, and very tender to the touch, and the man was already feverish and quite delirious. Clint worked on the four soldiers all afternoon only stopping for a cup of coffee or to rest for a few minutes between each patient. He ate a hearty supper with his family and then went back to the infirmary where he seemed to be needed the most at the present time. Clint intended to stay the night on sick duty because he had some grave concern over the ailing man with the serious leg wound. If the medicine and procedures he used didn't work and take effect quickly, the young man could lose his leg from the knee down.

Clint stayed very busy the first few days, and Marcy and Beth only caught little glimpses of him for short periods of time when he came in at mealtime and sometimes not even then. Marcy realized he was doing the work he loved the most and work that he had wanted to be doing all this time. He was a good doctor, even though he had no real practice of his own yet. Marcy and Beth just had to learn to do without him being around as much as he was before they left the cabin in the mountains. Consequently, because of the confinement and no place that Beth could really get out and walk to like she had done back at the cabin, she was somewhat bored. She was certainly not allowed to leave the confines of the fort and go beyond the gates. One of the soldiers brought some flowers for her and Marcy, and this made her feel a little better and much happier in their confined, drab surroundings.

Marcy was teaching Beth to sew, and this helped pass some of the time away. It was nice having Mrs. Payton around too, as she was very helpful in many domestic situations. There were only three other ladies who lived at the fort, which were the wife of the colonel and his two nieces. The ladies enjoyed getting together to have tea, talk, and sew, or to just reminisce about home stories and travels.

One day, while having tea with the colonel's wife and his nieces, the unexpected happened. They heard the

MARLENE WISE

watchman holler, "Riders from the south coming." After a little while they heard the command to open the gates. The gates were opened, and seven men and horses and two pack mules and a wagon came through. They were dirty, unshaven, rough, and hard-looking men. They rode to the hitch and tied their horses speaking in loud voices almost as if arguing about something. The ladies could hear them in a heated discussion about obtaining their supplies and getting some food. Because of all the commotion, Beth went to the window to see what all the ruckus was about. She stood trying to focus her eyes and view the men that had just ridden in, but it was hard because of the swirling dirt and dust the horses kicked up. Soon the dust settled, and the men tended to their horses and then made ready to go to the trading post. One man removed his hat and flapped it across his leg to remove the dirt and dust, and as he did so, Beth turned white and began to tremble. She jumped away from the window, dropped the curtain as though it was hot to her touch, and stood with her back rigidly against the wall breathing in ragged and sharp amounts of air. She was trying to speak, but no words seemed to form or were audible.

Marcy rose from the table and went toward Beth. "Beth, what is it? What's wrong with you? You're as white as if you saw a ghost, and you're shaking like a leaf in the wind." But Beth could only shake her head yes, and with trembling fingers she pointed toward the window.

The colonel's wife, Amanda, came over immediately and said, "Here, child, you better sit down." Beth put her head down in her hands and began to weep and wail.

MARCY

Very concerned, Marcy gently shook Beth by the shoulders and asked her, "Beth, please, can't you tell us what the problem is?"

All Beth could say was, "The man, the man, he helped kill Mother and Father."

"What! Here at the fort? Are you sure? Are you sure?"

"Yes, Marcy, the two miners are out there with him." She moaned as she clasped her sister's hands together to keep her own hands from shaking so violently.

Marcy paced the floor and said, "I need to go check this out, but if it's them, the two miners from the wagon train, they will surely recognize me. They'll then know that we could testify against them."

Amanda said, "Wait, let me help you." She ran and wrote a note to the colonel. She asked for her husband to come quickly and to bring Dr. Brody with him immediately. Amanda opened the door and stepped out on the porch. She looked around and found no one nearby, but then she spotted a private headed for the barracks.

She looked in his direction and said, "Psst, psst, soldier!" He looked at her strangely, and then she beckoned him over. "This is very, very urgent. Please get this to Colonel McCord at once."

"Yes, ma'am. I will with all speed," he replied politely. He left immediately and then hurried toward headquarters with note in hand. The note was delivered with great speed, and very promptly the colonel and the doctor stood within the living room of his home. Clint was very eager to find out what the problem was because

245

MARLENE WISE

Marcy was nearly three months into her pregnancy, and he hoped it was not her that needed his services. Meanwhile, Marcy had taken Beth into the bedroom to lie down and rest, for it appeared it was more than the hot weather that was making her sick to her stomach and bothering her. It was her thoughts about these evil men who had returned to the fort as though nothing had happened that had drained her of all her strength and peace of mind.

Amanda revealed the tense situation to her husband and the doctor about the strange men that had just ridden in and then repeated what the girls had told them. The colonel asked Marcy if the identification was positive or perhaps the man just looked like this Matt. Clint said that he would go look, that it could be the same thieves who had robbed and burned their wagons too. "I will never forget the cold, uncaring face I saw up close that horrible day," he said through clenched teeth.

The colonel asked Sergeant Bracer to come with them and to bring about six or seven good strong men with him. "We are going to arrest those men who just rode in here. Where are they at now?"

"Well, I do believe they went to the trading post," answered the sergeant. The men rapidly walked across to the trading post and entered to do the job they had decided needed to be done. They looked around and spied the men at the far end of the room making orders for various things. One man was counting out money, and one was trying to sell some old watches and other items along with some pieces of jewelry. The colonel stepped

246

up and stated that it looked like they'd traveled for quite a distance.

The man with his back slightly turned to Clint stated, "We're miners from back in the mountains, and we just rode in to see if we could buy some supplies for the summer, if there were any to purchase." He also said, "We might even return in the later months and take the wagon train on to the Oregon territory."

But when he turned fully around, Dr. Clint Brody could then see his face clearly. He, like Beth, had gone white, white with rage all the way through his being, and he shook and trembled, but not from fright. He shook vehemently at what he felt inside and at what he was fighting to not do to this man. His vow was to save lives, not to take them, even though he knew they had done evil things. He had heard the hated name of Matt before, because Matt had massacred his family and others and had done the same thing to Marcy's family and friends. Clint looked at the colonel and then nodded yes.

In a loud voice, the colonel said, "Sergeant, arrest these men now, all of them." Two men at the end of the room drew their pistols. The colonel had drawn his, but not quite as fast as his opponent, and the bullet grazed the fleshy part of his left shoulder. Clint had nothing in his hands but his doctor's bag, and in his fury he suddenly realized that these men could not be allowed to go free without some punishment. They would never get a chance like this again when all of the men who had done evil, robbed, killed, and burned wagons would be together at one time. Something had to be done and now,

MARLENE WISE

but before he could formulate a plan in his mind, Clint threw his bag at the man nearest him and hit him in the chest, knocking the breath out of him for a minute or two. It was then he saw the barrel of a familiar-looking shotgun come around the door.

"Drop your weapons! All of you, and now!" They all looked up and saw Hank and more soldiers standing in the doorway and more at the windows. They knew they were caught like wolves in a trap, with no place to retreat or hide. Guns began to cautiously drop to the floor or were slid across the table. These men's reign of terror was soon to come to an end, and they never would be able to torture, kill, burn, loot, and cause havoc again. They would be put away for a long time. They would have plenty of time to remember all the crimes they had committed against their own kind.

Clint turned to Hank and said, "Boy, was I ever glad to see that familiar-looking rifle appear in the doorway. Thanks for bringing more help with you." Hank had seen the men ride in and had watched them very carefully. He too had recognized Matt and his men from the ambush on their wagon train two years ago. When he saw the colonel, Clint, and the sergeant and some men going to the trading post, he knew there might be some trouble. Matt was a cruel, vicious, and callous man thinking of no one but himself and what he wanted or needed. Hank had taken his trusty old shotgun and waited around to see if his assistance would be needed. He had no intentions of letting these marauders go free without punishment. They had to be brought to justice and made to pay for

MARCY

their wrongdoings and the sufferings they had made many go through, or they would simply continue their wicked way of life. All of their crimes were premeditated and well thought out, even who would assist Matt and his gang of thieves.

The men were rounded up and taken to the stockade on the fort grounds. It was later learned that these men had stolen supplies from army patrols and injured some soldiers with intent to kill them. It was decided the criminals would stay in the brig until the new wagon train arrived in August or September. When enough people arrived, a jury would be chosen and a trial would proceed so it would be a fair and just trial. The living witnesses would come forth and give testimony as to what had happened to them. The seven men were guarded heavily at the brig constantly. Clint knew that any chance Matt got he'd try to make a break for it and escape. When the men were taken out for any exercise or work detail, the guards were doubled. These men would not be afforded their freedom again so they could live off their unsuspecting and innocent victims.

Marcy and Clint talked about the train coming in a few months and how it would pass through before Marcy's baby was born. Marcy wished to go on to Oregon with the Paytons, but Clint thought it would be too difficult a journey for her to start out on. There was talk of sending Beth on with the Paytons where she could be in a different environment and go to school and have friends her own age. But when the subject was brought up, Beth became very sullen, weepy, and despondent, and she would not be separated from Marcy for any reason. The two nieces of Amanda's husband, Susana and Lorena, had done just fine out here. Amanda had been a schoolteacher before she had married the colonel back east and moved to the west with him. She tended to the schooling and social graces of the two young ladies. Beth would have it no other way; she desired to stay and be schooled by Amanda too. Also, she wanted Marcy to stay and be in a safe place when the baby was born. Hard decisions would have to be made by her family and friends in the later weeks.

The reverend and his wife were going to go on to Oregon, and Hank had decided to go too. He had decided it was time to start fresh and get on with his life. It would be hard to separate and leave these he had come to know as family, but lives had to move on and perhaps someday he might marry again and have a family. Clint was like a blood brother to Hank, and because they were very close, the separation would be very painful for him. The six of them had been inseparable this past year and had formed strong bonds with each other. They had shared the bad times, the good times, and the times when life seemed impossible and very unfair. Unless some unforeseen thing happened, then each family would go their separate ways with plans for their own lives and hope that someday they would come across their dear friends again.

DREAMS FULFILLED

The days around the fort were quiet and uneventful for the next two and a half months. There were always scares and stories of the Shoshone and Arapaho preparing for raids and attacks, but nothing ever happened. Of course, this became a greater possibility with the knowledge of an approaching wagon train. Somehow the Indians always seemed to know who was coming and going across the land. The Indians did not take kindly to the train coming across their lands because it angered them to see their food supply dwindle so rapidly for both them and their livestock. They felt that the white man abused the land, ruined its beauty, and brought them strange diseases that killed their people because they did not know how to fight these sicknesses. The white man had spoken with a forked-tongue many times, so the Indians had a great mistrust of them when they did speak. But they knew or had learned that not all white men were bad and behaved in this manner by saying one thing and doing another. However, it appeared to the Indians that the white

MARLENE WISE

man had an insatiable hunger and greed for what didn't belong to them. So in his desperation and gluttony, this sometimes brought about attacks by the Indians trying to keep what they thought belonged to them. There were recorded attacks by Indians on the emigrant pioneers, the army, missionaries, settlers, miners, trappers, and anyone else who seemed to bring a dangerous threat to the Indians and their only known way of life.

Clint and Hank had stretched forth their hands in friendship and help to the Indians that were close to them in the mountains. They both experienced a mutual bond created between them in many areas of life. They had no problems or discord with the local Indians or even Indians from neighboring tribes when they glimpsed the necklace Silver Moon had given to Clint; they knew of its meaning and why he wore it. Clint wore the necklace every day with great pride and also for some degree of protection, as it was also a sign showing his kinship with the other Indians. He had saved lives while at the fort due to Indian attacks. He felt in his heart that the attacks were because of the ignorance about each other's culture and beliefs. Many times the white man stepped on the sacred culture of the Indians and their beliefs without knowing they were doing so. Both wanted different things from the land and from each other. Clint believed there could be a balance and both could live together in harmony if both would just try to do so.

Marcy said she was an eyewitness to the balance of both parties getting along. She revealed that in the past months of life in those lower mountains with

MARCY

Clint, Hank, and the Paytons, both she and Beth had a firsthand account of life with the Indians, their customs, their people, and their generosity and even their love. Marcy had told Clint one time when they spoke of this very thing that if someone had told her this closeness could be so with the Indians, she would not have believed them. Marcy knew not all Indians were like this, but if given a fair chance, they could be. But her heart told her it would have to be fifty-fifty on the side of both cultures, a genuine desire to get along together. Marcy was quick to agree that since they had started on the trail, they had seen various lifestyles of the Indians, the good and the bad, the selfish and the generous, and the warring and peaceful.

Clint got his chance to prove this cultural balance one day in the hot, searing days of July. He was in the medicine room taking inventory of his medical supplies when he heard the guard in the tower yelling, "Indians coming from the north." The captain asked how many were approaching the fort. The soldier took his field glasses and spanned the land in the direction of the advancing Indians. "I see only three riding in, sir. There are others, perhaps twenty behind him, but they are not advancing, sir. The three are coming in alone," he reported. The captain told everyone to take their positions, for this could be a trick, so everyone must keep awake and alert. As the Indians approached slowly, the one on the far right raised an arrow with a white flag on the top. He waved it back and forth until they came to a complete halt not far from the main gate. The captain sent two men, Gruner

253

and Murdock, out to see what had brought the Indians to the fort. The gate was opened only wide enough for horse and rider to pass through. The tower guard continually scanned the land with his field glasses looking for signs of any movement or trickery and to watch the remaining Indians and their movements.

The Arapaho Indians raised their right hands in a gesture of friendship, and the soldiers in turn also raised their hands even though both parties carried their weapons with them. Murdock understood a lot of the Arapaho language and had learned to speak some of it. Gruner also spoke some Arapaho and some Crow. The Indians said, "We have come to talk with the white medicine man, Clint. We want him to make medicine and help one of our chiefs. Our chief is sick and might die if he doesn't get some help from your great medicine man. Great Spirit says white medicine man can help us." Gruner, a bit nervous and edgy, tried to watch the remaining twenty a little off in the distance and told the Indians to wait there. He and Murdock left them speedily and came back inside the fort. Clint was in the doorway.

The colonel and Sergeant Hawkins were saying, "We absolutely cannot allow this. It is too risky and would put a lot of lives at stake if this was a trick to gain entrance into the fort. If he goes and they harm him or kill him, then we have no doctor for our military men. If they attack us, then our men could or would probably die for lack of medical assistance. They could also take the women as hostages as they have done before."

Clint spoke up rather sharply and a bit testily. "I beg

your pardon, sir. I overheard your conversation, and your thinking is all wrong. You could save lives by assisting at this time of need. We must show our compassion; even though he is a red man, he is still a man just as you and me. You have a chance to show that you care, that you want peace, that you want to live together in harmony. I wish to go talk with them. Perhaps I can be of no assistance, but I would like to at least have the opportunity to weigh the situation for myself as the fort doctor," he snapped. He waited and looked pleadingly at the sergeant.

The sergeant said he and the colonel would have to talk about it before making such a serious decision. "I'll return and let you know what we have to say," the sergeant stated. Clint reminded them both that to waste precious time was wrong, and the wait might do more damage to the patient, making it harder to doctor him. He would not want to be blamed for the chief's death if he should happen to die, especially while they were waiting for an answer after asking for medical help. The colonel was very skeptical at first, but he trusted Clint with all of his heart. He had never met anyone like Clint before who was such an honest man, a great man of his word, a man with high values and morals. Clint was the most genuine and sincere man he had ever met in these parts of the country. He seemed to have the knack of knowing just what to do at the right time.

Clint said, "Colonel, I may have to bring the chief into the infirmary so I can better doctor him. May I go talk to them and see what I'm dealing with?"

MARLENE WISE

"Yes, but Gruner and Murdock go with you. We'll accept whatever decision you feel is necessary."

Clint made sure the necklace Silver Moon had given him could be seen under the collar of his shirt. He walked tall and proud out to the gate and toward the Indians. He talked with those who had come forward with the white flag, and they quickly revealed the story. Some of the Indians had come by some "fire water," and in a time of drinking and making merry, a wild rifle shot had been fired. It went through the teepee of Chief Tall Bear and struck him, lodging the bullet in his shoulder. He had the devil's heat in his body and had been sick for three moons now.

Clint told the Indians, "Bring Chief Tall Bear to me inside the fort and into the army infirmary." The Indians, expecting and hoping they could obtain some help for the chief, had brought him on a travois and were waiting patiently for an answer. Clint sent one of the Indians with the doctor's orders and information for them to bring the chief forward. As soon as word was received, the group of Indians gradually began a slow trek toward the fort dragging the travois behind them very slowly. They went at a very cautious pace hoping not to jostle the old chief in his weakened condition. When they reached the gate, the colonel requested that only the chief be admitted and the others to remain outside of the gates.

The Indians spoke among themselves and then to Clint; they agreed that they would return when three moons had passed again. Chief Tall Bear was then taken by the soldiers into the infirmary, and Clint began his

256

examination. The wound was nasty and jagged and looked as if someone had probably tried to remove the bullet and failed to do so. The site was badly infected and swollen, and the whole area around the wound itself had turned an ugly crimson. Clint knew he must do surgery immediately to take out the bullet, because the longer it stayed in him, the more chance of a severe infection or blood poison setting in and taking his life. The wound would have to be properly cleaned out and then cauterized to prevent further problems. Clint had done this procedure before but not when the wound had been so infected. Clint sent a soldier to fetch Hank, as he had helped him before and knew what to do, so he now needed his assistance again. Marcy could not be asked to help him in her condition; therefore, he felt it best not to have her in the room at this time.

Shortly, Hank appeared in the doorway with his rifle. "You won't need that this time, my friend. This is a different kind of work here with a different type of tool." He pitched him a long white apron and said for him to put it on. He administered the medication to put Tall Bear to sleep, and then the men turned him over on his stomach and began to work on the infected back. It was a long tedious job, and Clint could not be sure the steps he had taken would work at this point, but he had to do what he had learned and what he felt was best. All he could do now was hope and pray that Tall Bear survived the situation and the surgery. The surgery was finally done; now it was time to wait and see what the results would be, whether good or bad. But Clint prayed for the good and that the chief would survive and be able to go home and be with his family.

It was late in the evening when Tall Bear began to stir and make signs with his fingers and hands. He said, "I'm alive. I will get well and be strong again because you have the power from the Great Medicine Spirit. Great Spirit says he favors you, and he tells me you have a special gift of medicine in your hands." Chief Tall Bear, with a great sigh of relief and nothing more to say, closed his eyes and slept fitfully through the night.

By morning, he seemed somewhat better, so Clint had Marcy fix a hot medicinal tea for him, which he didn't wish to drink, but Clint made him. He told him that the Great Medicine Spirit said to drink all of it. Clint and Hank lifted him up a ways and handed him the cup. The chief looked into the cup strangely and a bit hesitantly but drank it down without a word. He was not really well enough to leave the third day. When the two Indians returned, they were allowed to see him for only a short while. Clint told them that he needed to stay three more days before he could leave and go back to his people.

But the Indian companions said, "We must all go today."

Clint turned and spoke brusquely, "No! The Great Medicine Spirit says he must stay here for a bit longer. If he leaves, it will anger the spirits."

"Okay, we will return in three more moons to take him back home," they agreed. Immediately they disappeared beyond the gates and rode slowly back to their village.

The sudden movements of the Indians coming and

going and being seen in out of the way places made the colonel nervous. He wished for all of this to be over and done because he had a very deep worry and fear that if Tall Bear died there would be retaliation against the fort. He shuddered at the thought of a fight as he now had six ladies to think about here at the fort instead of just three.

As time clicked away, Clint went about his work with urgency but with superior care and treatments. He tended to nothing really serious, only minor aches and pains and cases of dysentery and an occasional fever or bee sting now and then for the soldiers. He was happiest when he knew he was helping relieve the sickness and pain of others. He had wanted to be a doctor even when he was just a young boy and was always happy when he could help his father at times with small medical problems.

The third day again arrived, and Chief Tall Bear was sitting up and looking and feeling much better. After his sixth day, Clint was sure now that the old chief would be just fine. Clint stood across the room and stared silently at Tall Bear and Hank as they conversed. Clint beheld an old but strong man with a withered and wrinkled brown face. He knew Tall Bear had lived a very difficult life but had been an overcomer in the face of great adversity. He was a family man just like his well-known white "enemy." He had a wife and three children. He, just like any other husband and father, had tried to protect and care for his own family too. As the chief spoke with Hank, his dark eyes glistened and spoke almost as much as his verbal words, for Clint knew that he was a man of great wisdom and knowledge. As Clint watched him, he only wished that others would be as tolerant and try to understand the ways of the Indian as Tall Bear was about the white people and their desires and beliefs.

Clint suddenly heard laughter and realized that it had come from his patient and Hank. The chief called to Clint and beckoned for him to come closer to him, so Clint stepped away from the window and walked the few steps across the room. The old chief slowly took a medallion from around his neck, placed it in his left hand, and rubbed over it with his right as he said something in Arapaho. Neither Clint nor Hank knew exactly what he had said, only that it was an Indian blessing from the chief. He motioned for the doctor to bend down, and he almost reverently placed the necklace around his neck with great pride and happiness.

He then stated, "Never again will the Arapaho lift their hands in war against the fort." He then turned to Hank and took another necklace with a large bear's tooth and other ornaments on it and placed it around Hank's neck. He told Hank, "Never fear the Arapaho again as your enemy. As long as you wear the necklace, all will know the Great Spirit favors you and will know you as a kind, loving, and peaceable man and a great hunter of this land."

Soon they heard a light tap at the infirmary door. The sergeant had come to report that the Indians had returned to take their chief home, and immediately a big smile spread across the face of Tall Bear. As he walked slowly with his two young braves toward the gates, he

MARCY

paused and lifted his head. "Ah, how good to smell Mother Earth again," he said happily. "I have missed feeling my feet walking through the warm land, the smell and sight of trees, the great mountains, the waters and streams. I have missed the sight of the animals and especially the sight of the majestic eagle. I am grateful to be alive and in the country I love so dearly. Thank you, my friends and the Great Spirit," he said with a genuine tenderness in his voice.

The chief extended his long, thin brown hand out to the colonel in a hardy handshake of friendship. The colonel seemed surprised and was taken aback a bit at the gesture of the chief. Clint was greatly relieved to see the colonel's hand come up and grasp the chief's hand. While their hands were clinched, Tall Bear waved his left hand over the colonel and said, "You are a good man. May the Great Spirit watch over you and care for you and your family. We wish for no more war between the Arapaho and the soldiers. We must learn to live in peace and help one another as my doctor friend has done these past few days."

As the Indians left and the gates were closed, Colonel McCord said, "I wish all Indians had the wisdom and knowledge of Chief Tall Bear." He might not have to deal with the Arapaho, but there were other tribes that did not feel as Tall Bear, but perhaps Tall Bear could have some effect on them to try to live in peace. The colonel knew the other tribes were deeply angry about the white man's advance to the west and the infringements upon their land and way of life. The "blue coats" were

261

considered fair game by some Indians, but not all Indians were savages, just like not all white men were greedy and evil. Perhaps, one day, they could all live peaceably and understand each other's cultures, ideas, and beliefs.

Several days later, the Indians appeared again. The watchman shouted, "Indians coming this way!" Again everyone took their place. The women were told to stay inside and away from the windows. The soldiers took their field glasses and searched all around the surrounding areas again. "There are only five of them, and I believe they are Arapaho. They have large baskets on their horses," the watchman stated in a curious sort of way.

The sergeant again called for Gruner and Murdock. "Ride out and see what they want this time." The two mounted their horses and began to ride slowly out to meet the Indians with hands raised in a gesture of peace.

"Our chief has sent some gifts to your chief, and we wish to present them to him," they stated to the two soldiers.

"Follow us." They motioned.

They rode cautiously toward the gates and heard the watchman yell again, "Open the gates." Everyone gathered around the few Indians and their load of goods. They proudly presented the baskets of goods and bags to the colonel. They contained fresh meat, vegetables, and some large berries. One small bag was taken from the basket and passed over to Clint. As he opened up the little bag, he knew immediately what it was. It contained roots, leaves, bark, berries, and things for medicinal use that were found only in this area. This brought a smile to the grateful doctor's face because he was in short supply of some medicine right now. Thanks to the Indians, he could now make some of his own medicines as needed. Clint let his happiness be shown and shook the hands of the Indians showing them how pleased and grateful he really was. One Indian spoke to him in Arapaho and with hand and sign language. He understood enough to know that if he needed more roots, bark, or leaves or whatever, they would help him gather another supply of them. The colonel stood by in complete awe witnessing a sight that he thought he'd never see out here in this land.

Clint had brought more than medicine and a doctor's knowledge with him when he came to the fort. He had brought a new peace and friendship among the soldiers and the Arapaho, a feat which many thought was impossible and could never be obtained in their lifetime. It was now beginning to bring about a feeling of mutual understanding between the parties. The Indians turned and bid all a good-bye and left as quietly as they had come. Clint said later he would take some things to the Indian camp as gifts for them to show their thankfulness for their new friends.

For days, things were still and very calm with no raids, no uncertainties, and no critical medical problems for Clint, only hot, sticky, and sultry days of June and July that came and went. It was soon the latter days of July, and an unusual thing was beginning to take place. In the southwest the clouds were churning and brewing into ugly black and gray heavy clouds. If they continued to move northward, they would probably bring a heavy rain.

MARLENE WISE

Night fell upon the fort, and soon afterward bolts of jagged lightning began to strike nearby. The thunder roared like an angry lion on the prowl. Sometimes it seemed like cannon fire bursting wildly and loudly overhead in the far distant mountains. The wind whipped furiously and brought with it great drops of rain that could be heard as it struck any object in its way. The big drops of rain hitting the fort and the homes were a welcome sound. But, as time rolled on, they wished the beating sound would just go away. It became almost maddening to hear the repetitive sound over and over again. But the heavy drops fell all night and into the early morning hours. It was a blessing to have fresh rain water in the fort's barrels; however, when the rain stopped abruptly, it seemed very strange and peculiar to hear the eerie silence and peacefulness it brought again.

Whenever the sun came up, the soldiers rallied around, and almost immediately, they could see the sun glistening across the land, little dancing and shimmering beads of diamonds hung on to the sparse blades of grass and greenery found here and there around the fort. The fresh morning air had a clean, crisp, sweet smell to it that seemed to cleanse the nostrils when one took a deep breath. The earth had been cleansed and refreshed by the rain, and new life would soon shoot forth from the warm brown earth that had been touched by the graciousness of the rain when it was so parched and dry and seemed to be dying.

August was escorted in by Mother Nature with another refreshing rain. Clint said they were blessed by this unusual coolness. Everyone knew as the hot days approached with their dryness and sweltering heat, many would suffer from the intense heat and want a feeling of the cool again. The terrible heat wave was bad on man and beast and could quickly take its toll on both. Everyone always remembered August as one of the hottest and worst months of the year. The land was scorched, grass dry, the earth hot and cracked, and travelers were easily irritated by the blistering heat. It caused them to have an unquenchable thirst for a cool drink of water. There was always a shortage of fresh cool water for the livestock and man alike.

Marcy reminded Clint and her friends that God had always provided in a time of need and brought a refreshing and strength, and he would not fail them now. Marcy was thankful to be alive and have her dreams coming to fruition; she was thankful for each day that God provided for her and her family regardless of what type of weather they had. Life was good now, and she looked forward to the wagon train coming anytime.

MARCY'S DECISION

The Paytons and Hank had made their plans to go on to Oregon when the train came. But since there wasn't a doctor at the fort and with Marcy in her condition, the Brodys and Beth had decided to stay. Sometimes, Marcy found Beth sitting by the window doing nothing but staring out into space. Beth didn't really want to leave the security of the fort; nevertheless, at times, she longed to go to Oregon and live in a real town with a school, shops, a church, and the bustle of life. She only wished that her parents could have gone on to Oregon and that they could all be there as a family as they had all planned a year ago.

Clint was in the infirmary grinding and preparing new medicines when he heard the watchman's call: "Patrol returning." The patrol had packed enough supplies for about a week and had been gone for about that length of time. They could only carry about a week's supply of goods with them to not be burdened down in case of attack. They were going out to try to meet the wagon

MARCY

train coming in with the new doctor. He should have gotten on the wagon train at Cutter's Crossing with an army escort and supplies.

The patrol had indeed come across the wagon train, which would reach the fort in about a week or maybe less if all went well for them. The army had finally found a new doctor and sent him out to the fort on the wagon train. He was coming on in with the patrol with a minimum amount of goods, and the rest of his supplies and medical items would come in later on the train. As the doctor dismounted, introductions were made, and Clint could hear all about the new arrival, his travels, and his orders. At first, he felt a little hollowness inside, as he knew he would relinquish his duties soon and be replaced with the new army-appointed doctor. Soon he would not be doing the work he loved so well. He would of course stay and offer his assistance if permitted, because of Marcy. He seemed to be perplexed and a little more edgy now.

He met and talked with Dr. McLean for a long time as he relayed the whole story and told how he had received the gifts from Chief Tall Bear. Clint was well pleased and thoroughly amazed, as the new doctor looked at things much like he did. He was more than willing to help the Indians too, if his help would be accepted. He also mentioned the Indians' gifts of herbs, leaves, roots, and so forth. He relayed how the Indians could find these more readily than anybody else, as they knew the area where they grew in abundance. Clint told Dr. McLean, "The Indians will help you with a supply of medicinal items if your supply runs short."

267

MARLENE WISE

Excitement filled the air because the long awaited wagon train could be seen coming in the distance among the blowing dust. Old memories began to burn and light up the minds of all those awaiting the train. When the wagons arrived, they circled into two large groups on the outside of the fort while the gates were opened wide with guards close by, and the watchman remained on duty to report any suspicious actions. Even though there hadn't been any problems with the Arapaho close by, there were Cheyenne and Ute close by the fort who had not always been on friendly terms with them. The Cheyenne had given some serious problems before, so caution was to be heeded and guards were posted in strategic spots to keep a sharp lookout.

Some of the travelers headed for the trading post, some to see the doctor or to get dental service, some to the blacksmith shop, and some to socialize and share any news, even if it was old. The ladies came out to mingle and hear news from back home or about happenings along the way. Marcy spoke to several young women that were about her age who came in on the wagon train. Beth had already found a young girl a year younger than herself, and they were busily engaged in deep conversation.

Marcy looked across the way and saw a young woman heavy with child being fixed a place in the shade by her husband so she could rest. Marcy walked over and introduced herself to the young lady whose name was Emily Ann. She looked tired and worn from her physical heaviness with child and the hard travels. Apparently, she was strong and courageous, as she had come this far on her long journey. The more she talked with Emily Ann, the more she was convinced they should travel on too. Marcy found out that there were several women in the same condition as she and Emily. If these women could bear up under the load and make it this far, then she could do it too, no farther than they had to go now. Marcy explained to Emily that her husband was a doctor and told her what they had been doing at the fort for these past months. But Marcy told Emily Clint would no longer be needed since the new doctor had arrived to replace him.

"Oh, Marcy, we could surely use a good doctor to travel on with us," she suggested. "Some of these women will give birth this month and some next month." Marcy stated that if all went well she should have her baby in late September or early October. For many days Marcy had pondered the idea of leaving on the wagon train with the rest of their friends, but she just couldn't make up her mind. Marcy had told Clint she would stay, but she knew Clint would not be as involved in the medical work as he wanted to be. She thought a lot about the birth of their child, their safety, and about Beth and her needs. One day she thought about going, and the next she would talk herself into staying. But after talking with Emily Ann, she knew exactly what she wanted to do. Excited beyond belief, Marcy asked to be excused. Marcy said that she must go rest for a while but was really going to find her husband and did so as Clint was preparing to return to the infirmary.

"Oh, Clint, there you are. I must talk to you immediately," Marcy said with excitement in her voice.

"I will return shortly and then we will talk," he vowed.

"No! I must say my piece now," she said very sternly. Clint looked at Marcy somewhat shocked and surprised.

He backed up into the room and sat down on a little stool. "My Marcy, what is so important? What is it, Marcy? I must admit that I've never seen you with such urgency before."

"Clint, I want to leave with the train when it goes. I wish to go on to Oregon now," she said rapidly, as though she wanted to say it hurriedly so as not to change her mind.

"But, Marcy, what about the baby?" he asked.

"The baby will be just fine. Clint, there are other women on the train, at least four of them, who are expecting babies. They have come a long way, and they are just fine. Surely I will be able to make it for a month or so," she said with pleading in her eyes. "They have a doctor here now, and your services will no longer be needed. You could be of greater use on the wagon train and then set up your own practice when we arrive in Oregon. The army owes you some pay, and we have what was saved back for our trip."

Clint thought for a few minutes and then sighed. "If this is what you really want, Marcy. Have you spoken to Beth and discussed this with her?"

"She has met a new friend her own age from the train, and I'm sure she'll want to go too just so she can be with her newfound friend."

MARCY

Clint looked for the Paytons and Hank to tell them of their recent decision. He found them making ready their wagons for travel. He told them about their discussion and their fresh decision, and they were very elated and happy, especially Hank. Mrs. Payton said she would come help pack things for Marcy, as she should conserve all of her strength for travel. When Beth was told, she jumped with glee and was ready to start packing immediately. She was fully ready to go with no prodding or undue influence. Marcy hadn't seen her this enthused and happy in a long time, except when they had celebrated her birthday and Christmas back in the cabin.

The wagon master had told the people on the train that this would only be a short stop over for no more than one day or maybe two days' time if it was really needed. But he announced that with the crack of dawn, the wagons should push on to their destination in Oregon if possible. Everyone had pitched in and helped so that the doctor, Marcy, and Beth were all ready to go on time. Clint would not hear of Marcy walking very far at one time, so he insisted that she ride while he and Beth walked. This was not a problem for Beth, as she enjoyed walking with her new friend. They had lots to talk about and stories to exchange along the way. Clint was sure that the two of them wouldn't become bored or not have anything to discuss. It had been a long time since Beth had been able to talk or do anything with someone her own age, so she was enjoying herself immensely.

271

MORE THAN GOOD FRIENDS

Beth began to talk with her newfound friend. "I don't even know your name yet," she told the young girl. "We were in such a hurry to get packed and ready to go that I didn't even have time to ask you. We were the last ones to get our belongings together, as we had not planned to go at this time. But then, my sister changed her mind for some reason, and we had to pack in a great hurry, because the wagon master didn't want to wait for more than one or two days."

"Well, I know that your name is Beth, as I heard your father call you that," she said, smiling.

"Oh, that is not my father, but he seems like he is. My sister and Clint were married by Reverend Payton before we came to the fort. Clint has worked as a doctor here at the fort for the last few months until they could get a replacement," she exclaimed.

"Well, my name is Sally Brewster, and we came from Nebraska. My uncle and aunt were going to Oregon last year and had asked us to travel with them, but we didn't

MARCY

have enough money to leave at that time and told them we would probably come in a year or two. So this year, my father said that we had enough saved and we could purchase the things we needed to go west to Oregon," she answered. "He decided that we would go to Oregon instead of California, and maybe later we'd travel to California and try to find our relatives.

Beth looked very strangely at Sally and laughed. "What's wrong, Beth?" she asked with a puzzled look on her face.

Beth said, "This is very unusual because my last name is Brewster too. Everyone, at least my close friends, call me Beth. But my real name is Elizabeth."

"Oh, Beth, and your sister's name is Marcy?" she questioned her.

"Yes."

"What are your mother's and father's names?" she asked excitedly.

"They were Alisha and Stewart Brewster," she answered very slowly.

"Beth! For heaven's sakes! Alisha and Stewart are my aunt and uncle from Minnesota. They are who we are going to meet up with in Oregon after we get settled in when we arrive. Beth, that makes us cousins because my father is Stewart Brewster's brother. Your aunt and uncle are Hiram and Martha Brewster, my parents. I have a brother named Benny too. Beth, when you spoke of them a few minutes ago, you said, 'They were,' as in the past. What did you mean?"

Beth looked far into the distance with a wounded

MARLENE WISE

look on her face and told Sally that both of them had been killed by evil men. Sally suddenly fell into Beth's arms and said how sorry she was of all that had happened to her. Sally said that she didn't recognize her as her cousin as they didn't get to see each other very often. "We were all just small children the last time we were together in Minnesota. I can hardly remember many things about you at that visit. However, I've heard my parents speak of you and your family's name many times. Oh my, I can hardly believe my ears. You must come to the wagon and meet the rest of your family. You and Marcy both must come when we stop for the evening and have supper with us. I must run and tell my mother and father, for they will certainly be surprised at this news; however, Father will be sad about Uncle Stewart and Aunt Alisha. He only had one brother and two sisters, and now all he has are two sisters. We will see you in short time."

Beth ran to find their wagon a short distance up ahead. She ran beside the wagon and hollered for Clint to stop, and he slowed down a bit and then came to a complete stop. "I must get in the wagon and talk to Marcy."

"Beth, is everything all right? Are you okay? You're not feeling bad, are you? You look a little pale. Did something frighten you?" He stopped long enough for Beth to climb into the wagon.

She made her way close to Marcy's side. "Oh, Marcy! Oh, Marcy! You won't believe what I am going to tell you." Beth started and then stopped, and started again and stopped.

"Beth, what in heavens has you in such a dither? Does

this have anything to do with that girl you were walking with this afternoon?"

"Yes, yes, Marcy, that is what you will not believe." Beth was on the verge of tears now and was shaking. Marcy reached over and pulled Beth to her and held her tightly.

"You can tell me when you are ready, and I won't push you any further."

Beth, feeling the loving arms of her sister around her, sat for a few minutes more and then slowly asked Marcy, "Do we have an aunt and uncle named Hiram and Martha Brewster who lived in Nebraska?"

Marcy thought for a moment and then answered her softly, "Why yes, we do, Beth. But why are you asking about them now?"

"Because, because, they are here in a wagon on the train with us. Sally is our cousin, and she has a brother named Benny too."

"I don't remember the cousins too well, but I do remember Aunt Martha and Uncle Hiram. Beth, are you sure this is correct?"

"Yes, Marcy, and we are invited to go have supper with them when we stop for the evening," said Beth with her head hung low.

"Don't you want to go meet them? They have a right to know about Father and Mother," she stated in a hushed voice.

"Oh, Marcy, I told Sally what had happened, but I could not go through this again by having to tell Papa's own brother what had taken place."

MARLENE WISE

"Beth, you will leave it up to me, and I will explain all that is needed to know when the proper time comes."

It was soon late evening and time to head to the Brewster wagon for supper. Marcy took a few items to add to the supper meal as she felt strange that the cousin, Sally, had asked them without asking her mother first. Clint went along as moral support for both Marcy and Beth. As they approached their campsite, they smelled food cooking, and Marcy first noticed Aunt Martha at the side of their wagon at a small table making biscuits or bread. She then saw Uncle Hiram come from around the wagon and look their way. At first sight, Marcy stopped and almost felt like she wanted to faint. She could not believe her eyes, as Uncle Hiram was the very image of her beloved father, Stewart. For a minute, she was ready to call out to him thinking it was her father. Beth had stopped in her tracks and did not move nor budge. Her eyes were glued on Uncle Hiram, and she didn't look anywhere else. Both Hiram and Martha immediately ran to Marcy and hugged and kissed her.

"We would have known you were Stewart's child, as you look just like him. Here, come and sit down; you must be very tired and weary. Your baby is due soon, isn't it?" Clint looked and saw Beth still standing at the edge of the campsite looking very rigid and like she was in a stage of shock. Clint called to Beth and asked her to come over and sit by Marcy. As she started over to Marcy, Aunt Martha put her arm around Beth and welcomed her to their wagon.

Then Uncle Hiram walked over to her with his

arms extended and said, "Come, my child, you have been through a lot." Without reservation, Beth ran and fell into her uncle's arms. She seemed to be lost in time as she suddenly felt like she was in her father's arms, as often her father would say, "Come, my child," and hold out his arms to her. As she lay in his arms, she cried like she had never cried before until she was consumed with great sobbing and shaking uncontrollably. Aunt Martha brought a shawl and wrapped it around her. Beth finally began to calm down, and Aunt Martha asked if anyone was hungry.

"Come, let's eat, and then we can talk and visit some more. You can get to know your cousins better since you were all so young when we made the visit to Minnesota," said Aunt Martha.

Marcy said, "Well, we are going to have time now, because we know now that we have family right in our midst, and we can visit with each other in Oregon. And of course, Sally and Beth had already hit it off and made friends before they knew they were cousins. They'll have lots to talk about now, I'm sure of that." They visited for several hours, and then Clint said he thought he needed to get Marcy back to the wagon and into bed so she could get her rest.

"These last two days have been a little of a strain on her."

"Oh, Clint, I am—"

"Now, now, you have to listen to the doctor, right?"

"Well, it has been a very long and hard day, so we'll say goodnight and see you all tomorrow and catch up on all the news you have to tell us." Clint helped Marcy up on her feet, and they slowly sauntered back to their own wagon. Clint asked Marcy as they walked along what she thought about all of this.

"It just seems uncanny how our relatives would end up on this same train as us. I think it is just plain old providence that it would take place at this time. I am very happy for Beth's sake, as Uncle Hiram looks so much like Father and speaks like him that I think it will do her worlds of good to be around him as much as possible." Marcy paused and then said to Clint, "It's not that you haven't been like a father to Beth, because you have been, and she adores and loves you very much. You will never lose that with Beth. But it is good to have family close by and be able to share and have holidays together and so many other things."

Clint squeezed Marcy close to him and said, "Yes, Marcy, and of all people, I really do understand this better than anyone about family. That's why I am so anxious to be starting our own family. Family means so very much to me, to us."

SECOND CHANCE

Striker was tied behind the wagon, and he too seemed content that they were finally on the move again. Marcy sometimes looked back and watched Striker as he plodded happily along with them, and she wondered if he remembered any of the things that had happened to them. She sometimes let her mind wander and envisioned her father and Striker and oftentimes believed that Striker really missed her father just as she did. Her father had saved Striker from a severe beating and even death, and she felt there must be a close bond that neither she nor horse could ever easily forget.

August tenth dawned with waves of hot wind blowing in from the south. Even though it was still in the early morning, the heat was intense, and everyone knew the day would be a real scorcher. If all continued to go well, the wagon train should pull into Oregon territory sometime in early September. The next stop of any length of time would be at Fort Boise. Those who needed any supplies would be able to obtain a few things there for

MARLENE WISE

the remainder of the trip to go on to the area between Grande Rhonde Valley and the Blue Mountains. Soon after the stop at Fort Boise, the wagon caravan would enter into Oregon territory.

As they rode into the Blue Mountain lower area, everyone was taken aback and absolutely breathless at the beautiful sights they beheld. No one could believe that they had finally made it into Oregon. It had been such a long, hard journey, and now that it was over, it was difficult to fathom that they stood on the soil of Oregon, for which their hearts had yearned for so long.

As Marcy looked around and drank in this awesome and wonderful view before her, a little tear rolled down her cheek as she once again thought of her parents who lay in a grave far, far away. Her father had yearned to come to Oregon before he had been talked into going to California. She couldn't help but wonder what it would have been like to see the look on her parents' faces as they viewed this land for which they had so longed for. Her mind had been filled once again with various imaginations of the days that had already passed by. It was those days that had caused them to keep toiling, working, striving, and determining to go onward regardless of hardships and trying times that many times beset them along the way. There was not one family that had not had to endure many discouragements, hardships, fears, testings, and unmerciful bouts with the elements of Mother Nature that threatened the very life of every man, woman, boy, girl, baby, and the livestock.

Marcy was thrilled that she made the decision to go

ahead and come. Clint had delivered two babies, bandaged a twisted ankle, sewn up a cut on a man's forehead, and doctored quite frequently for dysentery and stomach problems.

They knew immediately when they crossed into Oregon territory. How beautiful! The evergreen trees were majestic and stately; the lodge pole pines were so tall they could hardly see the tops of them. This was indeed a forest of wonders where one could see little trails that led off the main trail and back into the woods. Some had already stopped along these trails and found what they were searching for in this area.

Somewhere between the fertile Grande Rhonde Valley and a beautiful clear and cool stream of fresh running water, the wagons drew up in the early afternoon to settle for the night. After camp was set up, Clint and Hank took their horses and went for a leisurely ride while Mr. Payton stayed to assist the ladies in case of trouble. The men's adventuresome ride took them into the woods about twenty minutes away from camp. As they paused to drink from their canteens, Hank asked Clint if he could hear a strange noise.

"What noise is that?" Clint asked.

"Listen, it sounds like the banging of a hammer off in the distance and voices off to the right like down in a hollow." They began to ride to the left upon a small wooded trail, and after some time, to their amazement, they came upon a little settlement of several cabins and a long building that had been erected just west of the cabins, and other buildings were in the process of being erected. The long building was sort of a trading post. After speaking with some of the settlers, they found out that supplies and goods were sent up the Colombia River every month. In the winter and very cold months, they usually double-ordered items to carry them through. Both men began to look around as they asked questions of those who lived there. The more Clint observed and talked, the more he smiled.

Looking at Hank with a big smile, he asked him, "Are you thinking what I'm thinking?"

"I think so."

Not too far away they could see a sparkling stream that ran through the property and were told by those who lived there that it was full of fish for the taking. They were told that sufficient amounts of deer, elk, turkey and fowl, bear, mule deer, rabbits, and other game for hunting and trapping were most plentiful in this area. One could certainly do well with traps from the Colombia River nearby and other streams and smaller rivers. If they trapped and got nice furs and pelts, they could be exchanged at the trading post for some supplies and goods. There was no denying it: there were plenty of trees and wood for homes, schools, and churches. There were still some beautiful flowers in bloom scattered here and there and in spots of shade hiding from the hot sun. Clint said this was probably a paradise for the leaves, roots, berries, bark, and items he would need to resupply his medical needs, plus he could always order and have them sent in.

Meanwhile, Hank dug down into the soil a ways and

MARCY

observed its rich dark blackness. He closely observed the wonderful soil that looked like it would grow just about anything planted in it. They still had a supply of seeds they had not used for this year. One of the families had a cow, and they could probably buy milk for the child, but in time Clint hoped to have his own milk cow and other livestock. With time and hard work, the men believed this settlement would grow into a prosperous town. They decided to go discuss their find with the others and get their input also. Some of the families with newborn babies might be interested in this find too. This new land was rich, rugged, and beautiful and had room for many people who wanted to make it their home.

Clint and Hank told of their find and asked the others about their feelings of settling here. Each family discussed their thoughts over their supper that night. They must give an answer to the wagon master before he pulled out early in the morning to go farther into Oregon as was planned.

It was decided that the Brodys and Beth, the Paytons, and Hank would definitely stay and build new homes. Later, Clark Weedman and his family of four, the Berrys, the Pringles' family of three, and the Blackmans' five had all decided to stay, and also one single man, Paul, in his thirties. Marcy was very pleased that her aunt and uncle and family would also be staying. It would be good to have family around as they started their new life. The total count added to this settlement would be twenty-two. There would be much hard work to do and not much time, but all of these families knew what hard work was

283

MARLENE WISE

and were not afraid to get involved. If they all worked together they could manage to get it done well before the cold weather. Clint, Hank, and Reverend Payton went to speak with the wagon master and advised him of their intentions. He was happy for them and gave them his blessings and good wishes.

Early the next morning after sharing some of their supplies of flour, sugar, salt, and coffee, the rest of the train pulled out and bid their friends adieu. In about a month, Marcy would have her baby, and Clint wanted her in a new cabin by that time, one of her very own. There were eight men and four already at the settlement. Twelve men could surely get a few cabins built in a month before the cold winter months would be upon them.

Sure enough, by the first of October they had several cabins erected, one of which belonged to Clint and Marcy. Marcy was elated to have her own house because on October 4 she went into labor. Marcy calmly called Beth and told her to run and find Clint, that it was time for the baby to come. This frightened Beth, and she ran wildly from place to place calling for Clint. Mrs. Payton sat by Marcy's side and held her hand and squeezed it as the pains came and bore down upon her, just as she had promised her earlier she would do. Mrs. Payton had a wash bowl set up with soap and water for the doctor and clean towels. She had gathered the needed supplies for the birthing of the baby. Mrs. Payton asked Marcy if she wanted her to call her Aunt Martha to come sit with her, but Marcy replied no. She would come by later. Aunt Martha had already spoken to Marcy about this very thing. Aunt Martha had promised she would cook the meals and help the family in any way that she could. She thought it a good idea to keep Beth occupied until the baby was born. Hank ran to retrieve Clint's medical bag, which had not yet been unpacked because he had not had to render any medical services in the last few weeks.

Marcy was nervous and frightened when the terrible pains came pushing down upon her. In her mind, she really wished that her own mother was there with her. She tried to relax and put her trust in Clint and Mrs. Payton, but it was hard for her, as every daughter wants her own mother at the birth of her first child. Her labor had started early in the morning, and their baby girl was not born until very late that night. Marcy was exhausted and slept much for the next two days. Marcy chose the name Annabeth Alisha. She named her after Clint's mother and sister and for Elizabeth, her sister, but also the name Anna was Elmira's middle name, and she thought it fitting for her to also have a name of her dear sweet friend. Of course, Annabeth's middle name came from her beloved mother, Alisha. Annabeth was a healthy baby and weighed seven or more pounds. Marcy would be up in a few days after she regained her strength and felt better. She never realized that having a baby was so much hard work.

By mid-October all the cabins were built. Corrals for the animals were started. A total of seven new cabins had been built to add to the four older ones. The little settlement now had eleven homes and a trading post. It was beginning to grow already, and as time went on, more and more would find their way to this settlement to make their home here as the wagon train came through each year and as others made their way up the Colombia River.

The settlement soon boasted a population of fifty-three settlers counting the newborn babies. The people decided that since they had a trading post, the makings of a small café, a doctor's office, a seamstress shop, a blacksmith shop, the beginnings of a lumber mill, and a church, this place needed to have a name. It was agreed upon after much discussion to call their new small settlement Second Chance. It seemed fitting as many had come to this place to start life anew. Hank even volunteered to make a nice wooden sign to hang at the entrance that would say, "Welcome to Second Chance." They were thankful they had been spared and given a second chance at life again. Many had not made it through their trip west and had to be buried along the way in some lonely spot that only God knew where to find them. Others, like Clint and Marcy, Elizabeth, the Paytons, and Hank had gone through much not knowing if they would survive. But they had put the past behind them and were grateful for a second chance at life. So to them, Second Chance seemed to be the most appropriate name for the new town that was growing day by day.

Marcy and Beth had reached Second Chance in a strange and perilous way with only half of their precious dreams. Back in another place similar to this one, they had left their beloved parents and the other half of their dreams buried deep in a cold, wild, and mysterious land

MARCY

called the West. The wrong trail, a bad decision to go to California, and evil men full of greed had led their parents to their deaths. Marcy, then a young girl barely seventeen, had thought that she'd never be happy again, but she had been wrong. Happiness had come to her again, and she had reached out and grabbed it and held on with all of her heart. Her old life lay behind her, and everything now seemed new and fresh, except for the buried memories that would forever be bound in her mind. New life or not, she knew there would be moments when these memories would flood her mind again and again. It was up to her as to how she let them affect her and her family. But in her heart, she felt that her own true happiness and new beginnings would start at this place called Second Chance, Oregon.